The Medic

Tales of
The Aura Weavers,
Book 1

LizAnn Carson

If anyone gets thanks here, it's the wonderful members of my critique group. Half the time my fantasy ravings leave you bewildered, but you plow through anyway, always constructive, catching what I miss. It matters. Thanks a lot.

LizAnn Carson

Prelude

Pacing the embarkation lobby just inside the forward hatch of the Eurocorp Adventurer, Doctor Constance Devereaux glanced at her chrono, more irritated than alarmed. She had won the last argument, but now wondered if it had been a Pyrrhic victory. Only two hours to lift-off and so far, no Pierre. No Omar. Where the *hell* had her husband and son got to?

The argument that night a month ago had been short, but vicious. "You're insane," Pierre had hissed at her from his slouched position on the sofa, one ankle resting on the opposite knee. He adopted a position of insouciance whenever she was angry, but a red flush marred his handsome, chiseled face. They fought their battles in lowered voices and hisses, and only after Omar was asleep.

"Hardly," she had replied, on her feet, arms folded. "Are you blind? The government's collapsed in Northam, their shields are down, their cities are in flames. We can't even see the sky because of the smoke. The public storehouses won't last the spring after the crop failure. Riots in Londres, epidemic in Ansur, the drought—"

"Oh, drop it." His sneer put the lie to whatever love had survived between them. "You've

1

become boring with your catastrophe theories." He had looked away, signaling his lack of interest.

"Your son went to bed early," Constance countered. "Aren't you even curious to know why?"

Pierre's eyes narrowed. He adored Omar but had always considered the ups and downs of his ten-year-old life to be Constance's province, not his.

She perched on the arm of the sofa, getting in his face. "I'll tell you why," she spat. "There was a demonstration near the shopping precinct. Riot police, arrests. Omar was there."

Pierre sprang to his feet and grasped her arm, hauling her up with him. His fingers dug in. "You let him go? You *bitch*! What kind of mother are you?"

She shook off his hand. "Don't be absurd. He walks home from school that way. A safe route. *As we agreed.*" She took a breath. "The point is, one of his friends got caught up in it. She was trampled. He saw it and tried to help, but the police dragged him away."

At that, Pierre had clenched his fists, but at least shut up. Later, over glasses of Malbec, they had managed a discussion of sorts, and by the end of it he had agreed – finally – to participate in the scheme to flee Terra.

*

Starships were nothing new to Constance. From her base at the Eurocorp South spaceport in France province, she had conducted post-flight clinics on dozens of them as the medic on call when the vast cargo transports berthed. Now, as she paced the Adventurer's embarkation foyer, crew prepared the tubby tourist ship for liftoff, seemingly en route to a Martian vacation outpost.

But the purported holidaymakers prowling the ship had a completely different purpose in mind. They'd scraped together the funds to put a down payment on the old boat, then rebuilt her to very different specs. The cargo bays held supplies not for two days, but for two years. Staterooms assigned to non-existent passengers stored the surplus. On the surface, the Adventurer passed the mandatory inspections, but it was insurrection, pure and simple.

Because Terra could not survive. Northam was finished. Stretches of the equatorial provinces of China Pacific Corporation hadn't been habitable in decades. With no economic potential, the other corporations had abandoned Afrique completely. And the revolution, as they called it, had arrived in Eurocorp. In light of Northam's fate, management governed with an iron fist; no thinking person dared step outside the rules.

Eurocorp had planned a voyage similar to their unauthorized one, only to cancel it in the face of political opposition. In desperation and against all legalities, she and her colleagues proposed to follow the sketchy trail of the early ships from centuries ago, to explore – with better technology – the possibility of a new, more livable planet. The Adventurer needed a medic, and she had signed on. Risky, but the sole viable means of escape from the approaching Armageddon.

Everything lined up, except for what she now recognized as her big mistake, a concession made in the glow of finally convincing Pierre. They had agreed that he would bring Omar to the Adventurer, freeing Constance to attend to her last-minute duties. Safe enough, she had thought, given Omar's eagerness to board the holiday vessel.

A different hum vibrated the plates beneath her feet. First officer Ben Albright's voice, with its harsh Angleterre accent, echoed against the hard walls of the featureless embarkation foyer. "On time for liftoff in two hours, twelve minutes. Be sure your stuff's stowed, folks."

Constance's screen blinked with a new message, from Omar. *Dad said we could get crème glacé. Love you.*

Her temper flared. They should be on board by now, and they weren't even at the spaceport yet. The *idiot*.

She shot back a text to both of them: *Hurry. Launch countdown begun.* Knowing Pierre, he would stall until the very last minute, just to set her nerves on edge.

She should have left Pierre years ago. She should have taken Omar and gone to her father's home and let Pierre stew—

"Looks like something's brewing."

Constance joined the ensign manning the hatch at the small window in the skylift tower. The spaceport lay below her, including a surging crowd outside the fence and fighting to get inside. The barriers held, of course, potentially delaying Pierre and Omar even more. If they got through at all.

She paged Pierre; he didn't reply. *Come quickly,* she texted. *Use the south entrance. Demonstration at the main gates.*

Dare she put her faith in a text? If she knew her husband – and she did, altogether too well – he had encouraged Omar to turn off his comm, sit in the hazy sunshine, and enjoy his ice cream as if the world weren't falling into destruction around them.

She paged the departure checkpoint, far below her. "Sorry, Doc," the official there replied.

"No sign of them so far." He sounded worried; Constance could hear rumblings from the crowd in the background.

Once again she had been blindsided by her husband's undoubted charm. What a fool she had been, trusting him to get their son to the spaceport.

An explosion rattled the tower. Off to the right, far below and outside the security wall, something flared. Given the drought conditions, a fire could spread out of control in a moment.

Another voice cut in. "Medic to sickbay. Code twenty. Medic to sickbay."

Training took over. Constance snatched up her bag and left the embarkation foyer at a run, heading for the medical facility on deck five. Code twenty meant a serious injury. With an effort, she forced her family from her mind.

*

In her tranquil clinic, ignoring the presence of a wailing teenaged girl in the waiting room, she found her senior nurse, Cerie, hunched over a gurney bearing a pimply, unconscious teen. Wheelz stuck out on his feet from the bottom of the gurney; no doubt the kid had been practicing a risky move in one of the featureless corridors. She flicked on the scanner.

Cerie recited the numbers scrolling on the monitor while Constance moved her hand-held over the teen. Concussion, not a bad one. The dumb kid had knocked himself out, but he would survive. Let him endure the killer headache; teach him a lesson.

The girl slouched in the waiting room howled, "He's gonna die, isn't he? You gotta do something, you can't just let him *lie* there."

What was she supposed to do, wave a magic wand and watch the kid spring back to perfect health? Constance sighed and returned the scanning device to its holder. "He'll be fine. Even better if you'd stop the caterwauling."

Mercifully, the girl settled into teary sobs, wiping her nose on the sleeve of her cheerful holiday shirt. Probably expected a vacation jaunt over school break, like Omar did. No point telling the kids they'd never go home again.

Constance consulted briefly with Cerie as she prepared to return to the entry port. A new, deeper rumble vibrated the floor, overlaid by Ben's voice. "Trouble. Sounds like we may need to make a quick getaway, so we're powering up. Everyone, report to your checkpoint and prepare for liftoff."

Constance looked at the speaker in the ceiling in horror. *Now?* No, impossible. They still had two hours. At least two hours.

Again, training took over. She collared the girl. "You, go to your family's quarters. Cerie, help me get this daredevil onto a cot. You know the procedures for securing patients?"

"I do." The younger woman rolled the gurney to the nearest of the five empty beds, and the two women transferred the kid. As Constance turned to leave, herding the damp girl ahead of her, Cerie manipulated the restraints over the inert teen.

*

Constance attained the entry port as the voice of Harry Belfontaine, the captain, boomed over the ship's comm. Tension underlaid his usual laconic cadence. "Okay, folks, here's the status. We've ceased fueling at approximate three-quarters capacity because of the risk of further explosions. The staff at the main gate say they may not be able to hold back the rioters much longer. And we think Eurocorp Command has caught on to our little scheme, because we've been ordered to stand down and expect a secondary inspection."

Then Harry laid it on the line without actually stating their objective: "We on the bridge are prepared to continue as planned. If you choose to remain in Eurocorp, disembark now. In fifteen minutes the skylift will be disengaged, and we go."

Left unsaid but known by every adult on board: if they were prevented from departing, anyone caught on the boat would be branded a traitor.

Constance felt her chest tighten in disbelief. Would Pierre get himself and their son there in time? Should she snatch this chance, abandon the four hundred plus passengers to travel without a medic? Even if she stayed, what were the odds of leaving the spaceport safely? A quick glance out of the skylift window told her the crowds had swollen while she attended to the kid in sickbay. A few had somehow broken through security and raced toward the departure lounge. One of the insurrectionists crumbled; a second later she heard a faint pop. If the mob managed to access the base of the skylift...

By instinct she raised her comm to page the departure checkpoint, then lowered it, numb with disbelief. Unless her family was already on the elevator as it made its last ten-minute trip, she would never see them again.

If she stayed behind, she would never see them again, either. As one of the senior officers and instigators of the plot to flee Terra, they would arrest her and... in today's environment, she might face a firing squad.

At the sound of running feet, she pressed herself to the wall. A family of four, panic etched on the adults' faces, bolted for the skylift. Once they had herded themselves into an elevator, an eerie silence blanketed the foyer.

She paged the captain's private comm line. "Harry, we can't go yet. Pierre and Omar aren't here."

He sighed. "I'm sorry. I can't hold—"

Ben's voice, loud in the background: "Bloody hell. The gates are down."

A clatter told her Harry had tossed his comm, without closing the link. Sounds from the bridge blasted through.

"*Captain Belfontaine, this is Colonel Josef Hernandez. I order you to stand down. Don't test my patience any further.*"

Harry must be yelling; she heard his voice through the ensign's comm. "Close hatch, *now*. Five minutes to lift-off."

Before the ensign could leap to obey, the final skylift disgorged two men and a woman in Spacecorp uniforms. They ignored both the ensign and Constance and jogged through one of the connecting portals, the look on their faces grim. In that moment she realized her decision had been made for her. The ensign shouted into his comm. "Three uniforms on board. Can't be sure but I suspect they're heading for the bridge. "

"*Shit*". That came through her comm from Georges Toit, head of security. "Confirm, bridge door secured."

"Secured, sir," came a female voice.

Another voice called off final checks. A woman replied to Harry's demand for information: "Coordinates programmed as far as zone three, sir."

8

The voice of Nicole Heidelberg, second officer: "Final skylift shuttle descending, skylift gantry sealed and released. Engine four online."

Zone three was Mars. From there they would be on their own, other than the reports from Northam's exploration pods, which their espionage system had uncovered, and fragmentary records from those early ships, so long ago...

From Nicole: "Engine 3 online." A pause, bustle and quiet voices in the background. "Engine two online."

Ben again, on the ship's comm: "All passengers, to your checkpoints immediately. Active crew, to stations. Someone find the Spacecorp interlopers and get them secured somewhere." Gone was any pretence this was a typical holiday charter.

Behind her the ensign thumbed his comm. "Forward hatch sealed and confirmed, sir."

"Engine one online. Ship fully powered, sir."

A string of voices sounded through the still open comm as others reported status: *Cargo hatch sealed and confirmed. Checkpoint twenty-three confirmed. Aft hatch sealed and confirmed. Checkpoint fifteen confirmed....*

"Best get to your security checkpoint, Doc," the ensign said.

Constance didn't move. Her plans, her family. Omar, her son...

Checkpoint five confirmed. Checkpoint thirteen confirmed....

The ensign took her arm, leading her gently but forcefully from the entry port.

*

A day later, after a rocky launch unsupported by ground control, Constance watched from her tiny stateroom window as the spaceport went up in flames.

Chapter 1

It couldn't be a more perfect spring day, and Constance was prepared to celebrate every sun-drenched minute of it as she stepped through the Adventurer's hatch and inched her way down the steep steps to the ground. The last time she had risked going outside, nearly two seasons ago by the time system on Newfoundland, the Aura enveloping the planet felled her so thoroughly she had doubted she would ever recover.

Newfoundland, accent on the middle syllable. Her home now, like it or not. Mostly, she didn't.

So far.

But oh, how she hoped Quinn's shield would hold. The shield meant freedom. She had been cooped up on the Adventurer, hiding from this thing called the Aura, while everyone else went about the business of establishing a colony around the ship. After two years in transit, it was hard to bear – but not as hard as another attack would be.

Quinn, a statuesque black woman – the only one Constance had seen so far, although when she tentatively broached the topic, she had been assured Quinn's skin pigment was common further to the southeast – was one of the famed Weavers, the men and women who, like Constance, had an innate affinity for the Aura and used it to enhance their natural talents. A Scribe, which seemed to be a catch-all term for any Weaver who couldn't be classified any other way, she had become a lifeline during Constance's enforced incarceration in the ship, as well as being her only hope for ever leaving it.

She and Quinn were of an age – around forty in earth years – and had discovered a shared love of science and research. Despite what Constance could only consider societal gullibility and mass delusion, Quinn was surprisingly down to earth. She endured a crippling foot injury, a seriously ill lover, and periodic bouts of homesickness without complaint. Following her example, Constance had stopped bemoaning her own situation. There was no reason. It just was.

When she cleared the steps, the ground underneath her boots felt springy with moisture and new grass. She resolutely put aside all fear of another Auric assault as she made her way from the vessel toward a cluster of buildings. It felt so good, so *right*, to walk on earth instead of the sterile corridors of the Adventurer.

Her brain remained on alert – that was only common sense – but so far, the agonizing pain and nausea hadn't slapped her down. And the air on her skin... by all the saints, how she had missed the feeling, the scent, of fresh air.

An unoccupied corner of her mind reflected on the word *saint*, which turned up frequently in Eurocorp, especially in place names. Part of some old religion, she had been told, and idly wondered how a saint got to be one.

Quinn probably knew. The woman was indefatigable in her search for information about their shared origin.

A crisp and lightly scented breeze filled her lungs. As she walked, she drank it all in, ignoring for the moment the myriad ways this planet wasn't Terra. Although surely the original settlers had brought seeds for food with them, the plants around her were as alien as the land itself.

And some of these plants became so-called medicines. Her experience suggested they worked, even as her logical mind defied the conclusions of her body. She would take her technological background, the machines that allowed her to diagnose and treat her patients accurately, over vegetation any day. No doubt some plants harbored useful chemicals, but in general she placed plant medicine in the realm of magic if not wishful thinking, along with such ancient techniques as homeopathy. With no way to assess potency, how could you effectively prescribe? But now the charge powering her diagnostic scanner worsened daily; yesterday morning she had found herself shaking the thing to remind it to do her bidding. Without her primary tool, what kind of a medic would she be? The damn thing couldn't be recharged; soon it would be useless. The local approach to medicine was the only remaining option.

Plants. She shook her head in disgust.

Quinn was a master at Aura manipulation such as the weave, as they called it, that energetically capped Constance's head and allowed her to venture outside. Quinn held herself regally, despite the shapeless linen tunic the natives all wore, and she could be intimidating. "Any little twinge, remember?" she demanded. "I need to know absolutely everything if the shield's going to be reliable. A leak could break the whole thing apart. Take your time."

Constance, who was far from incapable, had heard these words a dozen times already. But she bit back her annoyance. After all, if it weren't for Quinn, she might have remained imprisoned in the ship forever.

No twinges so far. No slight awareness, like early intimations of a head cold. She said so and received a nod in return.

The four hundred passengers and crew of the Adventurer had made significant changes in the half year since they had touched down. A large barn and numerous storage sheds lined a track heading north. Not far from the massive bulk of the ship, small buildings forming a residential compound huddled around a fire pit, although most people still chose to eat on board. A clear trail led to the southeast, presumably to the river. The livestock had been shifted from the holds to the planet. Dozens of chickens pecked around in an enclosure off to her right, and goats browsed freely. Fields had been fenced if not cleared, and she spotted Butter, Quinn's horse, placidly grazing alongside half a dozen cows. There would be calves in four months, thanks to artificial insemination. No way had they been willing to risk transport of a bull to the new planet.

The trail north led to Cann, the town nearest their site. Cann straddled the major cross-country track that ultimately led to the Motherhouse, where Quinn assured her she must go, soon.

Constance was in no hurry.

In the daylight, she could see circles of weariness under Quinn's eyes, rendered invisible by her dark skin in the artificial light of the ship. Her limp seemed more pronounced, as happened when she was fatigued. "Late night?" she asked.

"Kiril," Quinn said flatly. Which meant he had suffered an outbreak of the mysterious, Aura-caused disease infecting him, and Quinn had hauled him off to Cann, where she and Gwen, the resident Healer, had been up all night fighting it.

"What exactly are you doing to him?" Constance asked, not for the first time. They set off to circle the Adventurer, its gleaming, space-age body looking hopelessly incongruous in the bucolic pastureland.

Quinn sighed as she wielded her cane. "I don't think I can explain more clearly than I have already."

"Try." She was desperate to understand what she was being forced into.

"We tranquilize him, kind of like what you call hypnotizing, then I go in and—"

Frustrated as usual, Constance interrupted, "But what does it *mean*, 'going in'?"

Quinn hesitated. "It's so hard to explain. It begins with a trance, then—"

"Oh, no." Constance stopped, staring out at the fields and plows, the trace of the tree-clad river. "Don't give me other-dimension nonsense. I need something tangible. I can't see how it could work otherwise."

Quinn shot a look of forced patience at her. "Gwen got you through that bad episode. Was that intangible?"

"Power of suggestion. Placebo. Nothing real."

A hand landed on her forearm, gently. "No point rewriting history. We can talk it to death, but it won't change the fact that it worked."

Or that you're out here now. Quinn didn't say it, but Constance was sure she thought it.

More residences and outbuildings had been constructed on the far side of the ship. The

Adventurer's occupants were moving to land, to sod huts that offered larger if less comfortable accommodation. People scurried around, building a life. Building their future.

Out in the fields, one group determinedly struggled to dig out the thick grass and remove the stones so they could plant. Vegetables and lentils, to start with. Wheat, potatoes, fava beans... minor accidents and blisters were common now, but overall her co-passengers were healthier than they'd been, even before they left Terra.

Hard work. And now it was her turn, although the work would take on different dimensions.

Learning to be a medic without her tools. Learning the healing properties of the plants, how to process them. And how to channel this frightening, alien energy into something useful. In her dreams, she used it to recharge her scanner. Even though Gwen had successfully cured the sickness triggered by her last ill-advised venture outside, Constance refused to buy into any of the modalities that had been discredited long since on Terra.

And the thought of traveling to this Motherhouse place, a miserable sixty-day walk along dirty, dangerous tracks, scared her. At the Motherhouse she would be trained to use her Entrée, her personal access to the Aura, something she alone of all the Adventurer's complement possessed strongly enough to matter. To go alone, so far away from everything she knew... she shuddered involuntarily, earning an assessing frown from Quinn.

"Looking good!" The shout came from her right, out by one of the work crews. Harry

Belfontaine. After he transferred command of the Adventurer to Elspeth Gandsdotter, he had taken up civilian life with a vengeance, going native with the best of them and apparently loving every minute of it.

Constance waved.

"It's holding," Quinn yelled.

Harry dropped his shovel and jogged up to them. He reached for Constance, then hesitated and looked at Quinn. "Is this okay? I won't mess up your shield or anything?"

Quinn shot him a rare smile. "Not a chance. Go for it."

Harry picked Constance up and swung her around. He wouldn't have been able to do it so easily six months ago. She laughed out loud and punched his shoulder. "Put me down, idiot."

He beamed as he settled her back on her feet, but kept his hands on her waist. Harry wasn't the only crew member permeated with optimism these days; they all were. Hugging had become pervasive. "Everything's in place, now you're out of your prison. We cracked it, Doc! So, when are you leaving?"

The cheerful mood deserted her. She twisted free.

"As soon as we can get things arranged," Quinn replied. "I've sent for a Healer to serve as escort, she should be here in a nine-day or so. And we need to wait until a trading caravan passes through Cann. It's safer not to travel alone."

"So I've heard," he said. "They say they're defending against us. Seems we have red eyes and nine arms and instant destruction machines. We're going to take their women and kill their kids and... it's crazy."

"Weavers are spreading the truth as quickly as we can," Quinn said. "Problem is, few of us go as far west as this, much less all the way to the coast. And reports are mounting up that we aren't being listened to anyway. That's new."

"I'm sorry. For the unrest, I mean." Harry ran his hand over his crewcut and pinched his lips together. This situation had occupied a fair amount of discussion among senior staff, and frustration at being seen as dangerous warmongers surfaced regularly.

"Scarcely your fault," Quinn said. "And not the only problem we've faced in the last year."

"Still, it's not pleasant. I guess I'd better get back to work before they fire me." Harry gave them a brief salute as he turned toward his work mates. Constance noted the swagger in his walk, as if he relished every moment of the labor. Yes, coming here had been wise.

She and Quinn watched him cross the field, then they continued toward the river, the river she had yet to see, as she listened once again to Quinn's explanation of Aura-fuelled Healing.

Chapter 2

At the Motherhouse, nestled on the flank of the mountain range known simply as the hills, Dal had just emerged from a quick stop in the dining hall, grateful to escape the noise of the students gathered there, when his acute senses registered a presence. He turned to his right, scanning the slight rise toward the Bards' Lodge.

A man of patrician bearing with little tolerance for frivolity, Dal commanded respect throughout the community, but few made the effort to draw close to him. This suited him well; he preferred a small, but meaningful, circle of friends. The figure standing at the corner of the lodge, leaning against the stone wall, was one of the few who had breached his self-imposed solitude. A sturdy woman in a sleeveless tunic and long skirt, carrying a walking stick and wearing an odd, floppy hat, she showed no sign of moving from her resting spot, although she did raise a languid hand to wave in his direction.

That hat was so typical.

Bemused, he returned the wave, just as he noticed Arwen emerging from the administration building known as the Centra. She paused and followed his gesture with her eyes.

"She's back," Dal confirmed.

"Thank the Aura." Arwen had recruited her team of Scribes to track the woman's progress, as far as was possible, but Dal knew well that she had been concerned.

Being both a senior Weaver and deputy head of the Healers' Guild, he read both women accurately. "Leave her alone, Arwen. She's exhausted. And so are you."

"Irrelevant."

"It's not. You know as well as I do. Your last scan—"

"Meade's home. And that Terran woman, Constance," —her tongue stumbled briefly over the strange pronunciation, accent on the second syllable— "is on her way. Do you have any idea what this is likely to cost us, in time and disruption?"

Of course he did. Arwen's impatience was both well known and his responsibility to keep in check, at least for the moment. Perhaps tomorrow he could turn the situation over to the council? "It doesn't follow that you have to intercept Meade this minute. She's worn out, and she's been injured. Anyway, didn't I order you to take time off in the evenings?"

"I'll rest when our home is secure." Arwen assumed she would get her way – justifiably, as she was head of the Weavers' council and arguably the most powerful person at the Motherhouse, possibly in the entire Midland. Usually, she was right.

But Arwen couldn't see herself clearly. She had shrunk in the last year, grown frail. Dal frowned. "You make it impossible to take care of you, you know. Right now..." His voice trailed off as she turned from his diatribe and set off across the green. Irritated, he followed.

*

At the edge of the forest, beside the Bards' Lodge, Meade caught her breath as she studied the scene before her. She propped her walking stick against the building and squatted awkwardly, given the lingering stiffness in her right leg, to rub her fingers over a spicemint plant growing wild next to the foundation.

Nothing changed.

Not strictly true, she was sure, but so what? The bones were the same. She had been a Healer for over twenty years now, walking the roads and trails of the Midland, but coming back to the Motherhouse was always the same. Home. Nearing the end of a day balanced between the cool humidity of spring and the sultriness of summer, with sore feet and exhausted spirit, the very stones of the buildings welcomed her into their embrace. The four days from Stanstead to the Motherhouse had seemed interminable, even though they counted for little, given how far she had come.

Home. Taking a lungful of the pure mountain air, she began the final, shortest, leg of her journey, across the green and back up the far slope to the Healers' Lodge.

The last year hadn't all been fun. Not by a long shot.

Her own bed. A bath to soak her muscles – because while logic told her she was only in her mid-forties, surely she was getting too old for this distance of travel. Here were friends, colleagues, meals in the dining hall, picking the early mountain herbs... In no time at all she would be truly reintegrated.

And, she thought wryly no more than a handful of steps later, still miles away from the bed, the bath, the friends, because Arwen was heading in her direction. No sneaking past the Centra this time. Meade stopped and waited as the older woman reached her and enfolded her in a hug.

"My dear, you're here at last." The hug ended quickly enough, and just as well, because Meade didn't trust it for a moment. Arwen was no hugger; she wanted something.

Some things never change.

"Tired and footsore, but all is well."

"And your mission? I'm told it's accomplished?" Sure enough, Arwen stepped back, all business.

Meade nodded. "No one is going to find that cell. It's done."

"Excellent." Arwen, who was never stationary for a moment, started to turn away. "We have need of you here. Come with me and I'll fill you in."

Meade sighed and stood her ground. Defying Arwen was never easy for anyone at the Motherhouse, as most of them had been students during her tenure on council. But Meade had every intention of doing just that this evening. Not for nothing had she traveled the width of the Midland, all the way to the western ocean, accomplishing a necessary, but dangerous, task. "No, ma'am," she said.

Arwen turned and raised a gray eyebrow. Then, perhaps taking in Meade's general dishevelment and drooping shoulders, she relented. "Let the kitchen know, they'll hold a meal until you get cleaned up. First thing tomorrow, though. This can't wait."

Dal joined the little reunion. "It can. We have at least three or four nine-days before Constance gets here. Meade, what can I do for you?"

She reached out to him. "Dal. It's so good to be back."

He gave her his own version of a hug, superficially enthusiastic but with that little hint of drawing back she generally sensed in their interactions. As expected, he used the hug time to assess the residual pain radiating from the wounded leg. "Take my arm. We'll get you settled."

"Tomorrow," Arwen said implacably as Meade looped her arm through Dal's, putting more of her weight on him than she had planned to, but *oh*, she was tired. "Fill her in, Dal."

"Not a chance." As they moved away, she felt his breath on her head whispering his reply.

"Insurrection?" Meade whispered back, feeling her spirits lift. Dal had always been much too serious. He needed more lightness, more rebelliousness in his makeup.

"Absolutely."

As they reached the dining hall, Meade glanced behind her. Arwen had already disappeared into the Centra.

*

In a pale mountain morning, with none of the harsh light of the prairies, Meade stretched in the patch of sunlight warming her bed and snuggled lower in the covers. *Home.* Her reward for the long and perilous trek, the assignment so alien to her usual ways... and the saving of the Motherhouse, the Weavers.

After a delicious moment, she shoved the sheet back, giving the sun direct access to her skin, and propped on an elbow to study the man still asleep beside her. This was new, the only strange or unexpected aspect of her homecoming. Arwen's ambush, the scrumptious food, greeting the handful of friends they had run into as they climbed the slope to the Healers' lodge – those she had anticipated. Dal's Healing hands, working on her leg and then on her overall fatigue, were not anticipated, but also not unfamiliar. His exhaustion was. That fact, coupled with the subtle change in his sleeping face, erasing new lines of tension, hinted at the situation at the Motherhouse.

And yet all seemed peaceful. She could hear the usual morning sounds from the handful of Healers in residence, the shouts of apprentices out for a morning expedition of some sort. Their share room faced the wrong direction to receive aromas from the dining hall, but her stomach hinted at breakfast, soon.

Dal's eyes opened. He smiled at her, which also told her something she needed to know.

Why not? No need to rush to the dining hall, and Arwen... well, the more pleasure stored up, the better, though she couldn't imagine what Arwen wanted from her beyond a report on her year-long pilgrimage and the disposition of the power cell.

She leaned over, met Dal's mouth with her own, and abandoned herself to the luxury of loving, before the business of the day began.

Chapter 3

"You look better." Meade resisted the desire to squirm as Arwen scanned her. "Are you rested?"

She didn't doubt that Arwen knew exactly how she had spent the night – Arwen could be spooky – but played along. "Not completely, but it's good to be in my own quarters again."

Arwen's nod indicated her acceptance of the short summary. She had convened their meeting in the windowless conference room, not Meade's favorite, especially on such a perfect sunny day. The lack of adornment did serve to focus the mind, however. Daren, an older man who headed the Healers' Guild, was there, along with Dorcas, a Scribe of Daren's generation who was head of the Scribes' guild and usually played a part in whatever was going on. Hector, principe of the school, older than anyone at the Motherhouse other than Ezra, the Old Man, completed the odd panel. His presence puzzled Meade; did they want her to teach? She liked the kids, but...

Arwen called them to attention. "You heard about the ship that arrived from Terra?"

Terra, the mysterious planet that had been home to the two alien men, Joss and Kiril. She had met them both, had even assisted in their attempt to Heal Kiril from the energy infecting him, but wouldn't say she *knew* them. And now hundreds, perhaps thousands, of their countrymen had turned up...

Her route home had taken her via the north road, not the south, where the newcomers were said to have settled, so she hadn't laid eyes on them so far. "Rumors abound in the countryside," she answered cautiously, "but no facts. There's a lot of fear, towns barricaded, occasional violence. Even the sash isn't trusted anymore." She reached under the table and rubbed the ailing leg, which stiffened quickly whenever she sat for any length of time. "I assume they aren't really blue."

Dorcas barked a laugh. "They number about four hundred and are perfectly ordinary. Except two of them, and that's the problem. Because those two have Entrée."

Meade's brows rose. "Fully?"

"One of them, yes," Arwen said. "We can discount the other."

Meade's mind quickly sorted through the implications. "And this person... man or woman?"

"Woman," Daren said. "Her name is Constance. She's been working with Quinn."

"Her Entrée's strong," Arwen continued, "but there are complications."

Hector spoke up. "The Aura sickens her. Quinn thinks it might kill her, were she forced to spend much time unshielded."

Meade frowned. "The Aura's not as benign as we'd believed it to be, but making someone sick? That's unheard of, isn't it?"

Arwen reached for the tray that held the caff service and poured herself a mug. She sipped before answering. "Quinn thinks it's because she didn't grow up here, so her system isn't used to the Aura's presence. She's devised a shield, similar to the one that protected Bryar last year.

Without it... well, we don't know whether she'll adapt or not."

"Without the shield," Meade mused, "or if the shield fails, she's at serious risk."

"Until she acclimates, exactly." Arwen held up the caff pot. At their nod, she poured for Hector and Meade.

"And that, my dear," said Hector, accepting his mug, "is where you come in."

Alarmed, Meade sat up straighter. "Me? No, don't ask me. I'm sorry, but I can't travel to wherever she is. I don't want to, and I'm tired."

Hector reached across the table and put his wizened hand on hers. "No," he confirmed. "That's not the plan at all. Meade, for as long as we've known you, you've shown a specific attribute that we believe will be better, healthier, for Constance than anything else."

Daren spoke up. "You're of an age with her, but more, you are... blithe. Despite everything – and we know the last year hasn't been easy for you – you are one of the sunniest people in the guilds. And Constance is dark. There's little joy in her. The reasons are hidden from us. That grimness will interfere with her training, and based on Quinn's reports, she desperately needs training."

Meade clutched her tiny caff mug, frowning. "I know nothing about training. So what...?"

Arwen sighed. "It's straightforward enough. She's on her way here. Agnes is bringing her to the Motherhouse."

Meade silently absorbed the information. It made sense.

"First," Arwen decreed, "is simply to get her stable. And that's where you come in."

"You're assigning me... to be her friend?"

"More or less, yes," Arwen said. "She doesn't believe in or trust our work, so her powers terrify her, even the little bit she's experienced from within her spaceship. We need to convince her we aren't evil incarnate. It may take time to grasp the extent of the challenge she poses, time we can't afford to waste. We certainly can't turn her loose in the Midland. She's too powerful and has next to no control. Once she accepts the reality of the Aura, we still must stabilize her Entrée and train her."

"Not to mention lessening her sadness," Hector put in.

From then on, the meeting concerned strategy. Where to house Constance, how to assess her strengths, then lead her into the ways of the Aura, something that usually bloomed in a person around puberty and needed only direction. Constance called herself a medic, a healer of sorts for her people, and assumed she would train to be a Healer, but Quinn couldn't confirm this was the best path for her. Her exposure to the surface of the planet had been minimal, since her intolerance for the Aura kept her confined to the ship they'd arrived in, but based on Quinn's observations, her resonance with the land and plants – medicines – was nil. Perhaps once she no longer needed the shield? In the meantime, what to do with her?

Apparently, Constance's fate lay on Meade's shoulders. She settled in to listen while the elders surrounding her expounded on the challenges presented by this one lone, unhappy woman.

After far too much discussion, Meade escaped the meeting and positively erupted out the door of the admin building into the fresh, sun-drenched morning. Her thoughts about the stranger soon to enter her life would flow much better once she escaped the enclosed conference room. Breathing deeply of the air she had missed so desperately during her trek across the plains and the far-distant western mountains, she called in at the dining hall to claim an abricoe pastry, then headed past the amphitheater and along the trail to the river.

Chapter 4

She and Agnes had been on the road for ten days, days Constance would happily forget. The thought of at least another fifty did nothing to improve her mood. Daytimes, they plodded alternately through dust and mud; nights, they slept on hard earth, subject to every rock embedded in the ground, every bug, every unexplained rustle in the surrounding vegetation. The food was minimal and coarse. More than once she had watched – or tried not to watch – as the young man leading the trading caravan skinned some poor animal for their dinner. She hadn't had a bath, had barely been able to wash her hands. Water came from wells or springs along the track, medicines from whatever Agnes carried with her.

The caravan consisted of the man, his wife, his mother, and a covered cart pulled by an insolent donkey. Everyone emphasized the unknown threat of traveling alone, but for the life of her Constance couldn't fathom how this paltry support could defend them should they be attacked.

Attacked. Sweet dieu.

And always the implied threat of the Aura, the Motherhouse, lying ahead of her.

That night, as Agnes snored gently beside her, their companions wrapped in their blankets on the other side of the fire, Constance's world shifted yet again. She had woken, puzzled, to a sky awash with stars but no overt disturbance. She lay unmoving, wondering what could have interrupted her exhausted slumber.

And felt it. A tingle, faint, on the edge of her awareness. Not a physical sensation, exactly, but not mental either. Her muscles frozen, she waited it out, wondering if it would erupt into the violent illness that had assaulted her last autumn. But no, this was different. This was something... beyond.

With a gasp she sat up, eyes unseeing.

Quinn had predicted it, but she had shrugged it off. When Quinn first applied the shield, she warned her to expect nothing special for a while, while her body and mind adjusted to the Aura. But once she began to sense it from within the protection of the shield... Quinn hadn't been explicit, saying it affected each of them differently. The difference was subtle, but real. She merely offered, based on the experience of her friends Willow and Bryar, that life seemed less vibrant without the Aura, less rich and meaningful.

And now this. The tingling sensation didn't increase but didn't lessen either. It wasn't unpleasant. But the newness, and the wonder, and fear of what might come next, seized her. Carefully, Constance lowered herself onto her bedding, afraid to sleep, afraid to remain awake and alone, reluctant to waken Agnes. The Aura. Impinging on her consciousness.

Outside the campfire's perimeter grew an assortment of low-lying weeds; a few rose above the level of the stones surrounding the fire. Constance lay staring at their silhouettes against the dying embers, giving them no thought, until... as her weary eyes lost focus, a flare seemed to emerge from the tip of one of the plants. Then another.

Fire! Her first thought, as she jerked back to full wakefulness, was that somehow the cinders had jumped their stone barrier. But no; as her vision sharpened, she saw no change to the starlit camp.

But that flare was no flight of fancy. She hadn't imagined it.

Constance shut her eyes tight against any further tricks by the loathed Aura and lay awake much of the night, trying to will herself to sleep, or at best to keep her newly awakened awareness at bay.

*

Agnes, the next morning, sensed a change and demanded details before breakfast. *All* the details, of which there were pitifully few when Constance recounted her night. But it appeared to be enough for Agnes, who locked her in a ferocious hug. "Ah, now at last you'll begin to see. And to learn," she added ominously.

Constance turned away, intent on eating the pan cake Agnes had cooked. The thing was flavorless but provided nourishment and energy; she had long since given up on the idea that food need be palatable.

"But where to begin?" Agnes said, as if she still had an audience. "That's the question. Where do we begin, eh?"

Later, as they plodded on toward the road to Stanstead, Agnes said, "Hands, of course. We start there. Just you wait, girlie. You'll be amazed."

The new, vague tingling never left her. She ignored it. As she walked wearily on, Constance had exactly one wish for the Aura, for it to transport her, instantly and with no effort, from the dusty track to the Motherhouse. Since even she knew that was beyond its known capacities, she kept the wish to herself and listened attentively, exploring the various exercises Agnes threw at her, supposedly simple things like stretching and contracting energy between her hands – energy she wasn't even aware of, despite Agnes's insistence it existed. Nothing much happened that she could detect, but at least the lessons made the walk less stultifying.

*

Life improved, from Constance's perspective, as they drew closer to the road that would lead them north to Stanstead. Settlements became more frequent, places to barter for food or arrange a place to sleep. Agnes's sash won them more than one bed, of questionable cleanliness but softer than the stony ground; and her Healing resulted in meals they hadn't had to slaughter first. Progress was slower, but definitely more comfortable.

What she saw, in settlement after settlement, did little to inspire a love of the land. With the protection of the shield, she had spent time in Cann, the village nearest the Adventurer's landing site, but hadn't considered that it might be one of the more prosperous hamlets in the Midland. Most had fewer than a hundred residents, and all featured buildings that were little more than shacks, and a hardscrabble existence eked out from the stony soil and encroaching forest. She conceded that the people were generally healthy, clean – 'clean' being a relative term – and fed. But she couldn't imagine what gave them reason to go on. Yet cheer was the predominant attitude.

"Tis full enough bellies, the approach of Solstice, and the prospect of a good growing season," Agnes explained. Lately Constance had begun questioning everything, in parallel with the odd things going on in her consciousness. Her hands were most affected. The constant tingling seemed to center in her palms, and occasionally her fingers emitted those odd shafts of light she had seen first among the weeds around a cookfire, many days behind them now. Agnes assured her the energy was there constantly, it was her perception that was at fault, and that was the point of the exercises.

They had reached Poole around noontime, a town at the intersection of the track that had brought them from Cann and the north-south road – so-called road, Constance thought as she viewed the dirt trace meandering through the gently undulating countryside. Wide enough for two carts to pass, with grass growing between the wheel ruts... well, she could hardly expect these people to know about paving, could she? It was easy to imagine this road would be as much a quagmire as the one they were quitting, when a storm rolled in.

The town featured a pounded dirt plaza and several buildings made of stone rather than rough-hewn wood. In the middle of a workday, few people were about, but Agnes, her sash broadcasting her role, was hailed by the elderly folk resting on benches against the sturdier buildings.

"My knee's swole to twice its size. Perhaps a poultice...?"

"'Ave ya somethin' as brings down a fever?"

"'Appen you'll check on my granddaughter, she's that big with child an' rail thin otherwise."

Agnes set up in the town's healing room, a ramshackle wooden building adjoining the plaza. "Poole's large enough to have Healers' quarters," she said curtly, already engaged in the task of organizing her supplies. "We'll have a bed here, and food, but we'll work for it." She extracted a stone vessel from a shelf and set Constance to pounding into a powder one of the herbs she had collected and dried in the course of their walk.

That night they dined on a tasty stew of some kind of fowl with vegetables. Over the next day, Constance got a crash course in small-town medicine, Midland style. Although there was little sickness, there were many injuries great and small, pregnancies smooth or complicated, arthritis – to be expected from a life spent working as these people worked, day in and out – and a handful of cows, donkeys, and goats needing treatment. The sun lingered long at this time of year, yet it was past dark when she and Agnes collapsed onto pallets at the back of the healing room.

"Is it always like this?" she asked into the quiet.

"Nay," Agnes said. "The first day a Healer's in town, everyone wants a part of her. Then life settles down. In the normal course of things, we'd linger here three or four days, but... well, we'll be taking a detour. I've a mind to look in on Willow and that new child of hers. And you might profit by meeting Joss, hailing as he does from your world."

Weariness made Constance fractious. "How much of a detour?"

"Oh, a day each way perhaps. They've a life unlike what you've seen so far. And probably unlike anything you'd want for yourself, but you need to learn the options. And Willow may help with your early training, she being a skilled Healer herself."

Constance sighed. She had heard that note of resolution in Agnes's voice before and knew there was little point in attempting to dissuade her.

"And Hallan being a vacation town, they do say that Solstice is great fun there. It'll be a holiday for you."

Constance's ears perked up; this was her first hint of a resort on this hardscrabble planet. But she made no comment, shifted on her pallet into a marginally more comfortable position, and closed her eyes. Sleep came easily.

Until she was awakened in the early dawn by an indistinct murmuring, as from a long distance away.

The voice stopped, but not fifteen minutes later – by her reckoning, which was imprecise because on Quinn's recommendation she had left her comm, with its chrono, at the Adventurer – it picked up again. This time she thought it might be a man, but again it was much too distant for her to pinpoint the location or distinguish the words.

A mind can only handle so many unexplainable phenomena before it shuts down. "White noise," she muttered, and from sheer exhaustion sank once again into sleep.

Chapter 5

The north-south road snaked through rolling hills, vivid green pastures, and ripening crops. They had spent two full days in Boone after all, then set off on their own, the caravan having long since departed north. Constance and Agnes spent their first night in a much smaller town, which featured a simple, one-room hut for guest accommodation. When they entered, they found a pack already situated on one of the two pallets.

"Travelers' accommodation," Agnes said with satisfaction. "Not just for Healers. Whoever's here, we share. Looks like we'll have entertainment tonight."

Constance, nonplussed to find only one spare bed, asked, "How do you know?"

Agnes flicked a ribbon of fabric on the pack. "Red. That's a Bard."

And a Bard, Constance learned that evening, meant news, music and dance, acrobatics. She vaguely remembered Quinn's friend Bryar passing through Cann, but that had been long before she had been able to leave the Adventurer, so this young woman's performance would be her first experience.

And what a performance it turned out to be. The recitation of some long saga didn't interest her much, but when the girl picked up a lute-like instrument and began to sing, she found herself lost in the clear notes, the haunting melody. Agnes had to shake her arm to bring her back to reality when the performance ended.

That night, despite making a bed of a thin pallet on the floor, Constance slept soundly.

Early the next day, she and Agnes left the main road, turning onto a track running east toward the hills that had dominated the horizon. The trail was wide and well demarked, which was a relief; Constance had dreaded a one-person track with questionable footing.

"Do many people take holidays?" she asked.

Agnes grinned. "Mostly those within a few days' travel of some resting spot or other," she said. "There are hot springs at Hallan, so sometimes the hedge healers send patients. It's a pleasant town, small but fore-thinking. We'll get a room in the dormitory, hopefully."

Constance had raised a heel blister – another one; the things had contributed to making her walk a misery. "How far?"

"By tonight, I expect."

It became evident, as the light faded that evening, that Agnes was determined to make it to Hallan Hot Springs before they stopped.

The dormitory proved to be a motel-like building stretching along the shores of a lake that reflected a blazing sunset behind them. The place smelled of sulfur, but it wasn't overpowering. Constance stood in the doorway and laughed at herself with a tinge of bitterness. She had expected a Terran-style resort? Grimly, she surveyed her surroundings. On the far wall, a small, unglazed window looked out over the lake. The room contained two cots, shelves for their belongings, and a stand holding a pitcher and basin. Beside each cot stood a covered pottery basin. Stooping, Constance raised a lid; one sniff told her the purpose of the vessel.

She picked a cot at random and sat on it to pull off her boots and damp socks, sighing with relief as she wiggled her toes.

Agnes, ever efficient, tossed Constance's boots in a corner, clucked over her blister, and marched them both to the dining hall, which even at the late hour was bustling. Too tired to be other than obedient, Constance forced down a lentil dish. After finishing with a passable custard, they wandered to a crowded wooden platform built out over the lake

Agnes shooed away a gaggle of children, clearing a space, then said, "Get your foot into the water. It'll do more than my salves to soothe your sores."

Exhausted yet again, she settled on the edge of the platform, surrounded by holidaymakers, many of whom were exhibiting the joyous effects of alcohol consumption, and dangled her feet in the lake. It was warm, unnaturally so. But other than a little gasp of surprise, she made no comment, merely leaned back on her elbows, ignored her neighbors, and let her feet drink in the rich, sulfurous water.

*

The next morning, after another surprisingly good sleep, Constance willingly trotted out of town and uphill after Agnes, to a solitary cabin overlooking a perched lake. A woman with short, cornsilk hair stood in the open doorway watching them come. As they surmounted the last incline, she called, "Agnes!"

"Willow, my dear." The two embraced briefly, then studied each other, more assessment than connection.

"This trip has been hard for you."

"You're plumper than I've ever seen you. And my dear... your hair."

Willow blushed. "The weight feels good in a way. Maternal. As for the hair...." She shrugged. "Joss was pretty upset, but it'll grow back. Right now, it's just too much to deal with." She turned to Constance, hands extended. "Welcome."

Constance nodded and accepted the hands which, belying the woman's gentle appearance, were clean but work roughened.

"Constance," Agnes introduced her. "One of the new crop of Terrans, as I'm sure you've heard. I thought she should meet you before she sets out to be a Healer herself." She veered toward a flat, grassy area across the track from the cabin. "We're both worn from our travels. Give us a bit to recover, and we'll help out. Where's the baby?"

"Asleep, thank the Aura. He's good, though. Not too fussy at all. Sit," she continued. "I'll bring a tisane and some cakes. I'm not much at baking," she told Constance, "but there'll be Solstice treats in the market by tomorrow."

"Joss?" Agnes asked as she sank to the grass.

"Playing midwife in the barns. He should be home late afternoon."

The other woman's tone of voice rattled Constance. Despite her primitive cabin and near threadbare tunic, she radiated satisfaction. Probably the effect of new motherhood... but Constance didn't remember anything like this level of content after she had Omar. In fact, it seemed she and Pierre, sleep deprived, had done nothing but fight.

Omar. Her son. Over twelve years old now, if... She yanked her thoughts back to the present. Of course he was all right. By now he would be enjoying preteen activities at school, maybe starting to notice girls...

With a jolt she realized she no longer even knew what season it was back on Terra. And she would never know if Omar had a bright future ahead, or any future at all.

*

They settled on the flat, grassy space outside the cottage. Willow disappeared into the cabin, emerging with a rough plate holding pan cakes and jam on one arm, a sleepy, fussy baby and a rag on the other. She calmly nursed the child while she and Agnes chatted about people and events Constance had no knowledge of. Aware that she had been hustled away from the town before breakfast, she accepted a pan cake. It was made of a coarse ground meal and was edible with jam, just.

After they had eaten, Willow handed the baby to Agnes and offered the rag to Constance. It proved to be one of the shapeless tunics everyone wore. "Here," she said. "If you're anything like Joss and Kiril, you'll be more comfortable bathing with clothing on. Can you swim?"

Constance stared for a second while her brain struggled to catch up. "A little," she replied. Swimming wasn't considered a necessary skill in a world where all water was closely guarded, but she had made a couple of vacation trips to the sea; part of the holiday package had included swimming lessons. Still...

"You'll like this, then. Don't worry, it's shallow for quite a way out. I imagine you'll feel better once you've had a chance to bathe and wash your hair. I know it's the first thing I always want to do when I've been traveling. Go on, just follow the trail. And here's soap." She handed an orange bar to Constance, who stood and looked toward the lake. Doubtfully, she accepted the tunic.

"One other thing," Willow said. "It's heated, warmer than the lake in Hallan. There's a hot spring out in the middle. Trust me, you'll like it."

"Thanks. You're right, I need a bath."

"We'll join you in a little bit," Agnes said from her place on the grass, showing no inclination to move from the spot. Idly she shifted the baby onto her shoulder and patted his back.

Willow gave Constance a little shove, then settled next to Agnes. As Constance made her way toward the lake, she could hear them cooing at the baby.

Willow was right, she thought a few minutes later when, after ducking behind a bush to change into the sleeveless short tunic, she sank into the water. Despite the warmth of the morning, the heated water was pure bliss. It had been at least a couple of weeks since she had washed her hair, and her elbows were engrained with grime that hasty washes with a basin of cold water had been helpless to remove. Mustering courage and all she could remember from those years-ago lessons, she briefly ducked under the water, then grappled blindly for the bar of soap waiting on the bank and began the deliberate, blissful process of removing nearly sixty days of filth.

Agnes and Willow appeared on the little beach fronting the lake before she was ready to get out. Agnes stripped down and swam toward the middle of the lake, while Willow dangled the baby in the water. Content for the first time in what felt like forever, Constance floated on her back, watching the mare's tails drifting across the sky.

*

Two days later, alert and refreshed, Constance wandered the crowds in Hallan for Summer Solstice. This marked her first appearance wearing the light linen tunic that formed the basis of the Midlands' summer wardrobe, and she had to admit it was cool and comfortable. The local sandals, on the other hand, would take some getting used to.

The mysterious, distant voices no longer troubled her; she heard them only sporadically and was learning to ignore them. Agnes and Willow were off down a side street in the healing rooms, holding a clinic. Joss, the man from Terra, walked beside her. The baby rode on his chest in a sling; one of his big hands was always on the child.

Nothing, she thought, like Kiril.

She had come to know the other Terran from that ill-fated exploration pod, because he had turned up at the Adventurer, and from what Quinn said he was unlikely to leave again. He was wiry, edgy, opinionated, and very much in command of his world, whereas Joss, large and tanned with curly hair pulled back in a ponytail and an Aura-given ability to read animals, was a man of few words, at peace with his life and himself.

"I remember my first Solstice," he said now. "We were in Stanstead, and Kiril was still recovering from the crash. Bigger party than this one, better beer. I spent a lot of time alone in the woods that day. It's overwhelming, coming into a new culture."

His Northam accent tinged his speech, different from the one she had grown up with in Eurocorp but still a welcome taste of home. She nodded. "Finding your place."

"Easier for me than for Kiril," Joss said. They were strolling along the lakefront. Constance munched a fruit pastry. Joss held a mug of the local beer, but one sip had been enough for her to revert to sulfur-tinged water. "Northam didn't have the agricultural base we have here, or if they did, I never saw it. Technology's fine, but this is a better fit."

Joss, she knew, had spent most of the last two days with the cows and sheep. Just the day before, she had watched him feed a kid from a makeshift bottle, cradling the tiny orphan. He and Willow had an ideal life, she reckoned, work they loved in a community that valued them.

And the baby. They had named the child Kiril.

"Because he needs a legacy, too," Willow had said when Constance finally held the baby for the first time. "They won't have children, you know. There's too much uncertainty about that *thing* that's got its grip on him. He makes her happy," she continued with sadness in her eyes, speaking of Kiril and her close friend Quinn, "but I worry how long he'll be able to fight the demon off."

Or even stay alive. No one had said it, but Constance sensed the thought hovering in the air around them. On the other hand, Willow's man seemed destined to go on for a long time. Constance could imagine him turning his hand to whatever the town needed, whether it was in the barns or repairs to their so-called tourist infrastructure.

Music had started on the square, and most people moved in that direction. By unspoken agreement, she and Joss remained on the sidelines. They settled on one of the log benches fronting the lake and watched the dancing.

He chuckled. "Willow's tried to get me out there once or twice. Trust me, I'm safer with the cows."

Constance swallowed the last bite of her pastry and leaned back on her hands, lifting her face to the sky. The day was clear, almost without wind, and getting hotter by the minute. And she... well, it had been a long time since she had felt this level of content. Daily baths in the lake, decent food, and solid sleep had worked wonders.

"You're heading for the Motherhouse," Joss stated.

Her good mood evaporated. The mysterious, cold Motherhouse... why did she think of it as cold? Because it was further north, in the hills? Because its buildings were stone? Whatever, she shivered.

Joss chuckled. "It won't be so bad. Looking back, I guess it is primitive by Terran standards, but the food's great, the people support each other, and the training... trust me, it makes a difference. I'd have been a lot less freaked out at first if I'd had some background. This whole Aura thing is spooky."

"Still? But you've been here a couple of years now."

The baby grizzled. Joss's attention turned immediately and fully to his child, rubbing his back and humming what might be a lullaby, until little Kiril slept again.

Then he picked up the conversation as if there had been no interruption. "We're from technological societies. Do you think we'll ever *not* find the Aura spooky? The things the Weavers can do with it, and when suddenly you realize you can make something new happen yourself, just by using simple techniques.... Willow says you're strong in Entrée?"

"So they say." Constance longed to deflect the conversation, uncomfortable still with the weave encompassing her head, the simple magicks Agnes had tried to teach her as they walked.

"You'll adjust. And there's no reason you have to become a Weaver, although if you're as strong as Willow hears you are, you'd probably regret it forever if you don't. But when I started hearing the cows' thoughts... well, it wasn't fun. I found people I trusted to talk to, then I spent half a year training."

She smiled. "And saved a few sheep along the way?" She had heard about Joss from Quinn.

He grinned. "A few. But that first Solstice was tough. I was just beginning to sense the animals. Hell, until then I hadn't ever seen a cow, and suddenly I was in their minds. Talk about freaked out.

"It was worse for Kiril," he continued, reflecting, his eyes focused somewhere in the past, his hand gently guarding his son's head. "He was helpless with a broken leg, and none of this made sense to him. I'm glad he's where he is, but sometimes I miss him. Having someone around who knows where we came from...." A shrug accompanied by a wry grin told her the topic was closed. "This is home now. I wouldn't go back if we could. If there's anything to go back to. From what you've said, there isn't."

He couldn't know how his words pierced her. He couldn't know about Omar, left behind on Terra. "I'm wearing out," she said. "Too much sun and noise. I think I'll go lie down for a while."

"I get that. I'm going to drag Willow out of her clinic. She needs to give herself a break."

They parted, Joss shambling amiably into the village to find his woman. Constance made her way to the quiet and privacy of her room and collapsed on her bed. The heartache of losing Omar would never leave her, but at least she could mourn in private.

Chapter 6

Two days after Solstice, while the town of Hallan nursed aching heads and sore feet from the revels, Constance joined Willow and Agnes in the healing rooms. She would have been just as happy, truth to tell, wandering the lake shore; it felt like forever since the hours were her own, to use for whatever purpose she chose. But if she was to be a Healer, Agnes decreed, it was time she became an active apprentice.

"We need water," Willow called out. "And arnica." She was bent over a lad with a nasty, swollen bruise on his foot.

Water was easy; the healing room kept a cask of pre-boiled, purified water at the ready. Arnica... for what felt like the hundredth time that day, Constance stood in front of the racks of dried herbs. Although the language was sufficiently similar to her own that comprehension was rarely a problem, the writing on the handwritten labels was both faded and difficult to interpret.

"Top shelf, third from the left," Willow called without looking up. "Have you ever made a poultice?"

No, she hadn't. To be honest with herself if not with the two dedicated Healers working with her, she didn't much want to. She missed the quietly humming machines and chemical medicines from sterile facilities she was used to on Terra.

And she longed to dodge the smell emanating from the plant concoctions they used. Agnes and Willow appeared to thrive on it, taking deep breaths occasionally as if they couldn't get enough of the aroma. To Constance it smelled... not unpleasant, but not sanitary. Primitive.

The new reality. How many reminders would she need before it became familiar? In the meantime, she would learn to make the poultice.

Just as she began to apply the hot, wet herbs to the boy's bruised foot, the ground shifted. Agnes and Willow both looked up. Their eyes met. By common accord they lifted the boy from the examining table and installed him under it. "Come on," Agnes prodded, "you've been in quakes before. Get to safety."

The rolling became a severe jolt, taking Constance's feet from under her. She fell, grazing her knee, and dove for the safety of the space under the heavy table as, with a roar, the land lifted and tossed under her... and again, and again. She and Willow gripped the table's legs while Agnes held and partially covered the boy between them.

It was minutes later when Willow judged it safe to emerge from their tiny shelter where they lay like sardines while the building bucked and shook. The room, Constance observed when she risked standing on wobbly legs, was a mess. Dust from the rough-hewn walls covered everything, and a couple of the pottery containers of herbs had fallen, despite the safety rails holding them in place. Her poultice mixture was a greenish splat on the floor. From outside she heard shouts.

Willow darted to the door and looked around, then came back to the boy, whom Agnes was assisting onto the table. "That was a bad one," she said to him. "I think we're going to have more urgent need of the healing room than your foot. Take this." She used a scrap of fabric to package more of the arnica. "Take it home and get your mum to poultice it. She'll know how. *Not* a tisane. Can you remember?"

"Yes'm." Seemingly none the worse for wear, the boy hopped off the table one-legged and took off, hobbling. Constance couldn't help but observe that the Healers and the boy all showed more composure than she did in the face of the quake.

"If the mother could have done it, why was he here?" Constance asked.

Agnes gave her a look that told her she had completely missed the point of half the lessons that had made their long walk more interesting. "His mum hasn't the Aura. It'll work, but this would have worked better."

Of course. The Aura. Always the Aura.

"As well," Willow added, "arnica's not a medicine we like to have loose in the town. I know his mother and trust her good sense, but it's dangerous for general usage."

Her shaking legs and clenched insides weren't going to get the respite they demanded. Villagers began to appear at the door of the healing room, and for the rest of the day Constance had no time to contemplate the ways the Aura improved medical treatment. Willow and Agnes, helped by a woman named Jana, the village healer, calmly triaged and treated everything from a cut finger to severe concussion and broken bones, while Constance ran errands, boiled water, retrieved herbs, and once or twice assisted in restraining a person during a painful treatment.

Finally, nearing sunset, she and Jana were released to visit the dining hall and otherwise get on with their lives. All three healers, two with these special, spooky abilities and one without, seemed satisfied. Jana put a dab of an ointment in Constance's palm as they left and took one for herself. "This will feel good. Your hands must be chapped after all the washing."

Constance nodded and massaged in the cream. It did feel good.

They made their way to the dining hall. Cooking and serving had been shifted outdoors on the plaza until the large structure could be cleaned and confirmed safe. As she perched on one of the lakefront benches to eat her meal of steamed fish and vegetables, she mulled over her new predicament. If she resented the work she had undertaken to learn, what hope was there for her to ever find satisfaction in being a Healer on this benighted planet?

The voices kept Constance up that night. They still weren't clear, more like a faraway echo, the words indistinct. But she sensed an urgency underlying the murmur, one that set her nerves on edge and disrupted her sleep. Much-needed sleep, because every medic-trained instinct told her they were far from finished with the aftermath of the quake.

*

Agnes joined her for breakfast by the lake. She seemed preoccupied. "The quake struck harder further north," she said as she sat, holding a large bowl of porridge. "Word from Stanstead isn't good."

"Stanstead... isn't that where we're going?"

Agnes shoved a heaping spoonful of the glutinous stuff into her mouth. After she swallowed, she continued. "I'd planned to take you the shorter route, direct from Hallan to the Motherhouse. It's scenic, but more remote. We'd probably not see a soul. But now we'll likely be diverted." Another spoonful disappeared into her mouth. She actually seemed to enjoy it.

Constance ate most of her scrambled egg before she replied. "I still don't understand how you know all this."

Agnes studied her and frowned. Nothing ever was as it appeared to be, between Agnes and the Aura, and Constance worried about how much she saw beyond the obvious. "As you must know by now,' she said with visible impatience, "it's possible to exchange information. Most Weavers can at least receive a simple message, but only a few can transmit. Dal's in Stanstead, he was in touch with the Motherhouse last night. From there, Arwen and Dorcas sent out word to all of us close to the town. As for how...." She shrugged. "Best let the experts explain. I can't."

"I see." She knew without further consideration, although her heart sank into her stomach, that the voices she heard were Weavers speaking through the Aura. And she would wager they'd want to train her to hear them clearly, probably even become one of the voices herself.

Constance put down the toasted bread she had used to convey her egg to her mouth and looked around. The dining hall was doing a brisk business. Staff had been up all night, she speculated, cleaning, although most still preferred to eat outdoors. The day promised to be clear and hot; already the sun created a sparkling trail across the lake. It was still early enough that a whole chorus of birds clamored in the bushes outside. So normal. So... not spooky. But the way the Aura had attacked her, and the voices, and the hint of a glow of light she had been able to generate as they walked...

Spooky was the new normal. Get used to it, she lectured herself, then finished her egg and risked a cup of caff, the high-octane, caffeinated beverage brewed from a root that the entire civilization was addicted to. At least the stuff was served in tiny mugs, so she didn't have to choke down very much of it. The caffeine blast would help her get through the morning.

*

The voices hovered on the edge of her consciousness for two more days, days that found Constance spending hours in the healing room with one or another of the three healers in town, studying their techniques of tisane and poultice, aroma and salve. But there was free time, too; the other women seemed to sense her longing for solitude or, even more, something familiar to anchor her. Hallan proved to be a good place to recover from her trek, with its warm lake, trails that led through fields and copses, and peacefulness.

Then she woke following a restless night to find Agnes shoving her meager possessions into her pack. "You're awake," she pronounced. "Good. We need to move. Things have gone from bad to worse in Stanstead, and we're needed."

"How worse?" Still groggy, Constance swung her legs from her pallet and squinted at the other woman.

"Contamination of their well, Dal thinks. Not injury now, but sickness. We'll make time for breakfast before we leave. With luck, we can get some travel rations."

By then Constance was on her feet, pulling her limited possessions from shelves onto her bed for folding and packing. "So, we're not going to the Motherhouse?"

"No time. I'll meet you in the dining hall. Hurry."

Constance spared a second to watch Agnes's back as she strode from the room, pulling her rolling pack behind her, then sighed. Once again, her life was not her own. She finished her own packing and followed.

Chapter 7

The walk to Stanstead from Hallan generally required about four and a half days. Agnes was determined to accomplish it in three. There had been no time to bid farewell to Willow and Joss, whose cabin lay on the other track, the one leading directly to the Motherhouse. Constance almost thanked the fierce cramp she developed in her right calf after the first day's forced march; it meant she could move more slowly, chewing on the end of a stick Agnes handed her. It left a nasty taste but did reduce the pain somewhat.

No one, she noticed as they settled into the common rooms of wayhouses along the road, was going in their direction. One day out of Stanstead, they had been unable to find a room in the small village Agnes designated for their final resting place on the route, because of refugees from the town.

"Things must be worse than I imagined," Constance said as they joined a small camp of fellow travelers in a field and spread their bedrolls near their cook fire. She dropped onto her bedding and massaged her leg, which wasn't so bad as to hinder her movements now, but still twinged occasionally.

"Sleep well," Agnes muttered. "If I know Dal – and I do – we won't have an instant's rest after tomorrow. I just hope the Healers' lodge isn't full. At least it'll be sanitary. And it has its own well, so we'll have safe water, barring contamination underground. That's earthquakes for you," she grumbled.

Constance placed their pot of water on the fire to heat as she thought about what they would face tomorrow. As a medic, someone frequently in contact with extraterrestrial explorers, she had kept her vaccinations up to date. Uneasily, she suspected that gift from Terra might come in handy in the next few days.

*

Stanstead proved to be a town of solid buildings, a sensible municipal layout, and utter chaos.

Except...

"Where is everyone?" Constance found herself whispering as she and Agnes walked the silent streets toward the center of the town.

Agnes turned off the main road to the right, onto a smaller track that took them through... the suburbs, Constance thought with a hint of grim humor. Whitewashed walls, where they still stood, framed strips of garden as they passed building after building, most of them small, no more than one or two rooms. They dodged fallen masonry as they pushed closer to the center of the town.

So this was Stanstead. "It's smaller than I expected," Constance said, but she wasn't really looking around. Her focus was on the road, avoiding the rubble.

"Most live in the lodges." Constance caught the anxiety underlying the older woman's brief words.

As they turned to the left, Agnes released a sigh of relief. "There," she said, nodding. "The

Healers' lodge." Ahead of them stood a two-story building, noticeably larger than the others they had passed. It formed an el around a well-tended garden, with a smaller, one-story building comprising the short side of the el. Behind the smaller building, Constance caught a glimpse of a paved square. And she realized where the people were.

She left Agnes opening the gate to the garden courtyard and walked to the corner of the smaller building, hoping against hope that first glimpse had been in error.

Row upon row of pallets filled the square. The smell of feces was overwhelming, as were the sounds of moaning, crying, screaming... whimpering... falling silent. She could almost hear the silence of those who no longer cried. There must be... she counted rows, did a quick multiplication... a couple hundred people lying on the ground.

Several figures moved among the pallets. Others sat on the stone paving, bathing foreheads, holding hands.

What on earth would they do when it rained?

Agnes joined her. "Dal's there," she said, nodding toward a man just straightening up from one of the pallets. He shook his head and spoke briefly to the person kneeling at his feet. Then he moved on down the line. Even from across the plaza, Constance could see the slump in his shoulders, his weariness.

Agnes continued, "Over there's Cynth. I don't see any other Healers, though. Let's get our room and see what's needed."

Constance stood rooted, gazing at the plaza with a kind of uncomprehending horror. What were they contending with? Some kind of intestinal bug, like dysentery? Cholera? Neither had appeared in Eurocorp during her lifetime, so she had no experience of them. How could they possibly maintain anything approaching sanitary conditions? The plaza smelled like one giant latrine.

Agnes tugged on her sleeve and jerked her head toward the building behind them. Constance was just turning away when the man called Dal noticed them and waved a hand. Agnes returned the salutation and followed Constance away from the appalling view.

*

A day later, Constance had a much better idea of what they were facing – an epidemic of bloody diarrhea. Numerous dead, even more weak to incapacitation after the flux ran its course, which according to Cynth happened after three or four days – if the patient lasted that long. A team had scoured the lodges and private houses to be sure no one was suffering alone, but Constance had to wonder if they were any better on the plaza. Makeshift tents had been set up as defense against the sun, but the entire treatment team worried about rain, which was overdue. To further complicate things, aftershocks from the quake rolled through the town daily. The sounds of illness were punctuated by the occasional crash as another wall toppled.

Mercifully, the municipal building and the food hall remained stable. That first evening, after stilted introductions, she had challenged Dal. "When there's shelter, why aren't these people under it?"

He had looked down his nose at her, but even through her indignation she could see the exhaustion behind his eyes. "First, to support those who aren't sick. Second, a building could still come down. Anything else?"

When she was silent, he had turned on his heel and left her standing.

The dead were taken away. Constance didn't have the heart to ask where they were buried.

As well, she labored under an instant, intractable dislike for her new boss. Dal was distant, autocratic, dictatorial... adjectives piled up as she worked her way along one of the aisles between pallets.

"What do you expect?" Agnes barked at her. "He's in charge here. And look what he's up against."

"I know." It had only been a day, and already Constance wondered how long it had been since she had slept. She longed to call in at the food hall – not for the food, it was hard to maintain an appetite given the smell, but to rest, however briefly, out of the sun – but didn't dare. Work till you drop, she thought grimly. And then pick yourself up and do it again.

*

The well was boarded up, but still the sick arrived at the makeshift, outdoor hospital. The well at the Healers' lodge couldn't produce sufficient flow, so Constance was sent via donkey cart an hour out of town to carry buckets of water from a non-contaminated well. Back in Stanstead, Agnes gave her a blitz course in the chosen remedy and set her to work in the Healers' workroom, making a nasty drink from a mix of lookalike dried herbs. Without faith in its efficacy, she dutifully performed the hands-on incantation Agnes assigned her to boost the power of the herbs. She ferried the liquid to the three Healers, washed a constant stream of mugs, and when those tasks were up to date, joined the others in trying to get the liquid down the throats of the ailing.

A child died. Not in her arms, but near enough. Constance, shaken, ignored the others' disapproval and hid out in the room in the Healers' lodge she shared with Agnes, until she was calm enough to go back out into the scene of devastation.

Chapter 8

Meade sighed and kicked at the grass in the island between wheel ruts as she and Lamar drew closer to Stanstead. He walked well ahead of her, keeping his own counsel, while Meade dragged behind, wrestling with the situation, and even more with herself. Cheerful was as far from her mood as she had ever experienced.

Although the Motherhouse was shielded by centuries of Weavings, the damage from the earthquake was considerable. The high bank of the river to the east of the complex had collapsed in numerous places, in one case creating a cavernous gash in the landscape and carrying away a couple of stone outbuildings.

Worse, two apprentices had disappeared from the riverside trail, and were presumed lost in the maelstrom the river had become from the added debris. Even Bryar, noted for his fearlessness in the water, was unable to venture into the mad torrent in search of them.

One or two of the precious glass windows had cracked, something that had never happened before, and internal damage was extensive. Meade's desk had been overturned, one leg broken, sending ink over everything, and her bed had chased across the floor to block the door. She had been in the dining hall when the quake struck; it took assistance from two other Healers, one of them Lamar, to get into her room.

The Motherhouse would mend. From what she heard, she wasn't so sure Stanstead would. And, on a purely selfish note, the last thing she wanted at this moment was this four-day walk, followed by an epidemic requiring her Healing. Dal was well known for giving no quarter and working everyone to the bone, himself included, when the need arose.

And so, because she was fully aware of her reputation as a perpetually sunny, positive person, her present funk proved as much alarming as annoying. Where had her optimism gone?

Lamar was in his late twenties, an experienced, although still young, Healer. He was lean and fit. The sun had bleached his hair into a shifting field of browns and golds. With a touch of her usual irreverence, she reflected that if she had to trail behind somebody, he wasn't at all a bad specimen. But the thought cheered her for only a moment. She had another day and a half to plod through. The sun was at its hottest, and who could predict what awaited her at the end of the trek? She had only the scanty information Dal had transmitted; few Healers were good at sending messages through the Aura.

"Wait up," she called as Lamar rounded a bend and disappeared.

He obediently, but not happily, retraced his steps. "You okay?"

Catching the impatience in his tone, she debated saying nothing. But after all, you couldn't travel four days on foot with another Weaver without exercising courtesy, as a bare minimum.

"Well enough. I'm just sick of being on the road. And feeling... worried, I guess."

Lamar fell in beside her, moderating his pace. "No blisters? Shin splints?"

"No, nothing like that. It's just... it could be bad."

"Will be, from what little Dal said. Bad enough to damage the Motherhouse. Did you know there are cracks in the ceiling of the main healing room?"

"I know. Lamar..."

"Hmm?" She sensed his attention wasn't on her, but on the road, the destination, their next meal. To him she was merely an old, tired Healer he had been saddled with.

No, dammit. Stop that. She wasn't old, no more than fifteen years Lamar's senior, and if she was tired, she refused to show it. She had set a good pace so far and wasn't flagging, physically. "It's going to be a rough assignment."

He shrugged. "There'll be food and a place to sleep. We'll be okay."

"Stanstead used to be lovely. All those white buildings."

"It'll be rebuilt."

"Dal thinks the problem is the well. If it's contaminated..."

A note of impatience crept into his voice. "Then the town may not be rebuilt the way we think. Too many people live there for it to disappear. Give it a rest, Meade. You're getting on my nerves."

"Sorry." Cocky young whelp. But he was right. Really, there was no need to belabor the potential horrors ahead.

"Look, if you don't mind, I'd rather move on. I'll wait for you at the camp."

"Sure, go ahead." And she would arrive alone at the waysite they all knew, one day's walk from Stanstead. At that moment, it felt as if everything she did, she was forced to do alone. She was barely home after the long journey, all the way to the western ocean and back, to dispose of the power cell, occasionally with a caravan or another Weaver but mostly on her own. Once again her mood plummeted. She used to love being a Healer, but now?

With a weariness stemming from her heart rather than her legs, she hauled herself forward toward the waysite, purposely not thinking about the state of things ahead.

Chapter 9

Incongruously, it was a beautiful evening in Stanstead. The worst of the heat had died away, while a gentle breeze encouraged some of the stench to leave the plaza. For once, moaning wasn't the predominant sound. After a full day, plus most of the preceding night, of unrelenting toil, Constance could appreciate the quiet. Hushed conversation surrounded her as she sat slumped at a table in the dining hall, stirring fresh, raw milk into a bowl of the eternal porridge, the only food currently on offer.

She had gone back to the Healers' lodge to wash and change, dumping her soiled clothing in the hamper to be boiled. A thorough hand scrubbing, a quick splash of water on her face from the basin in her room, a tug of her brush – which she had brought from the Adventurer – and now here she was, hoping to get a partial night's sleep at least before another day of trekking to the safe well, simmering tisanes, fighting her gag reflex as she washed bodies soiled by their own waste, applying rags to foreheads, and helping those stricken choke down the nasty herbal remedies.

Dal sank into the chair across the table, jolting her out of a reverie.

Up close, she could see the depth of the dark shadows under his eyes. Although she hadn't known him prior to the catastrophe in Stanstead, she sensed the ubiquitous tunic and trousers masked a new gauntness.

Their eyes met for an instant, then he closed his. "By the Aura," he said, "I almost envy those poor souls out there. At least they're lying down."

Her professional experience kicked in. "You're going to be one of them if you don't rest."

"I know. But how do we stop, when...." He gestured toward the plaza, sighed, and attacked his porridge. The grimace accompanying his first bite confirmed for Constance that a few people, at least, shared her opinion of the stuff.

"We're on top of it," she said. "The numbers are down."

He swallowed. "But may not stay that way, not with the contamination spreading. There must be an underground connection to the main well. I estimate Stanstead's population will drop by a quarter before it's done. I've seen influenza and the occasional corruption of drinking water, but this is beyond belief. At least when Meade and Lamar get here, we'll have more hands. Any time now, I hope."

Meade and Lamar must be Healers, Constance concluded, and was vaguely flattered that Dal now considered her enough a part of his team he hadn't felt the need to elaborate.

Which was dumb. She had been a lot of things in the last few days – general dogsbody came closer to the mark – but Healer? Hardly.

"You've done more than you realize," Dal said, reading her thoughts. By now she didn't even speculate how he did it. "Even with your lack of training, you've been adding Auric energy to the water. Faint, but present. It makes a difference."

They ate in silence for a few minutes, although they could have talked about the work to board up the town's wells, the numbers of dead, the state of the crops and livestock... Constance had heard all these things discussed around her by the healthy residents of the town.

He finished before she did. As he stood, he asked, "How's the shield holding?"

The shield? It took a moment for her mind to catch up. For days, maybe weeks, she had scarcely noticed the Auric barrier Quinn had woven so carefully. Turning her awareness inward, she tried to find the faint pressure on her head.

"I don't know," she said finally, puzzled. "I guess I'm used to it. I can't sense it."

Dal stepped behind her and placed his hands on her head, without permission. She almost jerked away before remembering, in some far-off, exhausted part of her brain, that customs were different here.

"You don't sense it because it's barely there anymore," he said as he lifted his hands. "Probably it's been worn off by the demands on you in the last few days. Headaches?"

"No." If it was gone, she would really become one of *them*, these strangely endowed Weavers, no longer able to rely on the artificial barrier to keep herself separate.

"Good. Now, you have time before sunset, so I want you to get away for a while. Head west, the road crosses a ford at a bathing beach. Just be sure not to get any contaminated clothing in the river. People downstream use it." Then, effectively removing any personal concern for her welfare from his dictate, he added, "I need the team at top form. No one's going to take care of you if you collapse."

Fair enough. He had at least acknowledged her value and professionalism.

After Dal left, Constance stirred the gooey remains of the porridge, mulling things over. As a medic, she knew her place was on the plaza, easing as best she could the suffering around her. But she didn't feel like a medic anymore....

She jolted upright. The thought wasn't new, but it still had the power to agitate. If she wasn't a medic, what was she? Dropping her bowl at the hatch, she fled out into the comfort of twilight.

Chapter 10

Slowed by a catastrophe involving a sandal – his, not hers – Meade and Lamar didn't arrive in Stanstead until close to sunset. Footsore and irritable, appalled by the scene on the plaza, Meade stood in the upstairs hall of the Healers' lodge and realized that all three rooms were spoken for. She had hoped for privacy, but it wasn't to be. Two rooms appeared to have only one occupant, so she dumped her pack in the less pristine one, supposedly Cynth's. Lamar slouched on down the hall; he would have to share an obsessively immaculate space with Dal, a fate Meade didn't envy him at the moment. Then she headed off in search of food.

Dal spotted her, of course. She was no more than halfway around the plaza, holding her breath and turning her eyes away, when she heard her name, then rapid footsteps.

"Thank the Aura. It's good to see you, Meade."

"You too. But listen...." Better she say her piece before Dal set her to work, oblivious to her need for food and sleep. "I can't start right now. I'm dead on my feet."

Dal glanced at the ranks of pallets and sighed. "The dining hall's working on limited rations while we try to figure out how far the contamination's spread. Get yourself sorted out, and plan to take the early morning shift."

Meade glanced toward the dining hall, but her sense of duty prevailed. "Tell me about it. The transmission wasn't clear."

He ran his fingers through his short hair. On closer inspection, she had never seen Dal so disheveled, so frankly *dirty*, as he was now. Nor had she ever seen such severe markers of fatigue on his face, his posture. "We were getting on top of it," he said. "But it's spreading. The neighborhood wells are boarded up now. Little Hutt has the closest safe water, so we're running convoys."

"Boiling doesn't work? Maybe weave a template of some sort?"

"No time for experimenting with templates, and clothes are boiled, but we're reluctant to gamble on boiling for consumption. Constance makes two or three trips a day for water, and Marla's organized a rota for the town. For the first few days it wasn't an issue, then suddenly—"

He broke off, biting his lower lip as he turned to look at the helpless bodies on the plaza. "We've forbidden the kids to come, or people with kids to care for. There's a suggestion it may be contagious. We've been adamant about hygiene, despite what it looks like, but it's hard to enforce."

Meade produced a rare oath just as Lamar joined them. "Where do you need me?" he asked with no greeting at all.

"Same as Meade. Dining hall, then rest. The early morning shift begins before dawn, so someone will wake you. Agnes will be senior on that shift."

"Looks like a mess."

"It is," Dal replied shortly. "Best you can do right now is get ready for tomorrow. We're evacuating," he added, nodding toward the clouds amassing above the hills to the east. "We've been lucky so far, but the rain isn't going to hold off forever. The townspeople are clearing out one of the barns." He shuddered, no doubt thinking about the potential for further infection in a far from sterile environment, then took a deep breath and turned away, plunging into the maze of pallets, hastily erected sunshades, and anguish.

"You're heading to the dining hall?" Lamar asked.

"Hopefully, they'll have some food. It's long past supper."

"One of the locals told me there are no set hours anymore. People just eat when they can. Everything's fallen apart. Food, milking the cows—"

"And now we're moving everyone to a barn? Even with the cleanest cows in the world..." She turned away, heading for the dining hall.

"Guess we'll find out." Lamar followed her. Neither of them had anything more to say.

*

The day's heat had dissipated with the approach of night as Constance skirted the plaza to get to the Healers' lodge, resolved to grab a bar of soap and find this bathing place Dal mentioned. She strode purposefully, the promise of respite as reviving as the actuality promised to be.

As she reached the corner of the healing room, the single-story building forming the el of the garden, someone barreled into her, knocking her against the wall and leaving her breathless. But air or no, she reached out and seized the tunic of the small figure whose progress she had interrupted.

The two of them stood still, both glaring. A girl, she thought, filthy and underweight, perhaps ten years old. Children, other than the sick ones, hadn't been evident in the last few days, so Constance shifted from annoyed to curious. The child squirmed, fighting for freedom.

Constance's diaphragm regained its rhythm. She took a breath and said, "Oh, no. Hold it right there."

"Can't." The girl's effort to free herself became frantic.

"You can." Constance tightened her grip on the thin shoulder. "If it's so important, tell me. If not, you need a bath and food." Probably in the reverse order.

The girl was wiry and strong, and nearly impossible to control, but abruptly the battle stopped. The ragged bundle under her hands stood quietly, drooping.

Once I had a son. Constance held tight. "Tell me," she said gently. "You need help, that much is obvious. Why aren't you eating?"

"Can't," the girl muttered again.

"The dining hall's just the other side of the plaza."

After an uncomfortable silence, the girl shuddered, her whole body shaking. "Don't live here," she whispered.

What was going on? Who was this child, and where were her parents? "Your mom and dad... did they fall ill? Did they die?"

"Ain't got none."

Constance frowned. "No parents?"

She shook her head, barely, and fixed her gaze on the beaten dirt of the lane.

"Then why are you here? Where do you live?"

A miniscule movement suggested a point to the southeast, but Constance doubted her sense of direction. "Another town?"

"Yeah."

This was getting them nowhere. "Come with me," Constance said, asserting her questionable authority as the adult in the conversation. "We'll get you cleaned up and fed." She frowned at the anxious little face, eyes still focused downwards. "You're safe. Apart from the disease, there's nothing to hurt you."

"You got water?" Abruptly, Constance realized the girl wasn't whispering at all. Her voice was hoarse with thirst, and probably she was afraid to drink.

"Yes, I have water. Safe water." Constance risked removing her hand from the girl and gave her a nudge toward the Healers' lodge.

"You touch me, I'm runnin'. You got no right."

"But you've got the need. Come on." Wheedling, she added, "The water here is clean. It'll be okay."

But after a couple of steps the child stopped again. Her lips pinched together, as if screwing up her courage.

"Go on. Say it. What's the matter?"

Constance had to lean in to hear the struggling voice. "The others."

Blood really can run cold, Constance thought. "The... what do you mean? What others?"

A grubby hand twitched toward a hut at the far end of the garden. It had been the resident healer's home until recently, so Constance had heard. Renewing her hold on the child, she headed, not for the lodge, but for the hut.

The girl shouted, her voice hoarse to the point of croaking. *"No! I just wanna take them some water. You stay away—"* Without warning, she kicked out, landing a hard, dirty foot on Constance's shin.

It hurt, but not enough to stop their forward progress. "You get a grip on yourself," she barked. "I've got every right. I'm a healer, remember?" She had almost said medic, but the title would carry no meaning.

Nor, in her case, did healer. But that wasn't a battle to be fought right now.

"You touch 'em, I'll kill you. I swear it," the child rasped.

"I assume they're in as bad shape as you are." Constance's quickened her pace, hauling the girl along.

The child panicked and bucked, freeing her shoulder. Constance snatched her skinny arm and tightened her fingers.

"Don't you *dare!* I ain't gonna let you. You so much as lay a finger on 'em..."

But when the bid for freedom failed, she ran out of threats. As they approached the hut, Constance felt the tremble of fear under her hand. Rather than bulldoze her way into the shack beside the Healers' lodge, she granted the girl a pause. "Tell me your name."

Mute, the child dragged her toe through the dirt in the road.

"All right, you're Renee."

"Not."

"You are until you tell me otherwise. I have to call you something. Now, let's see what we have here."

In the building, which appeared to have been uninhabited for some time, were two more children, perhaps two and four years old, of indeterminate sex. Both huddled in a corner, and a smell of old diarrhea permeated the space. A quick touch on the forehead of the older one told her, first, that they were terrified of her, and second, that one at least had a high fever.

She left the children and dragged Renee outside. "Okay, here's the deal. They need a Healer, fast. I'm going to see who I can find. Upstairs in the lodge you'll find a table with a cauldron of water and some pitchers. Fill a pitcher and bring it down. I'll meet you here." She squatted so they were face to face and gripped the waif's elbows. "Have a drink yourself, but be sure to bring plenty for your friends. Do you understand?"

"'Course I do," Renee muttered, then straightened. "I ain't going back."

"Back where?" Constance asked, momentarily confused. Then she remembered something the child had said, that she wasn't from here. "No one's sending you anywhere. Just deal with the water. Trust me."

Constance straightened to find a strange woman about her own age entering the courtyard garden. The two women stared at each other for a moment.

"Are you Constance, by chance?" the newcomer asked. "I've been told to get some rest before the first morning shift."

"Meade?" Constance blurted. "Thank god."

Chapter 11

Instead of retreating to her room that night for much-needed sleep, Constance consulted with an equally tired Meade in the Healers' workroom, a cramped space with a large, wooden table in the center. The room held the memory of the many herbs processed there over the years; Constance, who had spent hours here creating the concoctions they fed to the sufferers on the plaza, sneezed.

"Wait till you get into the workroom at the Motherhouse," Meade said. "It's as if every Healing ever done lives there. Most of us love it."

"But not all?" Constance reminded herself not to be snarky. "Sorry. Long day."

"Me, too. And the porridge in the dining hall doesn't have a lot of sustaining power." Meade settled onto a stool, elbows on the table. "So, what do we do with them?"

Constance perched across from her. "Heather's fever is down anyway." They had alternated watching through the evening. Meade had attempted a Healing, although she reported she was too tired for it to be very successful. The younger two children had been assigned names, Heather and John, because Renee refused to divulge any further information – if she knew.

"And John's whining for food," Constance said.

"Gruel."

"Gruel." They had both ferried bowls of the stuff to the tiny cabin, which now was, at least, cleaner. It had been an exhausting evening.

"Where's Renee?" Meade asked.

"Last I saw, curled up in the hut with a blanket. She's much too thin."

"Her aura's disrupted." Meade arched her back, stretching and yawning. "I don't know why. Aura reading isn't my strong point. I kept her in one place long enough to balance her energies, though. That should help."

"She says she doesn't live here."

Meade shook her head, answering the unspoken question. "No clue. Stanstead's too big for us to recognize everyone."

"We can't let her roam free. There's too much danger of contagion now."

"I know." Meade idly traced a finger along the grain of the table's wooden surface. "Any idea where she gathered up the others?"

"No. But I'm glad she did, even if I shouldn't be. They're safer here than anywhere else in town. This epidemic's hit the children especially hard. We've lost so many."

"Do you suppose there are more wandering loose?"

"On the streets, you mean?" Constance frowned, thinking. "I doubt it. The kids have disappeared. I guess their parents keep them close to home now. I just hope no one's searching for them."

Meade sighed. "Dal would have a fit if he knew. Question is, when do we tell him? Would we put these children at greater risk if they become part of the system?

The women looked at each other across the table. They both understood the negative to that question.

"So..." Constance said.

"This hamlet with the safe well you get the water from... could we move them there? Would anyone take them in?" Meade asked.

Constance slipped from her stool and began to pace. "It's not close. I wish we could stretch the water supply from the well here in the lodge." Constance paused, then shook her head. "Never mind, I know the answer. It must tap a different aquifer, but it's a weak well."

Meade waited while Constance worked through her thoughts.

"The townspeople use a cart to fetch water. They might help. As for care... I don't know."

"Still."

The silence in the room was broken only by the occasional slap of Constance's sandals on the stone floor.

"Okay," Meade said with sudden resolution. "We're honor bound to tell Dal, and maybe Marla, but let's see how Heather is tomorrow and think about ways to put Renee to work. We can make some quiet inquiries about missing children. In the meantime, we'll keep them out of harm's way. No rule says they have to stay together. If we get permission, we could shift John in the morning."

Constance nodded. "I'll take Renee with me. She'd be an extra pair of hands. From what little she said, it's unlikely she's known around here."

"They must belong to someone." Meade sounded troubled, probably thinking the same thing Constance was, that these children could be orphans. Meade stood and made for the door. "I'm on duty at dawn. I'd better get some sleep. Good luck tomorrow, and stay in touch. I'll help if I can."

Constance dragged herself upstairs to the room she shared with the sleeping Agnes. Another day. Another complication. But those kids, they'd touched her.

Especially Renee. The little waif was on her mind as she slipped into sleep.

*

Constance woke earlier than she had planned, to a furor of raised voices below her. Dal and Meade, going head to head from the sound of it, with a minor chorus from Cynth, and occasional participation by voices she didn't recognize.

"Get her down here, *now!*" Dal roared.

Constance hastily rolled from her bed and pulled on the morning's tunic. She arrived downstairs to find Meade clutching a whimpering John, Dal red-faced, Cynth making pacifying, if ultimately useless, gestures, a young man – Lamar? – lounging against the far wall watching the proceedings, and a short older woman she didn't know at the foot of the stairs, her arms crossed. Constance's inner clock suggested it was dawn or later, but little light penetrated the stone-clad room.

"If I were you, I'd stop where you are," the woman by the stairs said. "It's out of control."

Dal caught sight of her and broke off his diatribe, turning his ire full force from Meade to her.

But instead of the rant she had steeled herself for, his voice was icy. "Can you explain exactly *what* made you think you have the right to kidnap Stanstead's children?"

Constance descended the last treads of the staircase and met him icicle for icicle. "Can you explain what makes you think this child is being kidnapped? And might I point out that at least he's healthy?"

"Needs changing," Cynth muttered. She took the squirming toddler from Meade and disappeared out the front door, calling, "We'll be in the healing room, when you've sorted this out."

Dal abruptly deflated and dropped onto the next-to-bottom step. "I'm sorry, Marla," he said to the woman beside Constance. "I don't have a clue what's going on here. I assure you it wasn't authorized, however."

Marla turned to Constance. "I'm the mayor. In theory, I keep order."

"How are you, Marla?" Meade asked in an abrupt change of subject. "I heard you were sick."

"I'm one of the ones lucky to pull through," Marla replied. "Still weak, but improving. Now, explain about the child."

Constance grabbed the conversational initiative. "We... I... found him. Obviously, we couldn't leave him to wander."

"We're looking for his parents," Meade chimed in.

"Found him where? Took him in where?" Dal's voice sounded as weary as his drooping posture suggested.

"Well..." Constance began.

Meade shook her head, signaling that the time for obfuscation was long past. "In the old healer's residence next door."

The implications sank in. Marla and Dal looked at each other for a beat, then Marla said,

"This child can barely walk, much less reach to open a door latch."

Silence. Nobody moved.

When it became evident no one else was going to speak, Constance asked, "Do you know the child?"

"Yes." Marla looked toward the door, reflecting. "Filip. One of four, no acknowledged father."

"Are they all right?" Meade interrupted. "Any sign of the disease?"

"I don't know. I've been out of commission myself." Marla tore her gaze from the door and frowned at Meade. "Tell me what you planned to do with the boy."

Meade was prompt. "Take him to Little Hutt when we go for water. And hope somebody will foster him until it's safe."

Marla sank onto the step next to Dal. "There are worse plans," she said.

"It's wrong," Dal shot back. "And it's not our responsibility. Not our choice to make."

"We were going to ask around first," Constance said. "Try to find the parents."

Cynth appeared in the doorway, Filip squirming in her arms. "Someone take him while I fetch gruel. He's hungry. I don't want to risk carrying him past the plaza."

Constance received the child, whose red face suggested the whimper was building to a howl, and handed him off to the young man; his sardonic gaze had begun to irritate her. Filip buried his runny nose against the young man's neck. The man's expression as he dealt with the frantic toddler almost made the whole scene worthwhile.

Dal sighed. "Tell me this much. How did Filip get into the healer's residence? And how many more are there?"

Constance had endured the cross-examination so far, on the theory that it was in fact right and proper. The child belonged to Stanstead, and if anyone in the lobby recognized him, so much the better. Heather fell into the same category; she would willingly give her up to scrutiny. But Renee?

Renee had said she didn't live here. Where, then? Might the jurisdiction of the town pave a path to safety? Constance had developed a sense that so far, the established order had been unkind, perhaps unsafe, to the enigmatic, passionate child.

But something told her that even if they all marched over to examine the human inhabitants of the old healer's residence, they wouldn't find Renee.

And so it proved. After admitting the existence of another child – Constance shot Meade a warning look, so Renee wasn't mentioned – the entire group crossed the garden in the courtyard and crowded into the hut.

Heather's fever had indeed broken in the night. With water and a little thin porridge, she looked substantially better than she had the evening before. A child of confidence and a great deal of self-possession, she stood from her nest of blankets on still-wobbly legs and presented herself to Marla. "I'm ready to go home," she said in a high voice. Then she glared at Constance, small fists on her hips. "And my name isn't Heather. It's Susun."

"Oh, my dear." Marla sank to her knees and enfolded the child. Above her she shook her head. Heather had no home to go to.

*

Mid-morning, Constance checked in at the barn now housing their patients. The cows had been shifted to another barn for milking, after which they would be fine in the fields. Stalls had been mucked out as well as possible, but a distinct odor of cow – and cow dung – still permeated the makeshift hospital.

The plaza was empty other than remnants from its former inhabitants, here a sunshade, there a pan, a rag.

Meade stood in the barn door, catching a breath of fresh air and shaking her head. "At least we could wash down the plaza, if we had enough clean water. With this dirt floor, the Aura alone knows what we'll do."

"Work harder to keep the floor clean in the first place," Agnes snapped as she crossed their path.

"And be grateful we're under cover," Meade added, ignoring Agnes's irritation. They were all on edge. Constance sensed that the full complement of Healers was past the point of being able to analyze, much less moderate, their emotions.

After a moment's chat with Meade, whom she barely knew other than their shared responsibility for the children, Constance left the barn. She collected her pails from a storage shed near the Healers' lodge, preparing for the first of her daily jaunts to Little Hutt, the hamlet with a safe well. Outside, full daylight revealed deep overcast skies and the certainty of imminent rain. Both the town and the Healers had positioned containers to collect the pure water.

A convoy of donkey carts waited to the east of the plaza, bearing empty casks to carry water back to Stanstead. Another cart had already departed for the ford, where Stanstead got water for washing. The river water was *probably* safe, Constance had been told, but there were other hamlets upstream, so how could they be sure? River water was boiled in great cauldrons at the rear of the dining hall before use. The carts would plod back and forth all day, keeping the town alive.

Marla stood by the convoy, Susun clinging to her leg and sniveling. The girl was to be taken to Little Hutt, in the charge of a neighbor she knew, while Filip was returned to his mother. Constance skirted the plaza to the rallying point, toting her bulky containers and wondering where Renee had got to.

But of the older child, there was no sign.

Chapter 12

A week later, give or take – Constance no longer kept accurate count of the days – the barn-hospital held fewer patients, and the healthy residents were tackling piles of rubble and dangerously unstable buildings. Procuring safe water still presented a problem, but at least the Healers had enough confidence in the town's water supply methods that she no longer had to go to Little Hutt several times a day.

The biggest change, from Constance's perspective, was Renee. The child had grudgingly let herself be taken to the ford for a bath and swim – a better alternative, Constance thought wryly, than being shut in a bathing room. Clean, in fresh clothing, with washed and combed – if uncut – hair, she looked much less like a homeless waif, more like a normal child with dark blonde hair and inquisitive brown eyes. Constance couldn't begin to guess her age but speculated that hunger and hard living had stunted normal maturity patterns. Skinny and underdeveloped, Renee could be anywhere from ten to fourteen.

But that was only the surface. Constance had seen the marks on the child's thin arms and back, marks suggestive of a beating with a stick or whip. In a flash of insight, she had said nothing, and by that one action she had won Renee's loyalty. The child followed her everywhere she was allowed to go – which did not include the barn, strictly off limits to everyone except the afflicted, the Healers, and Constance herself.

Marla had raised an eyebrow when presented with Renee, but despite quiet inquiries, no one had been able to identify her people. Constance sensed the child was starved for love. She wondered how on earth she herself had become a source of security, but accepted the girl's presence.

Having resisted every attempt to find her more suitable housing, Renee slept in the unused healer's hut, which had now had a thorough scrubbing courtesy of Constance and Meade's so-called free time. When Constance left the lodge in the morning, there Renee would be, waiting in the courtyard, perhaps prowling among the herbs – seemingly with some knowledge.

Contemplating the situation, Constance didn't understand herself. The last thing she wanted was to be burdened with a child, and yet, when the scraggly girl appeared at her side, ready for breakfast, she felt a lightening of her spirits.

She and Renee held to an uneasy truce, which involved Constance asking no questions and Renee volunteering no information. Their conversation concerned only immediate events as they ate in the dining hall – Constance was constantly amazed by how much food Renee packed into her skinny body – or bathed in the river. Where she was when Constance dealt with the work in the barn, she had no idea.

One late afternoon, released from her duties, Constance stepped out of the barn into the overcast day and stretched. She suspected rain would fall before evening, but no one would mind that; the dry spell had gone on much too long. The rain that had soaked the town soon after they moved their patients to the barn had been more than welcome, sluicing dust and germs from the plaza, feeding the crops, filling pots and cisterns on every surviving doorstep, but that was long days ago.

With nowhere in particular to go, she set off along a path out of the town, past paddocks where cows and sheep grazed. Destruction here was comparatively minor, and it would be a relief to escape the piles of rubble, not to mention the unavoidable noise of cleanup and reconstruction that permeated Stanstead these days. She idly wondered where her constant shadow had disappeared to; usually Renee met her soon after she left work.

She got her answer as she passed a sprawling cow pasture, about fifteen minutes from the town by her best guess. The child was in the middle of the wide dirt road, drawing... what?

Renee had smoothed out a patch of the track and constructed a picture that involved numerous circles and connecting lines. Roughly square, the diagram filled the cleared space.

Constance stopped at the edge of the work. Renee shot her an uneasy glance as she stepped back, so the diagram divided them by a couple of meters, and fumbled with the stick she had used to etch the lines in the dirt. She looked like she might bolt. Constance dropped her gaze from the girl to the diagram. Lines crossed each other. Some circles had several lines – connections? – going to them, while others skirted the edge of the diagram, solitary. One or two weren't connected at all.

"This is amazing." She didn't look up, sensing Renee's tension. "But what is it?"

"Nothin'." Renee sounded defiant. By now Constance knew that tone meant she was frightened. But why?

"Not nothing." She risked glancing at the girl. "It's a map of some sort, isn't it? But without labels, I can't imagine what." She returned to studying the drawing and spoke without looking at Renee. "I don't know what you've created here, but it's fascinating. Can you explain it to me?"

"Nah." Renee traced lines in the dirt with her bare toe. The experience of years raising Omar suggested Renee was worried she wouldn't meet approval for whatever she had done. "Just somethin' I like doin'. Don't mean nothin'."

"I think it does. I'd like to know."

Behind her, Constance sensed the arrival of the men come to take the cows into the second barn for milking; she ignored them, and Renee seemed not to be aware of their presence.

Then Renee took a deep breath and began. "This here, this is you." She pointed to one of the circles near the middle of the drawing. "And this is Meade, and here's Dal. And Meade and Dal, they get a line, and you get a line to Meade but not to Dal. And over here's the mayor, and she's got a whole lot of lines, and this is..."

Her voice grew in strength as she spoke. She used the stick to point out different people, different connections. Constance stood still and listened, astonished. There were at least thirty circles in the diagram, yet Renee remembered which circle represented which person. Even more fascinating was her perception of the connections. Her own circle, she noted, had few connections, whereas Meade's connected all over the place.

Lines dodged around the diagram, crossing each other. In a few places she saw evidence of an erasure. And Renee remembered it all, with no identifiers, not even changes in shape.

When the child wound down, she said, "Renee, this is remarkable."

She shrugged and kept her focus on the diagram. Behind them, the cows were now on their way out of the pasture. It was getting dark, whether from the cloud cover or sunset Constance wasn't sure.

"But the rain..." She hesitated. Renee knew as well as she that rain, or traffic, would eradicate the diagram.

"I told you," Renee said with an edge of impatience. "Don't mean nothin'. Just something I like to do."

From the village they both heard the bell, faint in the distance. Meals had resumed some regularity, with breaks from the insufferable porridge. Renee's head came up, her focus instantly on the dining hall.

"And that's okay? That it'll be lost, after all your work?"

Renee shrugged. "Sure. What else?"

What else indeed? They had no paper or ink, and Renee certainly couldn't read or write, or even hold a pen. For her, there were no other options.

"Hungry?"

The child flashed a quick smile.

"And..." How to put this delicately? "Are you okay to leave your work and go for supper?"

Forget the diagram. Renee danced right through the middle of it. "You bet." Without further comment, she took off down the road.

"Don't forget to wash your hands," Constance shouted as the child dodged the cows and bolted toward town. Renee was filling out; she didn't have the starved-waif look anymore. And that appetite...

Bemused, Constance studied the remains of the diagram one more time, wishing she had some way of recording it, then followed more slowly, confident she would find Renee in the dining hall.

Chapter 13

The sun was out in full force. Constance had spent the afternoon in a field west of town with Meade, harvesting a weed destined for one of the vile drinks they forced down the throats of the sufferers. The field was barren of shade, the weeds overgrown and irritating to her skin, the atmosphere sticky from the recent rain. Buzzing insects plagued her; in fact, everything about the experience made her yearn for the clean, streamlined rooms of her life as a ship's medic. At least it was a change, a break from the never-ending days, and frequently nights, toiling in the barn or the Healers' workroom.

Meade had confessed, as they walked to the field, that she had been assigned to help Constance adapt to life at the Motherhouse, a sort of special *project*. Although she recognized the probable benefit of having a mentor, Constance felt irritated. It wasn't Meade's fault; she liked the other woman. But still...

Despite her resentment and the pervasive sense of dislocation she felt in this land that seemed so ordinary but was in fact utterly alien, she had developed a new respect for the amount of sheer physical labor the Healers were capable of. The herb, which Meade identified as bilium, grew low to the ground; she groaned as she straightened her back. "You're enjoying this," she said accusingly.

Meade glanced up and grinned. "Most of us look forward to harvesting days. Working with our raw materials brings us close to the source of our healing abilities. And today I'm not complaining about anything that keeps me out of Dal's line of sight."

"True."

Meade stood in a single lithe movement. "This is enough for now. Your face is red. We can stop at the ford if you like."

Constance answered with a sigh of relief as she stood, her knees protesting, and scooped up her bag of loosely woven linen. Her skin itched as if she had developed contact dermatitis. Because of the temperature, her clothing was limited to a loose tunic, along with underwear she had brought from the Adventurer. Now she wished that, heat or no heat, she had also worn long pants.

It was less than ten minutes to the ford. As expected, Meade pulled her tunic over her head and tossed it on a bush, then waded in. "Boy, this feels good."

She still wasn't used to the Midland's custom of casual nudity, but walking back in wet clothing wouldn't be comfortable, so Constance resigned herself to the inevitable. Her tunic joined Meade's. The underwear stayed put. It would dry in time and provided a minimal nod to modesty. She joined Meade, sinking waist-deep in the cool water, then flopping back to allow her hair to float free.

After a few minutes relaxing in the shallows, Constance said, "This has to be the first leisure we've had since you got here."

"Makes it sweeter, doesn't it? I love Dal, but once he decides on something, watch out. He's a fabulous teacher, though."

"And he wants to see me," Constance groaned. "Suppertime. Does he ever smile?"

"Sure." Meade grinned, as if enjoying a private memory. "But he's taking this epidemic personally. It should have yielded to his determination by now. He's worn himself so thin, I don't think he could do an energy balancing at this point. A shame, because everyone on his team could use one and he's the best. But he's done so many, he's used himself up. Lamar says he's talking in his sleep."

Constance kept her distance from Lamar. She thought the young man mocking and emotionally disconnected from the crisis. But she didn't say so. By now she had worked out that relationships among the Weaver community tended to be complicated. For all she knew Lamar and Meade were lovers. Or Lamar and Dal. Or... Dal and Meade? Well, none of her business.

Reluctantly, the two women left the soothing river, donned their tunics and sandals, and plodded back to Stanstead. On the way, Meade explained what happened next. "There's a box kind of thing on the roof of the lodge. Some of the herbs go into it just long enough to wilt, which helps release their properties. They'll be for immediate use. The rest we'll hang up in the drying room just off the workroom. Once they're dried, they'll be good for a year or so."

"What I don't get," Constance said, "is how much you all love this. Not just the sweaty, dirty part, but the study. Learning how to use all these plants. Working yourselves half to death." She held out her hands, which were red and a little swollen despite the cool bath of the river. "I'm not a fan."

"That's because you're not a Healer," Meade said comfortably.

"Not..." That question again. In her bones she had already come to a partial conclusion, but no answer. She hated and distrusted primitive pseudo-medicine and felt no wish to pursue it, but if she wasn't a medic anymore – which she couldn't be without access to her modern implements and medicines – and she wasn't fated to be a Healer, then what was she?

"There aren't many options," Meade said, reading her mind, "but they'll figure out a place for you. You're not a performer, but you still could be a Bard, if you have any musical talent at all? Or recitation?"

Constance kept her eyes on the rough road, fighting a sudden vulnerability with not only her future, but also her essential nature, under discussion. "I can barely carry a tune. I spent a lot of wasted hours as a child learning piano, but I was never good at it. Wooden, the teachers said."

"I don't know what a piano is, but that seems pretty definitive." Meade kicked at a clod of earth as if it were a soccer ball, then paused to shake the resultant gravel from her sandal. "So, you're a Scribe. Scribes come in all shapes and sizes, skill-wise. Once Arwen's set up testing, they'll figure you out. And you'll feel a lot more grounded when you know who you are."

The encouraging words only served to sink Constance's spirits further. She hated the idea of anyone 'figuring her out'. "I'm too old for this."

Meade's face took on a thoughtful, faraway mien. "Me too," she said. "I've always loved just being alive, the study, the work, the travel, the people. Lately something's missing, but I can't put my finger on it. Ask around the Motherhouse, they'll tell you I have this reputation. Always positive, always happy. I don't feel very cheerful these days."

Constance presented the logical point of view. "How could you, with what we've been facing?"

Meade shook her head. "It's deeper than that. And I don't know why." She gave herself a full-body shake – reminding Constance of a puppy she and Pierre had given Omar, so many years ago now. "Never mind. Not like me to moan, and no point anyway. Let's just hope no new catastrophes get dumped on our heads."

They didn't speak again until they were in the workroom, and then restricted themselves to the commonplaces of herb preparation and life in Stanstead.

*

Dal was settled at a table in a dark corner of the dining hall when Constance tracked him down. Supper turned out to be a stew featuring shreds of a meat she couldn't identify. She sat across from her grim boss and took a bite before speaking.

While she chewed – the mystery meat wasn't exactly tender – Dal said, "I have a new assignment for you."

She swallowed. "I'm listening."

"Drop the attitude, Connie. I don't have time or energy for it."

"My name's not Connie," she snapped.

"Try it out. It's easier to say."

She looked up from the stew and inadvertently locked on his eyes. Deep brown in the gloom of the dining hall. Tired. And...

A jolt of electricity shot through her. Something she hadn't felt since those early days with Pierre, when...

Oh, shit.

They both looked away at the same time. Constance dropped her spoon.

Dal's gaze shot to her hands, shiny with the grease-based salve Meade had smeared over them. "What on earth have you done to yourself?"

In the time since she and Meade had returned from the field, her fingers had grown increasingly red and swollen. "Bilium," she said. It made handling the spoon challenging, but she gamely retrieved it from her bowl and took another bite.

Dal nodded. "Some people react this way, fortunately not many. It'll go away." His voice sounded stilted, as if he would rather not be speaking to her at all.

After another bout of chewing and swallowing, Constance nodded. "I won't go near that stuff again."

"The dermic reaction isn't triggered, or at least it lessens, once it's wilted."

An awkward silence fell between them. At last, impatient, Constance asked, "Another assignment?"

Dal paused, seeming to collect his thoughts. "Yes. You're taking a group of children to the Motherhouse."

"*What?*"

Dal nodded. "The town's been rounding up all the orphans and kids whose parents can't take care of them. Marla and I agree they need to be evacuated. The local hamlets can't handle the extra responsibility, given the extent of destruction from the earthquake. The Motherhouse is the logical destination."

"How many?" To her own ears, her voice sounded faint.

"Seven. The youngest doesn't walk yet. We've requisitioned a donkey cart and driver."

"And the oldest?"

"Eight or nine, I think."

Not Renee then. As she had almost constantly for the last few days, she wondered where the defiant child had come from.

"I don't do children."

Dal riposted impatiently. "You do now. Anyway, you're a mother, aren't you? Mothering skills are inherent once you've given birth. Or so they say."

Constance froze. "How did you know?" she whispered. She never talked about Omar. Never.

Dal shrugged. "It's in your energy. You'll learn to read auras once you get into formal training."

"There are no secrets on this miserable planet, are there?" she muttered.

Dal ignored that. "You leave the day after tomorrow. I've made a list of the children and a supply list, which you'll have to fill. It could be challenging, given the state of destruction, but do your best. Food and water are the most important, obviously. Lamar tells me the water supplies along the trail are safe, but for the children it'll be better – safer – if you carry your own."

Obviously. "Where are these children now?" she asked.

"In the leather workers' building. It wasn't too badly damaged."

Her stomach roiled; the stew lost its attraction. Constance stood. "Meade would be a better candidate."

"I need her here," Dal said, his voice flat. "She has competencies you don't."

His tone sent a chill through her. She made her way to the hatch, depositing her still half-full bowl, then outdoors. The plaza, washed, disinfected, and warmly welcoming in the evening light, felt almost like home. And now she was to be ripped away again, set on the road with a horde of children, trekking four days – if they were lucky – to a place where she would know nobody, dealing with... Oh, god. How was she going to cope?

Chapter 14

Constance lay wrapped in a blanket near the fire, wide awake and thinking that in the nine months or so she had lived in the Midland she had never wanted to arrive at the Motherhouse as much as she did now. She had dreaded it, resented it, held it in contempt for its teachings. But she had never longed for it. Traveling with a cartful of young children had taxed every nerve and mental synapse she possessed.

The kids didn't like being confined to the cart. Inevitably, whenever they stopped for a meal or at a waysite, the older ones took off like wild animals, desperate for exercise and freedom. The first night, Constance tried every game, every stratagem she had ever used with Omar to keep them under control. By the second night she let them run and prayed they would come back for supper.

Tonight, their last night on the trail, the sky was overcast, the ground spongy from rain earlier. A sheet impregnated with lanolin kept the damp away, but imperfectly. The smell of wet sheep, something she had never experienced on Terra where fabrics – and most meat, come to that – were synthetic, assaulted her nostrils. At least her charges had settled down at last; a faint, childish snore came from the back of the wagon. Across the fire, the grizzled donkey driver slept soundly, as he had the previous two nights. The donkey was tethered at a distance from the fire and seemed to be dozing on its feet. She alone was awake.

Or maybe not alone. Food had been disappearing from their supplies. Not much, but noticeable. And this was the moment to put a stop to it.

She disentangled from her bedding and donned her sandals. The camp was a clearing in deep coniferous forest, so it was easy to disappear into the trees while staying close enough to keep watch.

She waited... not so long; if her suspicions were correct, their invader was probably hungry. At last she heard a shuffling, as if small feet were working their way cautiously toward the wagon. Barely breathing, Constance froze in place.

The figure could only be Renee, front-lit by the remains of the fire. Constance waited until the girl was rummaging in a supply bag, making enough noise to waken the sleeping children – if they weren't so bone weary from their earlier mad gambol into the woods – before she inched her way across the clearing. She didn't try to catch the girl, but merely approached to within a couple of meters and said, "Hello, Renee."

Renee froze. She had stuffed her mouth with a piece of dried meat and was reaching in for more. Constance crossed the remaining distance between them and caught the girl's arm before she could react. But she kept her grip gentle. "Don't panic," she whispered. "Go ahead and eat. Then we'll talk."

Renee was no fool. She glared up at Constance, then nodded. Her hand came out of the food bag, clutching another piece of jerky, then she sank to the ground against a wheel, dragging Constance down with her.

Constance assessed the situation quickly. Renee must have been following the wagon, although her reasoning was a mystery. She was unwashed, exhausted, and... yes, scared. The tempestuous child was desperate. But what was her purpose? To go to the Motherhouse? She would bet Renee wasn't plagued by the Aura. She was too normal, too down-to-earth. Not a hint of the mystic. She waited.

Sure enough, once Renee had swallowed the massive bite she had crammed into her mouth, she muttered, "Couldn't stay there. They'd catch me sure."

"Who's 'they', Renee?"

The child manufactured indignation. "I told you, that ain't my name."

Later, Constance would reflect that the simple fact they both managed to speak *sotto voce* was the biggest miracle of the night.

"Then give me another one."

No reply. Constance waited a beat, then asked again, "Who's 'they'? Who's after you? And why?"

Renee developed a sudden interest in the ground. "Uncle," she muttered. Her voice sounded resentful, but Constance picked up an undercurrent of yearning. The trek hadn't been easy.

"Your uncle. Where are your parents?"

"Gone."

And that could mean anything, Constance thought. Did they die, or leave and abandon their child? Or were they still in the picture but had distanced themselves somehow? She suspected she would get no details tonight. And really, it wasn't the time or place. "Do you have any supplies with you?" she asked quietly.

"Blanket. Water flask."

"Let's go get your stuff. Then you can settle in with the others and get some sleep. We'll be at the Motherhouse sometime tomorrow afternoon."

Renee's voice rose in that split-second panic Constance had seen before. The muscles of her arm tensed under Constance's fingers. "Don't want to. It's all junk anyways."

"No water flask is junk."

"Leaks," Renee whispered.

"Mendable."

"Don't wanna. Don't."

Once again, the panic. Constance made an executive decision. They didn't need the child's equipment, and Renee didn't need any more grief. "Okay, that's fine. Will you settle in with the others? And not run away? This is the safest place for you, and I want you to stay here."

"Not with them."

"You did a good thing there, you know. Without you, she would have had no one." Not strictly true, but Renee needed something from her, and Constance wasn't sure what.

"Yeah, I know." Renee attempted to squirm away. "Not goin' in the cart."

Because of her need to be able to run, to disappear at will. Constance nodded. "Next to me, then." She stroked Renee's arm gently, then removed her hand. "Let's find you a blanket."

They had brought several spares, and as they huddled together like puppies at night, the young orphans generated their own warmth. Constance shook a blanket out and handed it to Renee, then led the child around the fire to a place near her own bedding. Nothing she could do about a ground cloth, but she suspected the space was drier than anything Renee had experienced recently. The old man across the fire grunted and turned over. The snoring child had fallen silent, and the world slept. Releasing Renee had been a gamble; she could bolt, could disappear into the darkness. But displaying faith in her was the best option, and anyway, Constance simply didn't have the energy to watch over her. So, she kept her distance as the skinny child made herself a cocoon and settled down, hopefully to sleep through what remained of the night.

*

Their reception the next day was, at best, not what Constance had expected.

From where she had been walking next to the bed of the cart, Constance surveyed the place that, presumably, would be her home for the next... how long?

They had stopped alongside a two-story stone building on their left, which looked down a slight slope over a green which fronted more buildings of similar construction. They ranged from one to three stories, the largest a two-story edifice with a single level sprouting off to the left, sprawling across half the length of the green. It was early afternoon, the sun baking down, and the complex was quiet other than faint ripples from a flute drifting from an open window above them. A couple walked across the green and entered a door in the central building, the only movement in the hot, quiet afternoon.

"You get off here," the donkey cart driver informed her. "Reckon you need to head to the Centra." At her blank look, he amended, "There. The big one. They'll get you sorted out."

The driver swung down from his seat and began dumping their belongings in a pile beside the building. Renee was already unloading the children, who, for once, stood silently, surveying the new surroundings.

"Where will you be? Are you leaving today?" Abruptly, the thought of being marooned here with no way to return to Stanstead struck Constance full force, as if the cart were an escape route to a way of life she at least was familiar with, even if she probably would never understand it.

"Going that way." The old man nodded at the track, which continued past the front of the building into the trees. "I'll put up in the village."

The village. This wasn't all of it, then. The Motherhouse complex, while solid and fairly extensive, could scarcely hold all the people needed to maintain a community here. It made sense, she supposed, that the workers would be housed separate from the Weavers.

The Weavers. And she was one of them, sort of.

Sighing, she nodded to the driver, thanked him, and signaled to Renee. "Can you ride herd on our charges while I go check us in, or whatever I have to do? Over there, I gather."

"Sure." Renee accepted the assignment as a matter of course and turned from her to the huddled group of cowed children.

Renee had been a godsend during the last day's trek, Constance reflected as she crossed the grassy slope toward the Centra. Behind her, she heard the rumble of the cart's wheels as the driver abandoned them to their fate.

As she approached the door, an older woman emerged and shouted, "Hello, the cart!"

The rumbling stopped.

"Thank the Aura I caught him," she said to Constance as if they had known each other for years. "The children are going to the village. He might as well take them." Before she could speak, the woman added, "We've fixed up a lovely creche for them and arranged for the village women to tend them. They'll be comfortable, and more at home than they would be here."

Constance found her arm in the possession of the woman's hand as she was steered back the way she had come. "But..."

"I'm Arwen. Relax, everything's under control."

When they got to the group of children, Arwen sank to her knees. "So, you're almost to your new home," she told them. "But there's a little more ride in the cart first. When you get there, you'll have tea and abricoe pastries. Sound good?"

To Constance's amazement, the children, every one of them, reacted positively to Arwen. Susun even stepped forward and announced, "Joel needs a bath. He stinks."

"We'll fix that. Let's go."

The donkey cart had passed the stone building, and the driver clearly had no intention of turning around and retreating the twenty meters or so he had gone since he had dropped them off. Arwen seized a pile of the bedding and miscellaneous possessions and marched to the cart, followed by the children, like ducklings, competing to see who could help most.

Except Renee, who slunk over to Constance's side and announced, "Ain't goin'."

She didn't hesitate. "All right. Stay with me."

Arwen seemed either not to notice or not to mind. In a twinkling she had the remaining

children in the cart – with her – and the entire
group was rattling down the trail toward the
village, leaving Constance and Renee standing
alone beside the small pile of their possessions.

Chapter 15

At the end of a long day, Meade kicked a pebble and thanked the Aura she had finally escaped from the barn. The building was high and airy, but the smell lingered nonetheless, and even with fewer sufferers the workload had been backbreaking.

Tired and hot, it seemed to her that the incessant busyness in the town resulted in no more than shifting piles of rubble from one place to another. Not true, she knew; what she needed was a walk in the fresh air, via a circuitous route first to the Healers' lodge for a fresh tunic, then to the swimming place at the ford. Cutting across the plaza would have been shorter and faster, but she avoided it these days. Something about it made her uneasy. Was it the number of lives that had been lost there, or the sheer awfulness of the Healers' work? Although her primary clan affinity was earth, solid and grounding, she also had an affinity with water and so wasn't immune to specters.

The northeast of town had suffered the brunt of the earthquake. Meade threaded her way past destroyed and condemned buildings, wondering how Stanstead would ever rebuild – but knew they would. She had dined the night before with Marla, Stanstead's indefatigable mayor, and saw in her the resilience that had marked the town, and the Midland as a whole, for as long as they had existed.

In the meantime, the few homeless children with nowhere else to go were safely at the Motherhouse. Meade wondered if Constance also felt safe there; the woman hadn't seemed connected or grounded at all during their brief acquaintance. No, definitely not a Healer, but what would the Scribes make of her?

Of Renee, that odd child who had attempted to rescue the children, there had been no sign.

She paused by the ruins of a larger one-story building and studied the man standing a little farther along the track. She had seldom seen that slump in his shoulders and didn't need to be closer to be aware of the deep lines furrowing his brow, the dark circles under his eyes.

He didn't look up as he said, "You're welcome to join me."

Dal's pain was deeper than a funk. Meade moved forward, picking her way across a small pile of rock and building materials that had slid onto the street, and wrapped an arm around his waist. "Can I help?"

He shook his head and managed a thin smile but didn't return her hug. "I'm just taking a break from it all. This was the wrong direction, though."

"Charlotte?"

He nodded.

Although never mentioned, Charlotte had hovered like a faint ghost over all their interactions since Meade arrived. She knew that Dal had spent much of his time recently in Stanstead, ostensibly training their new village healer and apothecary, but also fostering the relationship. Charlotte had been a weaver, working in the textile facility that now lay crumbled at their feet.

"I'm sorry." She tightened her arm around him. Dal must have been carrying the knowledge of his lover's death ever since the catastrophe began, adding to his burdens.

He took a deep breath and turned from the building. "It was over anyway. I'm not the easiest person to get along with, and given the amount of time I had to be away.... But she shouldn't have died like this. Where are you going?"

"To the ford." She didn't bother to explain why she was northeast of town, instead of west. "Come with me."

"I'll do that. I wonder..."

"Hmm?" She let her arm slip from his waist to hold his hand, interweaving their fingers, sensing he craved human touch just then. Dal tended to be aloof and seldom if ever showed emotion, but even he needed that reminder of his humanity occasionally.

He sounded determined, as if he had resolved to say what he had to, even though he didn't want to and resented the need. "Do you have the energy to do a Healing this evening?"

She made her response as light and nonchalant as she could. "Sure. It'll be good for both of us. This has been tough."

"You'll be able to go home soon."

His voice suggested he longed to go home as well. But that wasn't going to happen until the last remnants of the infection had cleared up.

They left the ruins of the textile facility behind, unconsciously speeding up. Meade sensed that any conversation about Charlotte touched something in Dal he would rather not explore, so she was quiet, letting him work through his feelings about the loss of his late partner in his own way. But once they reached the water, a popular place on this hot evening, and found a secluded spot a little downstream from the others, she studied him. Water wasn't Dal's natural element, he was almost entirely air, although his work with plant energies kept him connected to earth as well. But this hot evening he abandoned his body to the gentle flow, stretched on his back, eyes closed. He had lost weight. As a Healer, Meade read the markers of stress and incipient illness clearly enough. Yes, a Healing was needed, or Dal would succumb.

For some obscure reason, her thoughts flashed to Constance. She also was primarily air, but with hints of something Meade couldn't read. She wondered idly if these two wounded air clan people might provide mutual support, but didn't see how that was possible. They would merely reinforce each other's traits, and that was the last thing either of them needed. Dal needed...

Her. Tonight, she would offer more than a Healing. Once he was grounded again, once his energies were stabilized, she would boot Lamar out of the room he shared with Dal. She had known more passionate lovers, but there was a steadiness in Dal that she longed to see restored. This attenuated version made her nervous, as if the solid foundation of what made them Weavers had been compromised.

Chapter 16

A nine-day or so after her arrival at the Motherhouse, Constance surfaced from a decent night's sleep and stretched. Her suite in the guest lodge, which was situated next door to and slightly back from the dining hall, faced the green, so she didn't get direct sun first thing in the morning, but clear light through the unshuttered window was enough to rouse her. She turned on her side and considered what lay ahead.

Another day of Arwen's tests, designed to figure out how her unique access to the Aura worked. Everyone was different, but she seemed to be a mystery to them all.

Unique. Lucky her.

Another day with Dorcas, an older Scribe with hair going to gray and a weatherbeaten complexion, who had been assigned the thankless job – even Constance recognized that – of drumming into her the basics of Aura manipulation, so alien to her mindset they might as well have been in ancient Greek.

And free time, but without companions who understood her. No books, no concerts, no cafes. The complex comprised lodges for the different guilds, the guest lodge where she and Renee were settled, dormitories for students, work and study spaces, utility buildings of various sorts, the dining hall and the Centra. Cold stone, most of them, and insufficient to hold her interest for long. There was no peaceful river like the one in Stanstead, no ford to relax in, but rather a torrent that roared toward some unknown destination; she could hear it in the distance through the open window. Trails snaked along the river, up and around the natural amphitheater, and out into farming country and the village, both to the northwest. A massive rock outcrop hovered over the complex to the north, an outlier but at the same time anchored, as if it had been there since time immemorial. The sheer wildness and lack of civilization made her nervous; she rarely ventured far from the buildings.

She glared at the small desk tucked under the window, thinking about the seconds of paper – already used on one side – and her frustrated attempts to draw the weaving of yesterday's lesson. The simplicity of the techniques Agnes had struggled to impart during their long walk from the Adventurer seemed so basic now, such as holding plants to discern their uses, focusing intent to imbue them with greater healing properties – supposedly. Mind tricks, unlike Dorcas's elaborate exercises that inevitably left her feeling enervated and emptied.

Yesterday had been a mild triumph, in fact. She had – once – produced a light ball. It glowed with the intensity of one of the surgical bulbs in her old clinic and fizzed in her palm. In fact, its appearance had shaken her to the point that she had jerked her arm back and clenched her fist, thereby ending not only the light ball but any hope of creating a new one any time soon.

A crash next door indicated Renee was up. The child had agreed, grudgingly, to live in the guest lodge, but she seemed incapable of quietly opening a wardrobe to retrieve the day's tunic. Ah well, that was Renee.

Constance rose and began her own morning toilette. Renee presented an intractable problem. Constance rarely had a free waking moment without her presence. And while in some ways she enjoyed the girl's company, in others... well, there was just no room in her life for a child.

Another child.

This had more to do with her heart than her current circumstances. But she only admitted that late at night, when the unfamiliar stars reminded her how far away she was from Terra, from Omar.

Lessons provided a respite from the girl's presence. Dorcas had promised an intensive on light creation, so she would spend the hot day in the coolness of the Centra, in a workroom purposed for teaching future Scribes, which she guessed she was, or would be, since she didn't fit anywhere else.

It still rattled her to realize her medical career had come to an end.

Predictably, Renee met her at the door to the guest lodge, already in full flight. "So, I found this thing, and it's got somethin' in it but I don't know what." She fished a gnarly looking lump the size of her fist from a pocket and shook it, producing a faint rattle. "I'm kinda scared to break it open. But we could do it together. I can wait till your study's done."

"I think you'd better put it back where you found it. It could be poisonous or have stinging insects inside." Constance set out across the green, dodging a dozen loose sheep, natural lawn mowers. Renee stuck by her side like a limpet.

"I could ask one of the Healers. They know everything about stuff." The admiration in the girl's voice was palpable; Constance, for all that she would like to be free of Renee's constant presence, felt the rebuff.

"Then go ask. I'm no good for things like that."

Renee shrugged. "They'll sort out what you're good for."

Constance felt the offhand comment as another slap, implying that her possible worth was a mystery. But with a heaved sigh she accepted Renee hadn't meant it that way. It was encouragement, within the girl's scope of knowledge and confidence in the Weavers.

In the dining hall, one of the resident Healers joined them and seemed to enjoy Renee's chatter. Constance tuned it out. The girl was about the age Omar had been the last time she had seen him. It was hard enough to keep memories of him at bay, without making room for another child.

*

On her way to the teaching room, Constance was flagged down by one of the runner kids, the ubiquitous children the Motherhouse employed to carry messages back and forth, and told to go to Arwen's office instead. Constance hated reporting to Arwen. She, a mature woman, ended up feeling like a schoolgirl caught out in a misdemeanor. But she redirected her steps without demur and tapped on the doorframe before entering.

Arwen sat ensconced behind her desk, and Hector, the principe of the school, greeted her at the door. As usual these days, she sensed she had kept them waiting. She still hadn't fathomed how she was supposed to know when to be where in a world without timepieces.

Hector grinned. "No need to worry, my dear. Come, sit down." The portly little man ushered her in and gestured to one of the two chairs – straight back, no arms or padding, like almost every chair here – then took the other for himself.

No question why the kids adored him. She had heard he maintained strict discipline but had a knack for sensing when a school full of teenagers needed to blow off steam, judging accurately what was serious and what wasn't.

She sat.

Arwen looked tired. Even in the short time Constance had been at the Motherhouse, she could see the deepening lines on her face, the occasional slump in her posture. This was the most powerful person in the Midland, by all accounts. But at the moment she looked like a frail old woman.

Nonetheless, Arwen was all business. "We've been making some decisions on your behalf, which you may not like, but we consider essential to your continued wellbeing here in the Midland." She nodded to Hector.

He took up the narrative. "Every year we run a class in basic survival skills. I gather Agnes gave you some pointers on walking technique, so you didn't injure yourself over long treks. This class covers that kind of thing."

Arwen picked it up. "For example, how to snare a ground squirrel and skin it."

"And cook it." The two of them bounced examples off each other. Constance's head swiveled from one to the other while she tried to ignore a sick feeling growing in her stomach. The mention of skinning a squirrel didn't help.

"Edible plants. How to find them and use them."

"How to start a fire."

"Fishing. Do you know how to fish? Or clean a fish?"

Before she could shake her head no, Arwen picked up the argument again. "How to deal with basic health problems like injuries or infections. Even those who aren't Healers need to know these things."

"Building rudimentary shelters," Hector said. "You've seen the rolling packs most of us use. We don't carry much, but it's perfectly possible—"

"Wait." They stopped and looked at her. "This is a class for... what? Thirteen-year-olds?"

"Usually fourteen," Hector said. "Sometimes a little older. It depends on when we begin, and when they arrive here."

"And you want me—"

"To join the class, yes," Arwen confirmed. "We think you'll find it valuable."

She would find it somewhere between uncomfortable and appalling. Constance swallowed and said, "I can't see any point in lessons like that. I just want to get back to the Adventurer."

"Which is at least sixty days on the road," Hector said. "And once there, would you be a valued member of society? We've already determined you won't be a Healer."

"Do you even know how to cook lentils?" Arwen asked. "Do you know what a lentil plant looks like, or how to harvest it?"

Thoroughly upset now, she blurted, "I'd as soon never see one again."

Hector grinned. "A shared sentiment, I assure you. But lentils are a mainstay, there's no getting around it. I'm sure it's no different in Cann. You must know how to work with what exists here. There's no point assigning you to a kitchen if you can't tell a lentil from a fava."

"There's so much more," Arwen continued as if Constance hadn't voiced any objection at all. "Tricks of memorization. How to make paper and ink substitutes when you need them. Basic geography. How to dress. Nudity's acceptable in this part of the Midland, but that doesn't hold true everywhere. It'll be getting chilly soon. Do you know what sort of clothing you'll be issued? Could you work with raw wool to make it into a coat? Could you protect yourself from rain when you're still a day or two away from the next shelter?"

"Life in towns and hamlets," Hector said. "Political and social structures, and expectations, especially as you aren't a Healer. You have to earn your right to their hospitality, and that often means helping in the kitchens or the fields or the textile building. You need to assess your strengths and interests to volunteer appropriately."

Constance remembered the clinics Agnes had held in countless hamlets. She had been relegated to general drudge, running errands and assisting with more basic procedures under Agnes's supervision.

In short, she had been useless.

But to be demoted to a classroom full of children...

With that spooky way she had, Arwen divined her innermost thoughts. "You needn't have any more interaction with the apprentices than you want, but you may find them interesting, even fun. You need this, Constance. You're an innocent here, from an alien world we can't even imagine. Trust me, it's for your own good. Perhaps your own survival."

Hector became brisk. "Classes begin tomorrow morning after lunch."

"Accept the inevitable," Arwen said. "Questions?"

You're here to learn. This is part of the learning. Constance shook her head. She would survive it. She just wished some part of her life at the Motherhouse didn't involve surviving.

As Arwen stood, signaling the end of the meeting, she added, "One last thing. See if you can get Renee to come with you. We have no idea what she knows, but it certainly won't hurt her to learn. Not to mention the discipline of attending a class regularly."

Right. Renee. If she could even find the child, never mind bend her will to something as unpalatable as a classroom.

Chapter 17

Constance sat on a bench alongside the path that wound up the hill and around the amphitheatre before descending to the river. The bench was a little way above the Bards' lodge and the entrance to the track leading back to Stanstead. This location had become a favorite, being far enough away from the Centra that she felt safe from Arwen's scrutiny – an illusion, she knew, but a valuable one – and the forest at her back kept it shaded and cooler. She avoided the other end of the trail and the river in general, as the tumultuous flow made her nervous.

At her feet, Renee was drawing another of her intricate diagrams in the dirt of the trail.

In front of her, her hands were occupied with... well, nothing. Arwen had her trying to tie energy in knots. Instead, Constance's insides experienced the knots, but the energy... how was she supposed to know? It wasn't like she could dye the stuff red to make it visible.

The days since her arrival had overflowed with these impossible assignments, and now with the added burden of the survival class. She scowled, her arm muscles tensed in frustration. While occasionally she was able to relax into the tenor of her new life, more often the only positive she acknowledged about the Motherhouse was the food, simple, abundant, and readily available, a relief after the limited rations in Stanstead.

She dropped her arms to her lap. A breeze rolled down from the hills beyond the amphitheater before dying out, reminding her the food wasn't the only benefit. The availability of baths was another positive, as was the conifer tang scenting the hot, still air. A small suite of her own she could close the door on, and a comfortable bed. And maybe, maybe, the tally could include the ubiquitous linen tunic, which was soft and cool against her skin.

She would never love the hard-soled sandals, though, she promised herself in a flash of defiance.

Renee looked up. "How long to go to Hallan?" she asked.

"Two days and a little more, I'm told. By the direct route." Constance wasn't really paying attention, just parroting pieces of information she had gleaned over her time in the Midland.

Renee sat back on her heels. "Didn't know there was a direct route. Where's it?"

Pulled back into the present, Constance sighed. "I don't know. Probably somewhere south of here, since Hallan's south."

Then it occurred to her. "You're drawing a map."

Renee had gone back to her diagram. "Course. They're all maps."

And this time, Constance could understand it. She pinpointed Stanstead and roads meeting there, the Motherhouse, the village. Renee added Hallan and the road south. The road distances were approximately correct, when measured in days of travel. It was one of Renee's simpler diagrams, but the first she had seen in which the length of the connecting lines mattered.

Then her senses alerted her; someone was coming. Likely one of the apprentices, who had poured out of the lesson rooms onto the green a few minutes before. She estimated their ages at between twelve and twenty. Most of them lived and breathed their training with the enthusiasm of kittens attacking a new ball of wool. They were invariably polite and pleasant to her, even if she caught the puzzled looks as they tried to figure out what her role was. No one ever began training as a mature woman, it seemed.

It wasn't one of the kids, though. It was Meade, looking tired, hollows in her cheeks. She skirted the diagram and dropped onto the bench. "Home," she said without inflection. "Hey there, Renee."

"Hey." The girl didn't look up.

"Welcome back," Constance said. "Things are better in Stanstead?"

"Dal and Agnes are still there, but he packed the rest of us off. Did they give you a guest suite? I didn't pick up your energy in the Healers' lodge." Meade stretched, then slumped.

"I think everyone agrees I'm not meant to be a Healer."

"And that bothers you." Meade had her eyes closed now. Constance vowed to learn to relax so thoroughly, and so readily. One day soon.

"I'm a medic. It's all I've ever been. How am I supposed to find a new vocation at this point in my life?" Irritated, she threw it out like a challenge.

Meade didn't rise to the bait. "Purpose in life can be nebulous. Especially if you don't know what you want."

Constance didn't reply. No point, really.

A group of teenagers came haring along the track, jabbering, bare legs kicking up dust. Meade opened her eyes and sat up. Several of the kids acknowledged them, and one broke out of the pack to give Meade a quick hug. The group continued up the slope, their nonstop chatter fading. Like Meade, they had all avoided the diagram.

"Done. I'm hungry," Renee announced, standing and dusting her knees.

"Go get a pastry. Tell the kitchen I said it's okay," Meade said with an indulgent smile.

Renee raced off down the track without a backward glance.

Meade watched her go, then said, "She met us this morning on the trail. It's like she's everywhere at once. Is anyone keeping track of her?"

There was no judgment in Meade's voice, but Constance bristled. "Have you ever tried?"

Meade grinned. "I'd guess it's impossible. Where's she staying? Not with the babies, I bet."

Constance shook her head. "They're in the village. Still traumatized, but getting better. Renee's got a room next to mine, but she's some kind of free spirit. She keeps her promises, if she says she'll be somewhere, she's there. But she's careful what she promises. She needs to be in school."

"School's not common unless you're training to be a Weaver. What would the kids learn? They get practical skills by doing them."

"Of course." Kiril had fussed about that, back at the Adventurer. No ordinary people could read or write other than the archivists in each hamlet. There were no books, not much paper. Education was practical, based on survival. The world of the mind simply didn't exist, although everyone she met had a remarkable ability to remember and memorize, do mental calculations. The students here at the Motherhouse were the exception to the education rule; they were expected to master reading and basic numeracy. But Renee had no auric connection, no Entrée – Constance didn't know how she knew that, but she did – so she would be out of place among that tight-knit group of young people.

Meade gave her characteristic full-body shake, as if waking herself up, and said, "No doubt Arwen's got her claws in you by now. Inquisitions?"

"Occasional."

"Welcome to the club. Be patient, it's all in the interests of discovering your talents. You have them, never doubt. But they don't understand you yet." At Constance's appalled look, she laughed. "Arwen's got her claws in me, too. Everyone, actually. It'll be okay, I promise. I'm usually not intrusive."

"Everything is, seems to me," Constance grumbled.

"Has she taught you to shield yet?"

"No, but Agnes gave me some basics while we were walking. It helps," she acknowledged grudgingly. "But shielding's hard. It uses up every drop of energy I have to spare."

"You remind me of my first years here. Everything was hard. But for me, it was exciting, too. I'm sorry you haven't felt that excitement. It'd make your life so much easier. What are you working on now?"

"Knots." Constance raised her hands. "I used to do this when I was a kid. Rub my hands together, then feel the energy between them. It was much weaker, though. Sometimes I thought I was making it up."

"Weaving energy's fun. Let's see."

Meade leaned toward her as Constance performed the steps to create the flow between her hands, then began what she hoped would twist the flow so it would wrap around itself.

"I get it," Meade said. "Here. Try this." She shadowed Constance's hands with her own, leaning forward. "Pull a little here, try to keep the flow tight—" She broke off, grimacing. "I don't know what... ahh... *ahh...*"

Constance watched horrified as the other woman went limp and fought for breath. "Meade?" Shaken, she put her hands on Meade's shoulders. "Are you okay?"

Meade's body shook. "Get help," she gasped. "I can't—"

Just before Meade collapsed, slumping off the bench to the ground, Constance picked up a message in her mind: *Help me.*

She looked around frantically. There was no one in sight other than a Healer crossing the green. Too far to shout. But she had seen convulsions before, and this was beyond her ability to deal with alone. She knelt quickly beside Meade's quaking body, making sure her air passage was clear.

Then she ran.

Chapter 18

"In the name of the Aura, what have you done?"

Arwen's face twisted, rage tightening her eyes and mouth. From her seat outside the healing room door, Constance felt the fury viscerally. She had already had to flee once, seeking toilet facilities in reaction to the tension swirling around her – and around Meade. Even during the scarier moments of their flight from Terra, even the time baby Omar had fallen and knocked himself senseless, she had never been so terrified.

Now, as Arwen descended on her, radiating fury and power, she shrank back in her chair, her voice reduced to a whimper. "I don't know."

Beside her, Cynth, who had been standing guard to be sure she neither fled nor caused more harm, nodded. "She's telling the truth. She hasn't a clue what's happened. Status?"

Arwen gave her head a violent shake, as if she could dissipate her anger through sheer force of will. "No change. We can't understand it. Smoothing energy is one of the most basic things a Healer does – any of us can do it. But her energy won't smooth. We've straightened it out a little, but unbelievably, there's a knot in it. She can't function until it's removed. But so far, we haven't found a way."

Cynth made an ideal guard, Constance thought bitterly. She hadn't warmed to the Healer during their shared time in Stanstead, always sensing in her a coolness and a focus on her work that precluded more personal connection. Never unpleasant, but consistently distant.

"Take her to the conference room and send to the village for guards. I want her confined, and as far from Meade as we can get her."

No. This was wrong. Every instinct from her days as a medic on Terra rose in protest. "But I might be able to help." She stood, Cynth moving in tandem and grasping her arm.

Arwen was ice. "I think you've already done quite enough. We'll talk later and re-test your abilities. In the meantime, I want you out of here." Then she softened, just a bit. "We know whatever happened, it wasn't intentional. But until we disentangle this, everyone is better off with you safely confined." She nodded to Cynth, who moved toward the door, pulling Constance in her wake.

*

News arrived, when it arrived, in tiny chunks, mostly summed up by 'no change'. They had allowed her to leave the room, under escort, to visit the facilities. The water pitcher had been replenished, and a tray of food left sitting on the table for what Constance estimated must be a couple of hours. At least they hadn't brought lentils, which would have finished off her gut for sure.

The chairs in the conference room were adequate, but not really comfortable. The stone walls provided something variable to look at, however minor, but there were no windows. Other than the emissary from the dining hall and the grim-faced pair outside the door, she had seen no one, heard no sounds.

Around her, a dim, unchanging light filled the room. Where from? But Constance had recognized by this time there was little point in probing the spookier aspects of life at the Motherhouse.

Solitary confinement. They were trying to drive her mad.

The integrity of the few Weavers she had interacted with suggested this thought was frivolous. More likely, everyone was focused on Meade... as was she. The horrified look on Meade's face, the awareness that somehow the knot exercise had jumped from her hands to Meade's personal energy flows – *bon dieu*. She was starting to sound like them.

But the reality was, Arwen was right. She had caused the tangle in Meade's energy. It made no sense. It was ridiculous, impossible, this whole business of energies and auras, but it was the truth.

She paced, then kicked off the poorly fitting sandals and paced some more. When the unyielding floor began to bruise the soles of her feet, she sat at the table, longing for the familiarity of her life on Terra, and waited.

She had just dozed off, her head cradled in her arms, when the door shifted. A tiny movement, she thought through fatigued muddle-headedness, before it shut again. Then someone stood next to her, statue-still.

She dragged herself upright, shaking the wool from her head. "Renee."

The silent, unmoving child studied her with a frown.

"How did you get in?"

Renee shrugged. "Not so hard. Folks don't notice me."

That was true. Constance had marveled at the child's invisibility before now.

"I'm glad to see you. What's going on out there?"

Renee shrugged. "They say she's okay, just not right. Not convulsin' or nothin'."

Constance released a breath. "Good."

Renee took a step back and drew patterns on the stone floor with the toe of her sandal. "They're sayin' no one s'pected you could do stuff like that, on account of this thing you wore on your head."

The shield. She hadn't noticed it since some time in Stanstead, where Dal had told her it was almost gone. So now she could assume no barrier remained to defend her from the Aura. And this was the result.

"You need sumthin'? I can bring stuff."

A hug, she thought helplessly. But Renee kept a psychic distance around her at all times, avoiding anything that smacked of confinement. A hug was the one thing she couldn't provide. Despite their shared life here at the Motherhouse, she knew the child no better than she had in Stanstead.

"I'll be fine. What time is it?"

A meaningless question, she realized as soon as it escaped her lips. There was no timekeeping here, only vague estimates.

"Sunset just comin'. I reckon they'll be here to let you go soon."

"I hope so."

"Here." Renee dug in a pocket in her tunic. "This'll help you not think. My ma swore by it." She put a small, leaf-wrapped packet on the table. "I'll check now 'n then."

The words woke Constance fully up. "Wait. Your mother?"

The child bolted. Constance scarcely noticed the door slipping open, then closed. If she didn't have the proof of the grubby object on the table, she could almost believe the encounter had been all smoke and mirrors. Thoughtfully, she tucked the leaf-bound concoction into her own pocket, then returned her head to the table and allowed fatigue to overwhelm her.

Sometime in the night a Weaver she didn't know woke her up and escorted her to her suite. Neither spoke. Constance wondered if they would even tell her, were there a change. She fell onto her bed fully clothed and gave herself over to sleep.

Chapter 19

After that first brief, soporific sleep, Constance jolted awake, her mind spinning with fear and implications. Every fibre of her being wanted to run to the healing room, check on Meade, somehow help disentangle her energies.

Dieu! Could she really be thinking about energy flows? She needed her electronic scanners, those clean, efficient revealers of human life and health, not this irrational nonsense.

Superstition was the way of things here, though. The efficacy of auric energy still challenged her engrained belief systems, but she couldn't deny that, given the lack of basic medical electronics, the spooky techniques these people had developed offered the best hope for survival.

But Meade... Constance hadn't been doing anything, just playing around with a childhood game, reaching out with her imagination for some hint of connection between her moving hands. Nothing really there. And now...

When the sky began a pink tinge, Renee brought her a tray holding caff with unleavened bread and apricot jam. Like caff, the jam was ubiquitous, but would have been palatable had she been able to stomach anything at all. Renee disappeared almost as soon as she had arrived, only the tray on the desk proving she had ever been there at all. Constance nibbled a corner of the bread, hoping it would settle her stomach.

Not long afterwards, as the sun barely topped the hills east of them, the knock came on her doorframe. Her escort consisted only of Dorcas, offering no smiles and fewer words, merely placing a hand on Constance's arm and directing her to the Centra. They didn't go to the conference room but to a smaller one buried deep in the heart of the building. Constance paused at the door. No windows, just that eerie light. Stone walls and floor supported a ceiling woven from reeds or sticks packed with mud. An oversized wooden table stood in the center, surrounded by stools. Shelves and cabinets lined the back wall, laden with scrolls and pottery containers, each labeled in a swirly script she hadn't seen before and couldn't, especially in her current agitated state, interpret.

And Arwen. Arwen dominated the room. Constance felt the diminutive woman's presence right into her bones... and she didn't like it. This was beyond simply being aware of a powerful person. This was invasive.

Dorcas gestured her to a stool. She sat, despite an impulse to run, find Meade, or take the trail to Stanstead and never come back to this horrible, cold place.

But the vibrations from Arwen weren't hostile. There was a kindness there, a pity. Constance didn't indulge in pity herself, but just at this moment she was grateful for the sense that they probably weren't going to lynch her.

Arwen stood behind her, sending shivers up her back, and placed hands on her shoulders. "You aren't in trouble," she said, her voice matter of fact. "We know you didn't intend this. But frankly, we don't know what happened. We've never seen an effect on someone else's energy flows to equal this. You have more power than we ever suspected, and it's vital we both understand it and harness it. You can't risk being around others with this ability."

Never mind all that; it was nothing more or less than she had expected. "How is Meade?" she asked, twisting to look square at Arwen and in the process shaking free from those weighty hands.

"As well as can be expected." The answer came from Dorcas and was accompanied by a puzzled frown. "We've smoothed as much as we can, but the knot in her energy flow is causing emotional instability... and, unfortunately, prevents her from walking."

Constance gasped. "She can't—"

"No." Arwen resettled her hands on Constance's shoulders. "So, she's frightened, as you might well imagine."

Constance straightened; they wouldn't find her without backbone. They believed her to be the cause of this mess; even she couldn't deny that. If she held the key to fixing it, she would do whatever was needed. "What do you need from me?"

"I wish I had the answer." Arwen briefly tightened her grip, then released her and took a seat on one of the other stools placed around the table.

Dorcas paced before them, frowning. "And we won't know until we explore your abilities in much more depth than we have so far. It will be invasive, and it may be unpleasant."

"But we'll keep things as mild as possible," Arwen said. "The more you cooperate, the easier it will be for you. But I can't promise you comfort."

"Is there—?" Constance had meant to ask if she had a choice, but bit the words back. Of course there wasn't a choice. Whatever they believed her capable of, she – and they – had better figure it out quickly, or the potential for all hell breaking loose was much too great. Instead, she nodded, dumb.

Dorcas and Arwen exchanged a glance. "Have you eaten?" Arwen asked.

Constance shook her head.

Arwen made a brief gesture, and Dorcas tugged on what looked like an old-fashioned bell pull, the kind Constance had seen in an ancient castle once, when she and Pierre vacationed in Angleterre. The bell pull had the desired effect; within a minute a man poked his head in the door. Dorcas requested caff and tisane – had they noticed she shunned the black, bitter coffee substitute? – and the eternal abricoe pastries.

During the fraught wait for food delivery, Dorcas and Arwen settled at the table on either side of her and made determined conversation about anything and everything other than the one thing that must fill not only their minds but the very room. Constance ignored them. They wanted her to *eat*? The knot in Meade's energy flow couldn't be worse than the one twisting her stomach.

When Arwen's hand reached across the table and covered hers, she nearly jumped out of her skin. But something flowed through the touch; as her startled eyes met Arwen's, she realized that the tension clenching her was lessening, as if Arwen had transmitted some kind of calming energy—

No. Rationality was all she had left to keep herself sane. Reassurance was born from human contact, nothing more.

Surely nothing more.

A tap came at the door, followed by a pair of runner kids carrying trays. Constance had learned by now that the runner kids were village children who formed the second most reliable way to communicate around the Motherhouse, the first being – of course – spooky mind-to-mind messaging. Every common room in the complex had what looked like an old-fashioned bell pull; a simple tug produced a runner kid, ready to convey your message, day or night. They left promptly, and Arwen squeezed her hand before reaching for the caff pot. "Honestly. This morning will be much easier if you eat."

Dorcas poured from the pot of tisane and set the mug in front of her. "Believe it," she said.

Feeling trapped, but at least grateful for the lessening of the tension in her muscles, Constance reached for the mug. She did not, however, remove her other hand from Arwen's strong, steadying touch.

She suspected there was some sort of pacifying herb brewed into the tisane, because after a few sips she felt her equilibrium, if not fully restored, at least within reach. Food, however, proved to be beyond her.

Then the meal, such as it was, ended. Dorcas placed the trays with the remains of the repast in the corridor and closed the door with a thud that sounded like finality.

"Right," Arwen said, wiping crumbs from her hands. "Let's get started."

Chapter 20

The probing felt physical, occasionally jerking her body, pinching her insides. They focused on her Auric connection and ability to manipulate Templates, the most mysterious of Dorcas's lessons, intricate patterns of Auric energy that Constance had struggled, and failed, to diagram, no matter what her innate abilities might suggest.

Lunchtime came and went; neither woman let up. But the intensity lessened, making the remaining hour or so bearable, until finally Dorcas said, "No more. We'll learn nothing until she's recovered." And the torture stopped.

The last thing Arwen said, after instructing her on self-care for the next few days, was, "Acknowledge Omar. Life will be easier once you do."

On hearing Omar's name, the last of Constance's reserves deserted her; she sank to the cold stone floor and huddled there, shoulders heaving with the effort not to cry. After a minute, warm hands touched her and that soothing energy she had felt earlier seeped into her muscles, leaving her limp. Dorcas helped her up and supported her for the walk to the lodge.

Constance spent the rest of the day in bed or sitting in the chair, which she had turned away from the window, not eating, not speaking. Not crying or laughing or responding at all, despite Renee's constant provision from the dining hall, the tentative touch of a small – and surprisingly clean – hand on her shoulder, her arm.

Finally, around dusk and long after the bell had rung for supper, the stupor began to lift. Constance hauled herself upright and swung her legs off the bed, causing the small figure hunched over the desk to look up and grin. "Huh," Renee proclaimed. "Reckon you'll live?"

"Why wouldn't I?" Although when she tried to stand, her legs wobbled dangerously. "I need to wash."

"They're keepin' hot water for ya." By the time Constance was stable on her feet, Renee was there under her arm. "Come on."

A solitary bath? Pipe dream. The blessing was that the baths existed at all; the curse was that they were communal. Handling the stairs to the first level? Debatable. But it was time, and to her surprise, Constance found that the idea of a bath with her little helper in attendance didn't disturb her as much as it would have, say, yesterday. Between them they hobbled to the bathing room.

Later, after Renee brought her a belated supper, she flipped through the papers on the desk – surely she hadn't left them in such a mess. She might have known the child lacked the capacity to sit quietly by a sickbed. Her seconds of paper were covered with blotched and uneven attempts at using a quill pen – something Constance herself was far from mastering. And a couple of the sheets held more of Renee's diagrams.

"This one?" she asked, holding out a page.

Renee was hovering, twitchy with suppressed energy. "That's about the goats. See, this one, he's a big buck." She pointed to a circle near the center. "And he's got all these does. And then the kids, some of 'em are like this kind of horns, and some are like these." She gestured with her hands. "I'm talkin' about last year's, of course. See these two here?" She pointed to two adjacent circles. "They're gonna mate 'em, 'cause they make the best milk, so why don't they find a buck that'll give them the right milk in the first place?"

The question wasn't rhetorical; Renee wanted to know. It forced Constance out of her own head. "Perhaps they can't tell ahead of time? Or maybe it was an accident? How do you know the breeding history of the goat herd, anyway?"

Renee affected nonchalance. "I go down there a lot. There's a guy talks to me some."

Constance nibbled from the food the child had procured and listened to the flood of patter, amazed at the scope of the girl's inquiring mind. It was, she thought to herself, a surprisingly pleasant way to spend the evening.

*

"You look good."

Constance eyed Arwen warily across an excellent breakfast of eggs and newly picked tomatoes. The food grounded her, and a breeze through the open window above them in the dining hall refreshed her after a muggy night. "I feel all right," she conceded somewhat reluctantly. However good she felt this morning, the memory of the intense probing the day before wouldn't fade soon.

"I'd like to discuss what we learned." Arwen paused to nibble at the food on her own plate, a much smaller quantity than Constance had taken.

She doesn't eat enough. But the thought would have to wait. Arwen showed every sign of being a healthy, spry older woman, if perpetually tired. Constance had to assume if there were any health issues, the Healers moving in and out of the Motherhouse would have found them.

Arwen swallowed a bite of tomato. "Your skills are somewhat obscure. We think that because your connection hasn't been trained, it's been left to run rampant, so to speak. Strong lines that go nowhere, weaker ones that need to be enhanced. We can fix this, but it will take effort. Concentrated effort."

"Why am I not surprised?" Constance reminded herself she had come to the Motherhouse for that very training. Certainly, her energies felt scrambled enough to rival the eggs on her plate this morning.

Arwen grinned. "It'll mean doubling up on some of your lessons, pushing a little harder. We could continue as we are, but there's Meade. You're our best hope now."

Constance glared at her spoon – forks were in short supply in the dining hall for some reason – and put it down. "Remember, this all started because I couldn't master a first-year exercise."

"But you will. Don't forget that most first-year students have been playing with Auric energy for years. You instinctively suppress the Aura because it's hurt you before, and it changes your perception of yourself and your world. Once that's conquered... everything's going to be all right, Constance. I promise."

All right. What were the odds of anything feeling genuinely all right again? The hollow feeling that had haunted her ever since the Adventurer left Terra without Omar and Pierre flooded her. She looked down, quickly hiding the light tremble in her hands under the table and freezing her face into a mask. Actions she had used innumerable times over the years, keeping the grief inviolate, even to herself.

"For instance." Arwen reached across the table and placed both hands on Constance's upper arms.

And... something changed. It was nothing Constance could define, simply a slight shift. Instead of Omar, she thought of Renee, of Meade. Instead of allowing Omar's loss to define her, she felt as if... as if...

... as if the burden she had carried for years drained out through her feet into the earth beneath the dining hall.

She felt it as a physical sensation, an emptying.

And she didn't want it. *Omar.* She was losing her son... but was that truth? Wasn't he still there, wrapped in the familiar cocoon of memory and love?

She raised her eyes. Arwen nodded and removed her hands. "It's a start. Take this morning for yourself, but come to the workroom after lunch. Once things start opening, they'll move quickly. You'll have all the support you need, I guarantee it." She stood, gathering up her plate and bowl. "I'll see you later."

Constance remained anchored at the table, shaken by the unfamiliar, draining feeling, dealing with the hollow left inside, which was somehow, simultaneously, filled.

Renee, who had been banished to the students' end of the dining hall, appeared at her side. "You okay?"

Constance smiled. "I am. Tell you what, let's take the trail by the river this morning, shall we? See what we can find?"

Renee's thin face lit up. "Sure. I know where, it's like someone made it into a special place to sit and watch the river. It's got snails. Then we can go see Meade. She says it's lonely in that healing room."

Snails. Weren't snails a fascination to all children everywhere? Omar had... but no. Today wasn't about Omar. She smiled. "Grab a couple of pastries to take with us."

Constance studied the girl as she danced toward the serving counter and remembered the day they had arrived at the Motherhouse, how Renee had tended the children while she went to the Centra. Remembered the two children in the healer's hut in Stanstead, sequestered there by Renee to keep them safe. "Yes," she said to herself. "Let's do that."

*

Several days later, shortly before suppertime, Constance stepped out of the Centra, drained. She had failed to grasp the pseudo-science behind light balls but had once again created one, which didn't spook her quite as much as the one a few days before. Her resolve high, she turned her feet toward the healing rooms. It was time – past time. Since the accident, she had heard reports of Meade's progress, but hadn't dared visit herself. She and Renee had called in earlier, before lunch, but had been informed that she wasn't available. She had been taken somewhere for a Healing session, and a bath. No time for social calls – though she suspected Renee had spent at least part of the afternoon with the wounded Healer.

By now she knew of Meade's reputation: sunny, welcoming, always holding the best possible view of any situation. Even in Stanstead, Meade had managed to smile, never get overly discouraged, never snappish or grumpy. Even though everyone said otherwise, Constance clung to the notion that these character traits had carried over to the current mess.

She found Meade sitting in a padded chair on the covered porch above the herb-filled, sun-lit courtyard, a light linen blanket across her lap and a pile of knitting in her hands. Meade herself looked pale and had developed hollows under her cheekbones. The needles in her hands trembled slightly. She looked up when Constance approached but offered no smile. "Don't want to spend time with the cripple?" she asked, her voice flat.

"What?" Constance stopped at the base of the porch. "I... of course I want to see you. We came by earlier..."

"Renee told me."

"It's just... I've been hearing—"

"Reports." The knitting dropped to Meade's lap. "Oh, I'm the subject of numerous reports. Only I can't read them myself anymore. I access them and they're tied in knots, or my eyes are. Do you have any *idea* what that does to your head?"

Constance lowered herself onto the edge of the porch. Her fault. The result of her bumbling.

Meade sighed. "I was happy once," she said. And then said nothing more.

Constance looked down, letting her toe trace patterns in the grass much as Renee did when she was frightened. She swallowed. "I never meant this to happen. I was just trying—"

"To do a student exercise. Do you think I blame you? No one blames you." Her hands returned to the knitting, the wooden sticks clicking rhythmically as she spoke. "At least I have enough wits left to carry on a conversation, as long as I don't try to think too much. It's funny. In Stanstead – no, before Stanstead – I thought something was missing from my life. What a joke."

The knitting sailed into the courtyard. Constance gasped at the violence in Meade's throw. But when she stood to retrieve the tangled bundle of threads, Meade said, "Leave it. Who knows, I might stab myself with a needle. Why go on living like this?" She closed her eyes.

The depth of pain in her voice woke a remnant of the medic Constance had once been. She mounted the porch, dropped the yarn, and took Meade's hands in her own, resisting the other woman's instinctive recoil. "Tell me what I can do and I'll do it."

After a moment's resistance, Meade's hands turned to grasp hers. "Be patient? I hate this. I hate depending on others to move around. I hate being nasty and angry. I hate the way the Aura is all messed up in my mind. I understand what's happened, but... oh, hell, Connie. I don't know what to do."

That nickname again. This time it didn't chafe.

Her throat too constricted to speak, Constance used an edge of her tunic to blot the tears that coursed down Meade's cheeks. After a minute she swallowed and mustered medic-engrained reserves to speak calmly. "I'll come every day. We'll find a way to make you better. There *has* to be a way." To her horror, she felt her own eyes filling; she, who prided herself on her detachment. But she forced herself to continue. "When I first got here, I left our ship and the Aura almost killed me. I was bedridden. Weak, nauseous, blinding headache. Then..." She hesitated as the memories flooded back. "Then Gwen took over, she's the resident Healer, and did some of her energy magic, she said she linked with Quinn's energy to get through the ship's shielding, and I was better. Quinn's Weaving let me leave the ship. So I can understand, sort of, what you're going through. It's all so complicated, but there's a solution in there somewhere. There must be. And we'll find it," she concluded with a resolve she didn't truly feel or believe. But it was vital that Meade believe it.

*

Later that evening, Dorcas appeared at her door and gave her a rare smile of approval. "Well done. Meade hasn't cried since the accident. Whatever you said or did, you released something that's been locked up. It helped."

"Thanks," Constance muttered. However positive the result, to her it felt like another chain binding someone to her. More than ever, she wanted to be left alone.

Chapter 21

"Have a lookit this." Constance had been studying yet another weave pattern that afternoon, but glanced up when Renee waved a diagram under her nose.

A nine-day had passed since the start of her intense training. Although horrendous at first, already she sensed a shift to something more settled, more focused. Her mind seemed sharper, and even her body felt stronger. Her skills... well. But she could make a light ball reliably now, and the day before, to her own amazement, she had moved a pebble across the desk without touching it. Student exercises, but they encouraged her.

In her spare time, she visited Meade, although each encounter was more frustrating than the last. Despite that early connection in Stanstead, Meade now shunned her support, even tentative efforts at friendship. As often as not, Renee came with her, or was already there when she arrived. Meade had some kind of bond with the child that Constance couldn't fathom and didn't try to interfere with, since it was obvious they both benefitted. She ignored the occasional twinge of jealousy at the understanding flowing between the crippled woman and the girl.

The change in the weather helped. Constance detected the first hints of autumn in the air. While she couldn't look forward to a winter in this place of stone and isolation, the freshness of the cooling air revived her spirit, making her think of potages and toasted cheese.

She shook off her thoughts and turned her attention to Renee's diagram. It was a mess. Blots, lines drawn then scribbled out, one whole section with a giant, irregular X through it, but with lines and arrows seeming to direct to the other side of the sheet. "Can you understand this?" Constance asked cautiously, well aware that Renee could be prickly when questioned.

This time she got a pitying look, with an undercurrent of impatience. "Look. This here's the kind of cloud that's real thin and gets itself into tatters. And here's where it's just like a blanket, all gray."

Sure enough, this time Renee had added little sketches inside each of her bubbles, from puffy shapes to flat lines. The connectors included arrows. "So this means one comes after the other?"

"Course it does. What else? And then here's those giant clouds that come from the hills and 'get thunder, and here's..."

Her grubby, and now ink-stained, finger pointed out the different shapes. Constance followed the rambling explanation with half her mind. There was no doubt Renee was proving to be an excellent observer of nature, with a unique way of making sense out of patterns. The diagram, if copied out clean, would be a work of science as well as art. But she had already been forced to lecture about overuse of paper, because there just wasn't that much of it. Even the seconds, back sides of apprentice exercises mainly, were in demand; at times Constance felt slightly guilty about helping herself to them, even for her own studies.

But Renee had to learn. Just like Constance's errant energies, in a way; if Renee's unique observational and organizational skills were channeled, who knew what might be revealed?

Or suppressed. Training Renee would require delicacy.

And what were the odds of accomplishing anything formal? Training in the village offered only practical skills the child had already mastered or probably would never need. The apprentices' lessons involved energy manipulations, but Renee had no Entrée at all and would never belong to one of the Weavers' guilds.

Still... "May I borrow this?" she asked

And ran straight up against Renee's bullheadedness. "It's mine."

"True. And I'll bring it back. I need to talk to Arwen. If nothing else, we're running out of seconds."

"So? There's always the dirt." Renee shrugged. "It's not like they matter. Just sumthin' to do."

Constance shook her head. "They matter. Do you know anyone else who can do this?"

"Don't know anyone who'd want to."

Constance bit down exasperation in favor of a totally fake patience. "Look, Renee. You have something unique here. I'd like to..." What did she plan, exactly? Provide adequate paper and ink, certainly. But how to provide what doesn't exist? How to train when there is no master? "I want to talk to Arwen about how you do this. Perhaps she can help you do it more and better."

With a lightning change of mood, Renee grinned. "And you don't know what you're talkin' about, do ya?"

Constance grinned back. "No. But I'm not the right person to strengthen these skills. Arwen can help you."

"Yeah, sure." Renee's tone conveyed her scepticism, but she handed over the paper. "Whatever."

They left the guest lodge together. Renee took off barefoot down the trail to the village, Constance crossed the green to the Centra.

Arwen looked up from her workbench as she entered. "Just the person I want to see."

"Please no," Constance groaned. If Arwen was looking for you, it never presaged anything good, in her experience.

"No, nothing like that." The older woman waved a dismissive hand. "I expected you, that's all. Let's find refreshment, shall we? Then you can tell me why you're here instead of working on your exercises."

"Renee interrupted me."

"Ah, that child." Arwen led the way out of the cramped workroom, along the bare stone corridors and out into the sunlight. "A tisane, I think. We're both a bit jangled."

After a silent foray into the dining hall, they returned to a bench outside the Centra, mugs and small nut pastries in hand. "So," Arwen said with a hint of a sigh, "What's Renee up to now?"

Constance swallowed a bite of the pastry – hazelnuts? – and narrated the events earlier, finally producing Renee's diagram.

Arwen leaned over the paper with interest. "I think she's got that line wrong," she commented, then was silent for a few minutes while she studied the picture and Constance traced back the questionable line. Arwen was right, as far as she could interpret weather conditions. But given the complexity and what appeared to be a timescale attached to the style of the connecting lines – something she hadn't noticed at first – it was hardly a demerit. The work was amazing.

"According to this," Arwen said, "we can say that today's weather will bring high cloud within a day, and probably a thunderstorm within two days – from the west, not the east. They're usually not as ferocious." Sure enough, the eastern thunderstorm symbol had been drawn larger. "Interesting the way that the weather diagrams from the east, from the hills, almost feel sinister. Or am I reading something into the diagram that isn't there?"

As she had been taught, Constance paused to assess her own reactions before speaking. "No. I don't think you are."

"So, what do we do?" Arwen asked.

"I don't know. That's why I'm here."

"Unfortunately, we can't let her have any more paper. She's using up our supplies as it is."

Constance nodded. "But it's bigger than just finding her something to draw on. She's got a unique mind."

"And it would behoove us to train it. I understand that." Arwen stood, brushing pastry crumbs from her tunic and clutching her still half-filled mug. She brandished the diagram. "Leave this with me. I think I know a candidate to take her in hand, but I can't make promises yet."

Constance also stood, nodding at the paper. "She wants that back."

Arwen's smile was almost mischievous. "Tell her to come to me."

Constance chuckled to herself as she walked away, anticipating how any meeting between Arwen and Renee might go.

Chapter 22

"That man's here."

At Renee's laconic statement, Constance straightened and looked over her shoulder to the door where the girl stood, following those actions with a groan as her back protested. How long had she been hunched over her worktable, staring at the weave, anyway? She had begun to feel as if she were lost in it, traveling along the threads deeper and deeper into the mystery of the mind.

Renee remained by the door, scowling, arms akimbo. "You hear me?" she demanded, dropping her air of sophisticated indifference. "I said, he's here."

"What man?" As happened far too often for her own comfort these days, Constance found her mind following three paths, the weave, the mysterious man, and evidence that Renee was approaching her teen years. Menarche. How on earth was she going to handle that? Not the birds-and-bees part, Renee undoubtedly already knew the facts, but the psychological and hormonal changes inherent in the girl's approach to womanhood.

"That bossy one in Stanstead. He got a right to be here? Yeah, I reckon," Renee answered herself. "They say he teaches the 'prentices. So I guess he's gonna be around awhile."

"You mean Dal, I expect. He's here? Did Agnes come, too?"

"Dunno." Clearly the older Healer was of no interest to Renee.

"And this concerns us how?"

Instantly defensive, Renee retorted, "You don't have to be so grumpy about it."

Suddenly aware of her own weariness, Constance stood and shot a glance at the window. She had been so wrapped up in the weave she risked missing supper. "You're right. I'm not grumpy, just overtaxed. Have you eaten yet?"

Renee was already out the door; nothing interfered with her appetite for long. "What's that word? O-ver-taks...?"

Constance caught up, pulling her door to behind her, and reminded herself of a personal promise to pay more attention to the girl. "It's a fancy word for working too long and too hard. Tell me what you've been up to today."

"Been in the village. Harvest, everyone's busy, there's so much to do. There's gonna be a party. I don't like parties," she said as if it didn't matter. "And they put me in charge of the little kids, the ones we brought and a few more. We had this soup for lunch with egg in it, it was weird..."

Renee prattled on as they crossed the green to the dining hall, while Constance reflected on her throwaway comment: *I don't like parties*. What did that mean, with regard to the child's background? The bruises were gone, the scars had faded, and Renee had filled out; she was no longer the skinny waif who had sequestered two other children in a hut. One thing she was sure of, Renee had been abused. Parties might be a negative memory, if they had ever happened at all in the girl's short life.

Another thing to sort out.

At the door to the dining hall, Renee got swept up in a group of new apprentices who probably were about the same age as she was; Renee's actual age remained a mystery. Grateful for the break but feeling light-headed, Constance collected her food – a small meat cutlet, vegetables, potatoes – and settled down to a solitary meal while her mind struggled to completely disentangle itself from the weave she had been studying.

Ground, she grumbled to herself. She hadn't gone through the process of grounding herself in ordinary reality before she and Renee left her room for the dining hall. Now she was paying the price. Yet another lesson learned.

*

Next door in the Centra, Dal faced Arwen across her workbench, allowing his face to reflect his displeasure. "You are aware I've only been home for half a day?"

"You've had time to bathe and check on Meade. And presumably you've already reviewed the lesson plans for the fourth years. You can't claim exhaustion."

"I think I can. Meade gave me a tongue-lashing."

"Fair enough," Arwen said, backtracking. For a moment he foolishly thought she would let him escape. But as was often the case with Arwen, it proved to be a false hope. "I have a new assignment for you. An experiment, really. It concerns Renee."

"Renee... that child Meade and Constance found? What does she have to do with us?"

"I don't know. And that's why I need your help."

Dal stared. Arwen was at her most infuriating when she became enigmatic. For her to admit not knowing anything at all was sufficiently unusual that it caught his interest.

"You can't really think... oh, come on, Arwen. Me, with an undisciplined child? Especially one with no Entrée. Isn't Constance taking care of her?"

"Constance has quite enough on her plate," Arwen said calmly.

He sighed, making sure Arwen heard. "Tell me what you want me to do with her. And why."

Succinctly, Arwen outlined Renee's odd talent for organizing facts. To conclude, she placed several of the diagrams, provided by Constance, in front of him. "I don't know where this is going. I do know that she sees things we don't, in ways I don't understand. She's attached to Meade, but Meade's skills are largely restricted to Healing. Where Constance is concerned, she'll be able to sort all this out, but not yet. She's incredibly powerful, but her energy's still wildly unfocused, so we're pushing her training as hard as we can. Besides, there's an emotional involvement there, although she doesn't acknowledge it yet."

Dal picked up the papers and studied the rough, intricate diagrams on them.

Where on earth had the child learned this?

Reluctantly, he looked up and met Arwen's steady gaze. "I see your point."

"You're the most logical person I know. If anyone can train this talent, you can. There's no time to lose, though. She's hopelessly undisciplined and inclined to dismiss the diagrams as unimportant. But there's more here... there are connections on these pictures that defy my ability to understand where she got her raw data."

Dal nodded, once again absorbed in the drawings.

"So." Arwen's voice had that sharp, wrap-up-the-meeting tone.

He looked up. "So."

"You'll do it."

Wearily, he conceded and gave her a grin. They went a long way back, he and Arwen. She knew him well. "There's a choice?"

"You don't want a choice."

"I demand right of refusal. When do I meet this paragon?"

"Tomorrow. If we can find her."

"Oh, great," he groaned.

"Join me for supper?" Arwen slid from her stool.

Recognizing her victory, and that he would have no time at all to recover from the grueling experience of Stanstead, he nodded and followed her from the room.

Chapter 23

Dal met the girl two days later. Renee had exhibited a remarkable ability to recognize potential limits to her freedom; in that time, Dal hadn't once laid eyes on her. Arwen finally had tracked her down in the village and asked one of the burly farmers march her back to the Motherhouse, under strict instruction not to let the girl out of his sight. Renee had proved to be both chameleon and escape artist.

Now the child stood, surly and scruffy, across a table from him, glaring. He, Arwen, and Constance had agreed that Renee would not do well in one of the windowless workrooms in the Centra, and nobody wanted to impose an unwanted study regimen in her room. As a compromise they met, this sunny early autumn morning, in the guest lodge lounge. It wasn't a bright space, but at least there were windows.

Faced at last with the reality of the child, Dal did a quick scan of her mind – Renee seemed oblivious – and concluded that she was both annoyed and scared. Why scared? He had listened to Constance's summary of what little she knew about the girl and was inclined to agree; Renee's early life hadn't been easy.

"Those're mine." Renee stared at the papers under his hand, resting on the table they had positioned by the window.

"I know." Dal kept his voice neutral.

"I want 'em back."

"You'll get them back. Why do you want them?"

The question caught her by surprise. Dal was impressed that she pondered the question before answering. But then she only said, "'Cause they're mine."

"Do you need them? To keep track of the information you've recorded, for instance?"

"Naa. I can do 'em again."

"Then why are they so important to you? Constance tells me you used to draw them in the dirt."

"Sure." She looked at him defiantly. "Still do."

"You can't keep those."

"So?"

"So, what's the big attraction, Renee? What makes these more important than the dirt ones?"

Quivering with frustration, the girl looked on the verge of tearing up. "They're *mine*."

Again, Dal gently touched the girl's mind. For a moment he almost forgot what he was looking for. The inner workings of Renee's mind were beyond anything he had ever experienced. But there was time for that later. "Ahh. Because you don't have anything else that's yours. Is that right?"

Renee looked down. "None of yer business."

"Fair enough." He stacked the few pages, tapping them on the table. "I'll put these here." He followed the words with action, placing the sheets midway between them. Renee moved with the speed of a snake, snatching, but he left a heavy hand weighing them down. "We'll talk. I give you my promise that when we're done, you can take them. But I need you to listen and answer honestly when I ask a question. That's the deal. Agreed?"

She continued to mumble. "Don't see why you wanna keep me here. Who cares about your dumb questions anyway?"

Dal played his trump card. "Meade might."

Renee's head came up. She said nothing, waiting.

"We believe," Dal said carefully, "you might be able to help her. You know how unhappy she is."

She stood stock still. Her eyes never left his face.

"Did you know," he continued casually, as if it didn't matter, as if being witness to Meade's pain over the last two days hadn't wounded something inside him, "that people have patterns, too? Every single person. That's what's twisted in Meade. Her pattern is tangled up. And you are an expert at deconstructing patterns, even without more training."

"De-con…?"

"Deconstruct. Breaking down a pattern into its individual pieces. If we can deconstruct Meade's pattern, figure out how the twists go—"

In a lightning change of mood, Renee went from withdrawn but curious to belligerent. "You know I can't do that. I ain't got that Entrée stuff like the rest of you."

"No. But with one of us, perhaps we can work through it. Meade needs you, Renee. That's the best reason I know for you to help. The chance you can help Meade."

The girl turned away – she had yet to sit down – and paced furiously the length of the room and back. "Don't think I can trust you," she announced when she finally stopped by the table.

"I don't think I can trust you, either. You haven't exactly proven yourself trustworthy."

He felt the emotion like a blast. *"That's a lie,"* the girl shouted in his face. "I did everything. I got those other kids in Stanstead away, and I kept 'em all safe comin' here, and I help Constance and I feed the goats and—"

Dal retreated. Challenging Renee's reliability was a kneejerk, based on impatience more than reality. "You're right. I'm sorry." He left it a beat while the child thought. Her face betrayed puzzlement. Was it possible no one had ever apologized to her before? "Help us, Renee. Help Meade. With your gifts... well, you could be a powerful person, if you wanted to be."

Renee made a rude noise. Dal nodded. She wanted freedom more than power. Any attempt to contain her would inevitably end in failure.

"Renee?"

Another manic circuit of the room, then the girl pulled up beside his chair. "All right, I'll do it. But don't you dare touch me. And you give me those. Now."

Dal immediately handed over the pages. Renee flipped through them, her tense face softening as she reviewed one, then the next. Then, praise the Aura, she sat across from him and said, "So, Know-It-All, what do I gotta do? Can we have some food first?"

To his surprise, he found himself smiling. "I've brought buns and tisane. Nobody functions well on an empty stomach."

This, he thought, might not prove to be such a bad assignment after all.

Interlude

Clouds striped the sky. Constance fought a wind that sent early fallen leaves scudding across the green. She had been in the Centra since breakfast, and still there was work to do, but she had progressed far enough in the lesson that Dorcas had permitted her to complete it in the refuge of her room.

Life had settled into a pattern as autumn chased the warmth of summer away. Constance found herself resorting more frequently to a wool shawl procured from the textile building and wondered about warmer covers on her bed. Whatever the amenities of the guest lodge, it was drafty and cold, the stone walls seeming to gather and store the chill. She had experienced cold before, of course, most recently the winter they had passed on the Adventurer where she was exposed to it whenever she encountered someone fresh from the outdoors. She had been able to sense it in their clothes, on their skin when they came in from whatever they had been doing out in the wind and snow; at the time, she hadn't thought that was strange.

There had been a massive party on the green just a few days before, celebrating equinox and harvest. She had had no idea so many people occupied the Motherhouse and its attached village

– or that they could drink so much, dance so wildly, make so much noise. Although she had enjoyed the performances of the two Bards currently in residence, the rest... well. She had retreated to the relative quiet of her own room... and then felt bereft, as if life was going on without her.

Which, she acknowledged, it was. She studied, visited the dining hall, persisted in occasional, unsatisfactory visits with Meade, indulged in walks around the environs, and slept, punctuated only by Renee's excited discourse.

Today, however, there had been no sign of Renee other than a brief sighting at lunchtime as the child flitted across the green. But Constance had long since given up worrying about Renee. She was a survivor. There was a subtle change in her though, for all she kept close to Constance whenever their workdays crossed. She seemed less... flighty. More focused. She refused to talk about her lessons, but she no longer needed prodding to place herself at Dal's table each day.

Safe in her room, Constance unloaded a tisane, already tepid, and a small bone-knit plant in a pot onto her table. The plant was a pretty little thing, low growing with succulent evergreen leaves. She had been told it bore delightful pink flowers late in the summer. Her task? To kill the plant.

Kill.

Constance refused to indulge in needless sentiment, but she was beginning to understand what the Healers meant when they talked about communicating with plants. They wouldn't consider it killing, but rather working with the plant to unleash its healing properties. From her greater scientific knowledge, Constance suspected those properties were locked behind cell walls, which needed to break – wilt – before the medicine could be released. To the Healers, it was mystical, a communion between them and the plants. The operation could be accomplished more readily – less personally – by placing the plant in one of the drying boxes on the roof of the Healers' lodge, but that wasn't the point.

She shook her head and almost absentmindedly snatched at warmth in the air, channeling it to the tisane. It was a handy trick, a mug of hot liquid could last hours. A minor triumph, and a practical one.

She kept the shawl over her shoulders, sat at the table, and studied the plant. It waited benignly, seemingly oblivious to its fate. Constance didn't believe it. The plant knew.

Renee exploded in. She never knocked, just assumed that if she needed or wanted to be somewhere, that was where she would go. "I need shoes," she announced as she flopped across the tightly made bed.

"I agree." Constance wrapped her hands around the tisane, shivering. Renee had brought the day's chill in with her.

"And pants," she continued portentously. "On account of, I ain't a kid anymore. Meade says I need to grow up."

You're mine, not hers.

Jealous?

Constance told herself not to be stupid. But when she asked, "Did Meade say anything else?" even she heard the tinge of acid.

"Nah." Renee lay on her back with one leg up in the air, examining a callus on the bottom of her dirty foot. "I reckon my feet'll get all soft, if I gotta wear shoes."

"If you don't wear shoes, come winter your feet will freeze off, I expect." Constance reached for the tisane and took a sip. Already cooling, but reheating it took energy, and when Renee was around she rarely had any to spare.

"Don't believe ya." Renee looked like she was settling in for the afternoon. The foot was back down, and the girl was wriggling into a nest, ruining the tidy bedclothes. Her face, after that declaration, became somber. Cutting through the energy, the sheer physicality of the child, Constance realized – something was wrong.

Renee might once have been reticent, but no more. Out it came: "My hair's no good."

"What? There's nothing wrong with your hair."

"Lookit." Renee rolled upright, grabbed a hank of her tangled mane, raised it and let it fall. "This isn't *serious* hair."

Serious hair? Constance put down her mug and turned her full attention to the girl. "You're already pretty," she said slowly. "You don't have to do anything to make yourself prettier. Except maybe wash your face more often."

She couldn't have said anything worse. Renee was on her feet in a flash. "I *knew* you wouldn't understand," she screeched. "Meade said you would, but you don't, you'll *never*."

Renee headed for the door, but stopped when Constance barked, "Wait." She spoke into a heavy silence, addressing the girl's frozen back. "If that's not it... you want to look more grown up?"

Renee spun. Her eyes shot fury. "You act like I'm just some pesky kid. Why can't you *understand*?" She reeled and this time made it through the door, leaving Constance stunned.

Her little girl was growing up. She was looking for stature, her place in the world. Why on earth had she posited a desire to be prettier? She knew Renee better than that, and wasn't surprised she was insulted.

Her little girl...

But why had she taken her concerns to Meade?

Abruptly the dart of jealousy was back. This time Constance acknowledged it for what it was. Renee was hers. Her child, approaching womanhood with her usual lack of grace. Constance supposed this was just the first of a string of tantrums ahead while Renee grew into her new stature.

The very thought made her tired. She glared at the little herb, as if it had failed to support her.

Then her mouth quirked into a half smile. If Renee was giving her fits, what would she do to Arwen, to Meade, to staid, stiff Dal? Life around the Motherhouse just might become very interesting indeed.

Chapter 24

It was, on the surface, a lovely morning. A gentle autumn breeze brought spicy, tempting aromas from the dining hall and brushed Meade's perspiring forehead as she eased to her feet. She balanced there for a few seconds. Then – she didn't collapse, exactly. It was more as if her legs lacked the will to stand. Once again, against her wishes, she found herself in the chair that had become her semi-permanent home on the porch of the healing rooms. On the way down, she knocked the knob of her elbow against the chair's wooden arm, sending a shaft of pain toward her shoulder. Her lips pinched tighter than they already were and her fingernails dug into the chair's arms, knuckles white.

"Good," Dal said. "Now, lift your left leg straight out."

"Why?"

"Meade..."

"I mean, why bother?" She changed the focus of her irritation from the chair and the sore elbow to the man tormenting her. "We both know it isn't accomplishing anything. I'm not standing any better than I was. Even when I get my balance, I can't recruit the muscles to walk. And I probably never will," she muttered in conclusion, half hoping Dal wouldn't hear, half hoping he would.

"I'm not arguing with you," he said.

His calm demeanor triggered a new thrust of annoyance. "You're so damned smug," she snapped, "but you don't have a clue. You're not trapped here—"

"Meade, just shut up, will you?"

His tone hadn't changed, but at the harsh words she gasped – and looked, really looked, at the man squatting before her. Dal was still Dal, but the gauntness imprinted by the ordeal at Stanstead had yet to leave his face. Dark shadows rimmed his eyes, and the expression in them was... haunted.

"I'm searching for changes," he said with slightly exaggerated patience. "When I scan your energy, I'm sensing any shift, any little relaxation in the knot. But for there to be a shift in your energies, you have to help."

"Nothing's happened so far. Why expect anything now?"

"It's data. I've come to believe that with Renee's help, we may be able to map whatever is going on. A map is no different from a weave, in its way." He stood and moved to the porch steps, where he sat and joined her in contemplation of the view. "It's our best chance, Meade."

Rather than responding directly – like by apologizing yet again for her sour mood – she said, "Renee's different these days. What's going on with her? Something about her lessons?"

He shook his head. "She's a sponge. Whatever the challenge, she's mastered it almost before I've finished explaining. I know what you mean, but there's nothing in the lessons to trigger the outbursts. No reason for her to be frustrated."

Meade toyed with the edge of the blanket thrown over the arm of her chair. "I'm pretty sure she's older than we thought. If her body's maturing..."

Dal nodded. "It's possible, and consistent. You and Constance will have to take care of that one. I'm not qualified."

Meade gave a quiet snort. No, Dal wouldn't have much patience with the vagaries of female biology.

He got to his feet and loomed over her. "Once more. Leg out, then in. Slowly, please." He held his hands poised to sense any change in her energy flow.

Still grumpy – but when wasn't she grumpy these days? – she paused, just to make her point, then lifted her left leg. Slowly, as commanded.

*

Later, back in her room, Meade sat at the desk and reached into her drawer for the crystal she used for meditation. It was half the size of her fist, bluish, of no value to anyone but her.

It wasn't there.

Frowning, she gripped the back of the chair to navigate the short distance to the bed, where she felt under her pillow and all through the bedclothes. Nothing.

She couldn't get down on the ground because she would never get up again, so she rolled from one side to the other, scanning the floor. She even peered into the skinny space between the bed and the wall, but there was no sign of the crystal.

Thoroughly shaken, exhausted and sweaty from the effort, she collapsed and lay still. It had been years since she had meditated regularly without her crystal in hand. Imprisoned as she was in a healing room when she wasn't in her own room in the Healers' lodge, it had been her constant companion. She hadn't taken it anywhere else, and the cleaning staff never messed with her stuff. It was just... gone.

*

In the Centra that afternoon, Constance sat at her assigned worktable and studied first the weave diagrammed with charcoal on the table, then the plant in front of her. Follow the threads, work the weave, form the energy and allow it to drop over the plant. She repeated the words like a mantra.

Poor plant. It was enduring her messed-up energy, and so far had managed not to die.

"Perhaps that's the problem," Dorcas said from over Constance's shoulder. "You really don't want to do this."

"Perhaps." By now she largely ignored the Weavers' spooky ability to read her mind.

"Let's try something else."

Dorcas crossed to the worktable and wiped away the weave with a rag. Then she drew a new one. It looked – familiar, in a strange way. As if it were the old one, only inside out. Which made no sense in a two-dimensional diagram. Constance frowned and let her mind trace the pattern.

When she thought she understood it, she looked up. Dorcas nodded, reached over, and partially snapped off a branch of the plant. "Fix it," she said.

Constance experienced a moment of panic, one she was all too familiar with as it visited her with each new exercise. Then she swallowed and turned her attention to the hapless bone-knit plant. The broken twig dangled from the main body of foliage.

"Since the energy of this plant is directed to mending, the weave should meld with its energy fairly easily," Dorcas said. "Just focus and take your time."

Constance did as she was told. Time, and physical reality, melted away as she walked the weave, building it with energy, directing it to the broken twig. As she finally tied off the energy, the injured branch moved, sort of jumped, but didn't re-attach itself. Exhausted, Constance drooped and let her head rest on her arms on the worktable.

"Wonderful. Almost there. It's approaching dinnertime, so stop for tonight. You channeled a lot of energy just now."

"Almost dinner?" Constance sat up and looked around, dazed. "But it's only mid-afternoon."

Dorcas shook her head. "Go on. I'll see you in the dining hall."

Stunned by the lateness of the hour, Constance slid from her stool and briefly touched the floor, grounding herself to clear the aftereffects of what she now realized had been hours in trance. Then she made for the Centra's main door. Her mind felt wrung out; she wanted nothing more than... well, she thought with a flash of amusement, a good sherry would be nice. But sherry didn't exist here. She would make do with a wash and a few minutes of quiet – unless, of course, Renee was around – before refueling at the dining hall.

*

After they left, the door to the workroom opened silently, and as silently closed a moment later. The bone-knit plant no longer rested on the worktable.

Chapter 25

No one crossed Arwen in this mood. Her hair, short and controlled, flared around her red face. Renee, usually indomitable, cowered on her stool.

The stool was strategic, Constance thought from her place on the sidelines. Although the girl was several centimeters taller than when she had been no more than a starving waif in Stanstead, still Renee's feet dangled well above floor level. No quick getaways this time.

Despite the outward signs of rage, Arwen's voice was measured. "Shall we make a list? Meade's meditation stone. My stole of authority. A packet of bandages for poultices from the healing rooms. Slates from the classrooms. The bone-knit plant. Do I need to go on?"

Renee had been studying her hands, clenched on her lap. Now she looked up and glared but said nothing.

"All things important to the people who use them. All trivial in themselves, not critical. Until the regulator on the boiler."

Constance's eyes widened. She was far from understanding the heating mechanism used for the Centra, the dining hall, and the guest lodge, but she knew the regulator controlled pressure, and without it...

"Do you have any idea how much harm an explosion might have caused?" Arwen continued through clenched teeth. "You could have killed someone."

Renee looked back down at her hands.

"*Answer me!*" Arwen bellowed. Everyone in the room jumped.

To Constance's astonishment, the hint of a tear appeared at the corner of Renee's eye. "Dunno," she muttered.

"You don't know?" Dal, who had been a statue in the corner until now, strode forward, his lips in a tight line. "Despite all the time and effort we've expended on you. The faith we've put—"

"Wait." In a lightning turn from her previous fury, Arwen's voice sounded subdued. "She's telling the truth, Dal. She doesn't know."

"She knows well enough what she's done. And if you think I'm going to waste any more time—"

"It won't be a waste. And while her actions are clear enough, to her the reason is a mystery. Isn't that right, Renee?" Arwen circled the table to Renee's stool, placed her hands under the still-skinny arms, and lifted the girl down. Taking her hand, she crossed the room to her desk and sat, drawing Renee to stand in front of her. Gently, she said, "Think, child. Your mind works in patterns. What pattern reveals itself here?"

"Dunno," Renee repeated, but her tone had changed. Her defiance – a fall-back position, Constance reflected – had vanished. Instead Renee sounded uncertain. She kept her eyes fixed on the floor at Arwen's feet.

"But you can find out." Arwen waved for Dal to back away. Once she and Renee were unopposed in their own bubble of space, she said, "Here's what you are going to do."

*

Constance watched, off and on during the afternoon, as the missing items appeared on the table in Renee's room next door. Her plant, somewhat the worse for wear as Renee had replanted it somewhere in a field, then had to dig it up again. The blue stone Meade cherished, the stole, the bandages. Several items from the kitchen, and a trinket from the Apprentices' lodge belonging to Amalie, the girl from the other side of the hills. The boiler regulator had been returned first and replaced; Constance already felt the slight extra heat the system provided.

Renee was silent during the process. Once the items were assembled, she muttered, "That's all." Then she added, "Go 'way."

Constance had expected this. "I'll call you for dinner," she said as she closed Renee's door. She fully expected Renee to disappear before mealtime, but she had to make the offer, assure the girl her support system was in place.

*

As she expected, Renee wasn't around when the dinner bell rang. But the next morning Constance tracked her down in her room, early. "Come on. You have a lot of work to do today."

"Don't wanna," Renee moaned from deep within the covers.

"You didn't eat last night. You need your energy."

In fact, Constance was mildly surprised to find Renee in her room. She had expected her to disappear for at least a full day, possibly more. She had obviously underestimated her grit. With a sigh, loud enough to express extreme displeasure,

Renee emerged, long legs first, from the bedclothes.

"I think," Constance said with a hint of amusement as she studied the dilapidated form, "you'd better wash your face and comb your hair before you appear in public."

Renee flushed beet red.

Wisely, Constance made no comment but turned to the door. "I'll wait. Don't be long."

Puberty. Back in her own room, she crossed her fingers that Renee would, in fact, turn up to go to breakfast, then quickly uncrossed them, scoffing at herself for resorting to a relic of a more superstitious age, even if out of habit rather than belief.

Then she paused, thought about the last few nine-days, and re-crossed her fingers. Just this once, just in case.

Chapter 26

The next afternoon brought excitement and novelty to the green. Standing there, held by a tall, dark-skinned man with grizzled hair, was...

A horse?

Constance paused at the door of the dining hall and stared. Horses were rare enough in Eurocorp, but Quinn's had been the only one she had seen in the Midland since she arrived.

This one was jet black with a white blaze on its nose and one white front hoof. Renee, barreling out of the hall behind her, stopped in her tracks. "What's that?" she whispered, as if to speak aloud might dissipate the animal into the ether.

"A horse."

"But where'd it *come* from?"

"I don't know. The man might be a relative of my friend Quinn."

"Don't know no Quinn."

"A Scribe. I knew her back at the Adventurer, where I come from." Constance consciously forced herself not to whisper, although even to her the appearance of the horse seemed just short of miraculous.

Arwen had emerged from the Centra and now stood chatting with the newcomer. It was obvious they knew each other.

Renee left Constance's side and crossed toward the beast, entranced. She followed at a little distance.

"Excellent," Arwen said, acknowledging them, and put a hand on the girl's shoulder. "Ifram, this is Renee. I think she'll fit our needs very well."

He gravely offered a hand to the girl. Renee eyed it suspiciously, looked at Arwen, who nodded, then accepted his hand. The shake was a mere formality, not enough to deflect her attention from the horse.

"Here, try this," Ifram said. Instead of releasing Renee's hand, he carried it over to the horse's shoulder. The horse stood obligingly still under the caress. Renee's expression suggested she had entered a new, enchanted world.

"Now this," Ifram said. He released Renee's hand and used his own to stroke the horse's nose. "Try it. She'll let you."

From the moment the horse turned its head into Renee's hand and nuzzled, the girl was lost. Constance, standing next to Arwen, saw it happen. Privileged girls back in Eurocorp sometimes rode horses. For her part, she had never really understood the attraction. Now, she saw it in action.

"We call her Socksy. The kids named her," he added with an embarrassed shrug. "She's tired now, but come to the village tomorrow and you can ride her."

"Ride," Renee echoed. From the expression on her face, the heavens had opened and angels had sung, like in the old legends. Her eyes dancing, she looked away from Socksy to Ifram. "Really?"

The man smiled. "Really. Arwen told me you might be interested in taking care of her. It's a lot of work, though."

"I ain't afraid of work."

"We'd best get Socksy over to the stable," Arwen said. "She needs to settle."

Renee's attention flitted rapidly from the mare, to Ifram, to Arwen. "I'm goin' too."

Arwen gave one of her rare smiles. "Yes, I daresay you are. Ifram, would you care to join me for dinner this evening?"

He shook his head and rubbed a hand over his hair. "Thanks, ma'am, but I reckon I'll stay in the village. I've got acquaintances there, from when I brought Butter."

Butter, Quinn's horse, now lived with Quinn at the Adventurer. She also had developed an attachment to an animal.

Ifram led Socksy toward the trail leading to the village, Renee excitedly chattering at his side. Constance remained with Arwen until the two turned the corner and disappeared from sight.

Arwen lifted her brows. "I believe Dorcas is expecting you?"

She nodded, failing to muster enthusiasm for Dorcas's mental poking and prodding. Not when real life was happening right here, before her eyes. But, she conceded with an internal sigh, such was her life, just as Socksy now seemed to be Renee's.

As she turned to leave, she felt Arwen's hand on her sleeve. "Before you go, though, come with me. I want to show you something."

Constance trotted obediently to Arwen's office, judging it a more comfortable option than contending with Dorcas.

"Dal gave this to me. Have a look." Arwen sat behind her desk and offered a paper.

Constance accepted it and glanced at it... then looked more closely. "She did it," she murmured.

"She did. She's worked through what possessed her to take all those items. Not to mention the increased intensity."

The diagram showed it all. Wavy bubbles for feelings, hard lines for events, more connections than Constance could hope to sort out in a quick perusal. She put the sheet on the desk. "I don't think I had this level of insight when I was her age."

"You probably had a support structure you trusted. Hopefully, Renee will come to trust hers as well. Furthermore, with this development, I think our concerns about Renee have found a simple solution."

As Constance turned to the door, Arwen spoke again. "Now, you'd better get to Dorcas, before she arrives to drag you off. Patience has always been a challenge for her."

The women exchanged a smile. Constance had never hoped to hear Arwen speak so honestly about her deputy's personality, and felt of a tiny part of the tension, which never completely left her, release.

Chapter 27

Constance sat on the bench overlooking the amphitheater, site of the appalling misadventure with Meade, and experienced a rare moment of peace. The day was perfect – a high, clear autumn sky, leaves on the few deciduous trees around the Motherhouse beginning to turn, that undefinable scent to the air that presaged winter. She had always loved autumn, perhaps related to the excitement of getting back to her studies. Summer felt like a suspension, autumn a renewal.

The seasonings the cooks baked into their pastries were different from the ones she was used to, cinnamon and nutmeg and cloves, but they carried the same feeling with them. There had been a pie made of some sort of root vegetable, similar to a yam, for dessert at lunch. Usually Constance skipped the sweet, but this time she had indulged, and was glad of it.

As well, Renee had settled down. After an understandable withdrawal, shamefaced, into herself following the return of the stolen items, she had devoted herself to that remarkable diagram, and Constance had seen little of her. Now, she saw even less as all the girl's free time was taken up by the horse. But no one doubted where she was, and her scant time with Constance was marked by somewhat better manners and less impetuousness than before.

Towering conifers formed a backdrop to the bench; she leaned back, tipping her head. Already they emitted a scent reminiscent of Yuletide candles back on Terra. Once, she had heard, people cut down trees and decorated them in their homes. Amazing, to think there had been so many trees they could be used in such a frivolous way.

Her reverie was interrupted by someone making no attempt to disguise his approach. She straightened and watched Dal climb the slope, wasting no time, his face as usual set in grim, unwavering lines. She nodded, assuming he would carry on around the trail that looped the amphitheater, but instead he sat, uninvited, beside her. "It is nice, isn't it?" he said, although he gave no indication of agreeing with his own statement. "I've long favored this time of year."

Information she had no use for. She nodded and gazed ahead. Down below, a group of older students engaged in some kind of ball game that involved tackling and shrieking. Hard to believe she had been that young once.

"Renee's doing well," Dal continued, staring out over the Motherhouse complex, "but she needs to learn discipline. You can help with that."

She ignored his demand for her assistance. "She's better. More focused. No one can fault her care of Socksy."

"True, but to the detriment of her other assignments."

"Which, I gather, are now directed to helping Meade."

"She needs more training. And she hasn't shown up the last few days."

Constance shrugged. "It's an infatuation. I'm told young people often develop a passion for horses. Get her attention and she'll be back at her studies."

"I'll be restricting horse time if she isn't." Dal's voice was all hard edges.

"Do you expect... will there be something to help Meade soon?"

"Perhaps. But don't expect to be part of the team."

Constance bristled. "Look. You know it was an accident. If I can help—"

Dal's prolonged sigh made her feel like a student who should have grasped a fundamental concept long ago, but for some reason resisted learning. "You're a beginner. An apprentice. Get that through your head. Your skills just aren't refined enough."

She faced him, fighting down anger. "Not to manipulate Meade's energy, no. But to support Renee with the mapping, yes. I know how her mind works better than anyone—"

"Other than me. Because I'm the only one taking a methodical approach to the challenge."

Constance's patience snapped. "If you bring your insufferable arrogance with you, you'll get nowhere."

Startled, Dal turned on the bench to face her. She met him glare for glare. "I have advantages you can't hope to share when it comes to understanding her mind," he said, his voice unyielding.

"And one massive drawback."

"And that would be?"

"You're a man," she snapped.

Somehow that fact carried more weight than she expected. They both fell silent, locked in each other's gaze, exactly as had happened so many nine-days ago back in Stanstead. Once again the awareness of Dal's essential maleness coursed through her.

He broke away first, standing and crossing the path to stare out into the distance. After a pause, he asked, "You think of her as a daughter, don't you?" His voice carried none of the near hostility they had veered so close to only a few seconds before.

She hesitated, allowing the silence to settle. Her daughter? Hers, anyway. She had never put it in words quite so... so committed.

Her daughter. Suddenly, her relationship with Renee had become all or nothing. Step up to the plate... an old expression from Terra, probably from Northam; she had no idea of its original meaning, but certainly it was about doing the job, making the commitment.

Omar...

Renee...

The two children danced in her mind, the son she would never see again, the... daughter?... she now seemed to have adopted.

"Yes," she said.

The silence stretched long, neither of them looking at the other. Then Dal nodded. "That's good. As a Healer, my assessment is that she's pre-pubescent. Behind in her development, probably from hunger and poor treatment. But the way she's growing now, she'll catch up soon. She'll need you."

He turned to her. "I agree to you helping with the mapping. I'll be in touch in a few days, once she's absorbed the insight from Arwen's assignment." He scowled. "Which, incidentally, is setting back the timeline for Meade's Healing, but there it is."

He gave a curt nod and headed down the trail toward the Motherhouse. Constance remained on the bench for a few minutes, trying, and failing, to sort out her thoughts. Beneath the revelation about her relationship to Renee, she fumed that he dared to assume the right to give her permission to do anything. Then she, too, rose and returned to her work.

Interlude

Renee had been gone all day. Reports placed her in the village, where Socksy and a new litter of piglets would be more than enough to hold her attention. But when she wasn't home for supper, Constance became worried.

"Calm down," Dorcas told her as they crossed paths in the dining hall. "She's fine. We've got Marie keeping an eye out. And Tomas will walk her home, as always."

"Still..."

"Eat your meal. And plan to do a deep meditation tonight. You've got a big day tomorrow."

A big day indeed. Dorcas intended her to walk a weave for the first time, and the idea of relaxation was a joke. Even apart from Renee's conspicuous absence, Constance was a wreck. Alone at her table, she nibbled her cutlet – perhaps nuts but certainly not meat – and did her best to still her mind.

Before she returned to her room, she stopped at Renee's door and knocked on the frame. From within she heard a sound that might have been Renee's customary 'yeah?' or might have been a whimper.

"Renee? Can I come in?"

Interpreting the resulting mumble as a positive, she pushed the door open and stepped into Renee's room.

No light had been lit, but even so she could see that something had changed. Something...

She crossed to the bed where the girl sat slumped over her crossed legs and lit the lamp on the nearby desk with a gesture, a skill she was inordinately proud of.

The long tangle that usually shrouded Renee's face was gone. Her hair now framed her face instead of cascading down her back.

Everyone from the Motherhouse made the short trek to the village for haircuts, where several of the villagers were skilled – relatively skilled – with haircutting razors. Constance had yet to see a pair of scissors in the Midland.

The girl squirmed, then collapsed sideways, hiding her head as much as she could with her arms. "I hate it," she wailed.

"I don't. I don't think I do anyway. Come on, get up. Let me see."

Renee allowed herself to be pulled upright. Her face was streaked with tears. "They all laughed. They said I looked like a girl. They didn't mean it good." Another tear leaked down her grubby cheek.

"'They' being boys, I assume?"

"Yeah. We were looking at the piglets, and they all just..." Finishing the sentence proved to be too much. Renee collapsed in tears.

Constance gathered the distraught girl in her arms; unexpectedly meeting with no resistance. "I *hate* it," she said between gulps. "I don't wanna grow up and hafta do this stuff".

"There's no stopping the growing up part," Constance said gently. "But what you choose to look like is up to you. Let me see, properly."

Reluctantly, Renee left the nest of Constance's arms and sat straight. Her eyes were frankly pleading for approval.

"Meade says I have a pixie face, and I should have pixie hair. What's a pixie?"

"I don't know." Constance pushed damp, short locks from Renee's face, finger combed it... and marveled. "Meade's right. It suits you. You look good, truly." she said, continuing to work her fingers through the new style, which draped, shiny and thick, over her hands. "Boys know nothing," she added. "Especially if you've always been one of their group. They'll get used to it."

"Ya really think?" The tears stopped. Renee swallowed, hard. "I'm scared," she said, barely audible.

"Don't be. In fact, I know it's a bit late, but let's go see if we can get in to visit Meade. Right now. She'll want to see you."

"But if she doesn't—"

"She'll like it. We women know these things." She stood and hauled Renee up with her. "And you're going to love it. Lighter, easier to care for – just wait."

They found Meade in the healing room, and she came through, as did several of the apprentices they passed on the green, who were loud with praise. By the time Constance saw Renee snuggled in bed, she was confident the girl was, at that moment, scornful of the questionable taste of the boys in the village and fully embracing her inner woman.

Boys, she thought as she returned to her own room and bed, watch out.

Chapter 28

"I'm not ready." Constance heard the pleading note in her own voice and hated it.

"You are. Just around the Motherhouse to start with. I'm impressed, actually," Dorcas said. "I never thought you'd have the discipline to progress so quickly."

"But this... I can't do this."

"You already have, in a small way. We just didn't put a name on it."

The two women sat together in their workroom, tucked against a side wall of the Centra. The room held little, just a table, a couple of straight-backed chairs. At least a window provided natural light, although it was too high and small to offer a view.

Constance swallowed. She had largely put aside her contempt for what, deep inside, below the level of logic, she still believed to be non-existent powers based on imagination rather than science, but this was a step beyond simple acceptance. This was conviction – and faith.

"Walking a weave isn't all that complicated," Dorcas said. "I'll provide a tether, and you won't be expanding the weave or going beyond where I can pull you back if I need to."

The room was chilly; autumn had rolled in with a vengeance. Stinging rain in the night had turned the green into a quagmire and chilled the stones of the walls. Constance pulled her wool shawl tighter around her shoulders. She wasn't prepared for this.

"You know the technique, and you're familiar with the basic weave. You'll be perfectly safe."

Walking a weave represented a major step, something apprentice Scribes didn't attempt for several years into their training. To do it safely, her mind had to be open to Dorcas, while at the same time completely attuned to the gossamer threads of the weave. Later, when she was accepted as a full Scribe, she wouldn't need that tether, although it was foolhardy to attempt a major Walking without it.

She sighed. It wasn't as if Dorcas and Arwen hadn't already invaded her most private awareness. And hadn't she been building toward this point for months now? All it took was courage... and releasing her last resistance to the power of the Aura.

"Let's review. The weave is..."

"Energy," Constance replied.

"It looks like..."

"Thin filaments. Getting finer near the edges."

"You maintain contact by..."

They had been through this catechism so many times, Constance had it by rote. "Concentration. Focus."

"And if you lose contact?"

"You crash out." At Dorcas's raised eyebrows, she elaborated, "You come out of the trance."

"And find yourself..."

"Wherever you were when you lost contact."

Dorcas nodded. "Which is why Quinn's journeys worried us so. She could have been stranded anywhere on the planet, at any time in history." Her friend Quinn was known for taking risks, and her colleagues at the Motherhouse weren't happy about that at all.

"I will anchor the weave," Dorcas continued, "and I'll be in your head to talk you through it. It's a small weave, so you won't leave the environs of the Motherhouse. Nowhere near the river or the woods. You're not going to drown or find yourself stuck in a tree."

Despite herself, Constance smiled. "I'd better not."

Dorcas shot her an answering grin. "Let's do this."

*

Preparation was simple enough. Under supervision, Constance built the weave, creating the energy pathways that would support her in her walk. Not that she could see them, but somehow Dorcas knew when it was correct and stable. Then, using the techniques she had practiced for months, Constance slipped into a trance state. She became aware of Dorcas's voice in her head, coaxing her toward the weave.

And there it was, hovering like a living thing over the green and the amphitheater. Diaphanous, with one corner pegged down to a place in the Centra. That would be Dorcas, providing an anchor as she had promised.

Now, project yourself toward the center of the weave. Not the edges, it's not as robust there. Go.

She had tried to get an explanation of how to do this projection thing, but the words didn't make sense. Now they did. Without effort, she found herself above the amphitheatre, looking down at the complex, then far out over the river toward the hills, northwest toward the village. To the south she could see a trail snaking through the countryside, probably toward the small town where Willow lived. She tried to remember the name of the village and felt her concentration slipping. Beneath her, the weave trembled.

Concentrate.

Shaken, she followed Dorcas's instruction. The weave stabilized.

Move around. You need to learn to navigate. Be careful not to get lost in an intersection.

The threads of a weave took you to different places, in time and space. At the intersections you could change your focus, take yourself in a new direction depending on how far the weave stretched. She feared the intersections but found it straightforward to pass them by. One day, perhaps, she would be able to visit the Adventurer on a weave, see how her colleagues and friends were coping in this new land. For now, she prowled the complex, enjoying the perspective of the Motherhouse from above. A group of apprentices gathered around a teacher, she thought it was Hector, but it wasn't always easy to identify people from directly above them. Dal she recognized, though, squelching across the green from the Centra to the healing rooms. Going to spend time with Meade? She was probably on the porch, but Constance couldn't see through the sloping roof.

Renee shot across the green, heading for the path to the village. Her heart hiccupped at the sight of the gangly child, now becoming a teenager, a woman.

Constance gasped as she felt the weave fray around her.

Focus.

Heart pounding, she tuned her mind back to the weave.

Come back now. Gently. You've been gone long enough.

She realized abruptly how tired she was. Following the instructions drilled into her, she let herself slip from the weave to her starting point, the chair in the workroom. Almost like going down a slide...

And then she was sitting at the table and Dorcas was snuggling her shawl closer around her, putting a mug of hot tisane in her hands.

*

"You did that weave thing today," Renee said, sounding nonchalant. Her eyes, sharp on Constance's face, gave her away. She was interested.

Constance nodded. She had spent the afternoon wandering around the complex in the cool, damp air, challenging her mind to come to terms with the major event of the morning. Renee had found her at the natural bench by the river. The previous night's rain had transformed the flow into a mad torrent, which frightened Constance and thrilled her in equal measure. Her hands rested on the stone of the bench; for the first time she fully understood what the Weavers meant by grounding herself in the earth. Her mind couldn't quite let go of the exhilaration of soaring over the Motherhouse, supported by a fragile cobweb.

Not so fragile. But risky enough for all that.

"What's it like?" Renee settled on the damp ground, ignoring the likely saturation of her tunic and pants. She propped elbows on the bench and gazed up at Constance. Her face and hair were clean. With her proper haircut, Renee was transforming before her eyes into a very attractive young woman. But did anyone care about such things here? Not at the Motherhouse, unless perhaps among the apprentices…

She popped her thoughts back to the immediacy of the girl beside her. "Flying, I suppose."

"Like when I ride Socksy."

Constance's head jerked up. "You're not taking her out of the corral, are you?"

"Well, sure." Renee shrugged. "'Cause she needs exercise, doesn't she? When she gets movin', it's kinda like flying. But you gotta stay alert."

Constance swallowed down her trepidation. They had a bond, she and Renee, however unlikely. Better to build on it. "On the weave, you never let go of control for even a moment, so you can't really take time to enjoy it."

Renee nodded. "Dal's always on about controlling your mind. Seems obvious to me."

Constance allowed a small smile as she looked down at the earnest face. "For you, perhaps, because your mind is unique. Most other people daydream, shift from thought to thought without meaning to."

"I do that." Renee sounded offended. Constance wondered how much Renee longed to be like the other kids, not the apprentices so much as the ones from the village. She spent enough time with them, working with the animals, learning techniques for growing and storing crops.

"Do you? You always seem focused to me."

"Nah." Renee stood and walked toward the bank overlooking the river, plucking the wet tunic away from her backside. Constance felt her heart hiccup as the girl approached the edge. The bank appeared stable, but the scar upstream where it had collapsed during the earthquake was warning enough; this was dangerous territory. Renee wasn't much of a swimmer, and today the river displayed a dangerous violence.

Renee grasped a slender branch and swung from it, sending a shower of yellow leaves over the ground. She studied the water. "You ever watch how it goes?" she asked. "When it hits a rock or a branch or something, it changes so it isn't going straight anymore. It goes up and down instead. And it gets stuck at the sides sometimes."

Constance just smiled and nodded. There was no point in tracking every one of Renee's analyses. There were too many of them.

Renee turned from the river and sat next to Constance. "So, you can really do this? Dal can't. He told me. Not Meade neither. It's just the Scribes who get to fly."

"I'm not a Scribe yet. I haven't even been able to heal the heal-all plant."

"Still."

It was sinking in that Renee was impressed. Constance suddenly felt warmth sweep over her. She hadn't fully come to terms with the notion of the girl as her daughter, but it made Renee's interest – and implied approval – doubly sweet.

Chapter 29

Constance was unwinding in her room from a day spent mainly in a confrontation with the poor heal-all plant when she became aware of a disturbance. She stood, stretched, and peered out her window. Below, two men and a woman, all in filthy, threadbare clothing, were crossing toward the Centra from the trailhead to Stanstead, buttonholing anyone they came across. At this time of evening, just before dinner, there was no shortage of subjects. Whatever they were after, their voices were strident with demands. Constance caught the occasional word, enough to tell her they were looking for someone.

Interesting. The few people who visited the Motherhouse usually came to spend time with family living here, or to trade. They stayed in the village or the guest lodge, had formed relationships with the residents, and generally were welcome. This group brought in a decidedly different air.

Mildly curious, and hungry, Constance wrapped her heavy shawl more tightly around her shoulders, readying herself for dinner. She knocked on Renee's door on her way out, but there was no answer.

By the time she got to the front of the Centra, Arwen and Hector had engaged with the small, angry group. Arwen waved her over. "These people are looking for a girl they claim was stolen from them in the earthquake." Her eyes flashed a warning.

Careful what you say.

Abruptly, Constance knew.

For once she was glad of the spooky way the Weavers, especially the Scribes, got into her head. But the caution wasn't needed. The newcomers were belligerent, unsavory – beyond the usual grime of travel – and doing nothing to further their cause, whatever it was. She resolved then and there that she had never heard of any missing child, had never come across a runaway. She shook her head, indicating no knowledge, and stepped back.

"We got a hint, see," the older of the men said. He stood braced with legs apart. He held a knife, not unusual for a traveler on the roads of the Midland, but the way he passed it from hand to hand implied a threat. "That she might be hidin' hereabouts. See now, she's my brother's kid."

The woman spoke up, shoving greasy hair back from her face. "She's ours by right. We got the job of raisin' her when old Jarek died. Left her with us, he did. She owes us, all we've done for her."

"And we want her back," the man concluded. The third member of their party, a younger man, crossed heavily muscled arms over an equally developed chest and watched, silently. A light flickered behind his eyes that Constance didn't like. Clearly, Hector and Arwen caught it also. The child they sought wouldn't be safe with these people.

Arwen sighed; Constance was aware that she was tamping down her temper. "The child's name and age, please?"

The woman spat on the ground. "Girl's name's Nada. She'd be about fourteen now, I reckon. Small for her age. No looks to speak of."

Of Renee's immediate safety, Constance had no doubt. Quite apart from her ability to disappear at will, she had friends in both the Motherhouse and the village who would never let her be discovered by this disreputable family.

"No," Hector said. "I head the school, and I assure you there is no one who meets your description. I know every child here. We don't have your niece."

"I think we'll just have ourselves a look around." The knife moved from hand to hand.

Arwen said, "Most of the buildings are off limits, but you are welcome to join us for a meal before you leave."

"Ain't leavin' tonight," the younger man spoke up for the first time.

"As you wish, of course. You're welcome to camp at the waysite a short distance back toward Stanstead. Feel free to take water and trail provisions with you."

Arwen didn't invite them into the guest lodge. Good. The longer this confrontation lasted, the more Constance's sense of danger spiked.

"You best understand," the younger man said, his face hard, "we don't tolerate nobody workin' against us. We're gonna find our girl."

"You back off, Jimmie," the older man snapped. "I'll do the talkin'."

"You won't find her here," Hector said calmly.

The knife rested in the older man's hand as he puffed out his scrawny chest. The look in his eyes was chilling.

Constance became aware of a disturbance in the air; someone was manipulating the Aura, and on a larger scale than she had ever experienced. She looked at Arwen and Hector's placid faces, then glanced around to see Dorcas and Kalia, another Scribe in residence, watching the group intently.

"Constance, come with me, please. Good day to you," Arwen said to the newcomers, then started toward the door to the Centra.

"Just you hang on there," the older man barked. "We got rights to our property. We ain't finished here."

Arwen turned, her face a mask. Whatever was happening in the Aura, she was a part of it, Constance was certain. "I am. Enjoy a meal if you wish. Then I recommend you start for the waysite. Night comes early this time of year."

By now several Weavers had gathered around the newcomers, effectively forming a barrier to keep a group of ever-curious apprentices at a distance. Constance found it easy to lose herself in the gathering before slipping away and following Arwen into the Centra.

Safely in Arwen's office, the older woman collapsed into her chair, although the slightly blank expression never left her face. "We're building shields around the buildings," she said. "They won't get in. Where's Renee?"

Constance shook her head. "She wasn't in her room when I knocked."

"She's cagey. I expect she needed to be to survive with them." The contempt Arwen put on the last word positively curdled the air in the room. "Don't worry. They aren't getting her. No one's going to admit they even suspect who she is, not with their behaviour. Did you see the look on that boy's face? He knows full well she's coming of age. She wouldn't be safe, even apart from the kind of abuse we know she's endured already."

The remote expression abruptly left Arwen's face, and the disturbance in the Aura settled down. "There. That's done. They won't be able to get into any of the buildings in the complex except the dining hall. They'll approach and lose the inclination to enter. It's a major work, and I doubt we'll be able to keep it active beyond overnight, but that should be enough. I don't want to compel them to leave yet, but I will if I have to."

Dorcas slipped into the office, her usually placid face grim. "They've opted to eat. We've forbidden the apprentices to talk to them, and Hector warned them not to hassle our students – not that I think they'll pay any attention. But the students are no fools. Nobody's going to say anything they shouldn't. A lot of them may choose to delay their supper until our guests leave – I noticed there wasn't the usual stampede for food. Could be their smell put the kids off?" Dorcas smiled. "Any thoughts about where our girl is, Constance?"

She shook her head. "I doubt she's in the complex. Meade might know."

"Go ask. I'd like to find out. I don't need to remind you to avoid them. If they sense you're hiding something, it could get tricky."

Constance nodded and excused herself. From the Centra's main entrance, she saw no sign of the people who had come to steal Renee away, so she slipped out, turned left, and bypassing the dining hall she made for the healing rooms.

Chapter 30

Two days later, there was still no sign of Renee. As far as anyone knew, the unsavory family had left the day after the confrontation on the green. Renee's prolonged absence was worrisome but not frightening, because there were signs. The girl had gone to ground, but clean tunics disappeared from the textile building regularly, and two days ago some of the paper seconds and a pen vanished. She was safe, somewhere close, and getting on with her life in her own way.

At least she was eating. Constance had called in at the kitchen to make sure food would be available, even after hours, to find that the kitchen staff already had plans to assure Renee's well-being. Most of the food disappeared, but no one saw the elusive girl.

"A bit like Tai, when she was younger," Bryar commented. He and Tai were at the Motherhouse on their way to Hallan for a visit with Willow, then along the main southern road to Quinn at the Adventurer. Constance felt a twinge – no, make that a bolt – of jealousy when she heard their travel plans. She let it go. The Motherhouse was her fate, and now her home. She had almost become accustomed to the cold rooms, hard beds, and long days spent mastering skills she had once denigrated.

She knew better now.

Bryar, a Bard, planned a performance in the dining hall that evening. Constance would attend, of course, although she found the long recitative pieces, which everyone else met with wide-eyed wonder, tedious. Her hope was that the promise of entertainment would draw Renee from wherever she was hiding.

"She can take care of herself," Arwen said, not quite dismissively but without overt concern. "Relax."

Constance snorted at that.

Arwen laughed. "Ah, motherhood. Go back to work, Connie. She's fine."

Connie? That name again. She had set Dal straight when he dared to use it. This time she just didn't have the energy. Nicknames implied – friendship? Did she want friends here?

Later, Dorcas fussed at her. "How do you ever expect that poor plant to heal? Look, it's formed scar tissue over the break. You'd best start over." She reached across the table in their workroom and snapped another branch.

Constance, feeling sorry for the plant, brushed it with her hand... and the newly broken twig straightened and fused.

"Ha," Dorcas said. "I knew all that practice would bear fruit sometime soon. I don't suppose you want to try to kill it now?"

Constance shot her a withering glance. "It's like a friend. A comrade in arms."

"Take it out somewhere along the trail and re-plant it, then. It won't be happy in that pot over the winter. It needs the cold."

As if it wouldn't get plenty of cold in my room.

After finding a likely spot along the trail leading to the village, she dug a hole with a spoon she had purloined from the dining hall and tucked the plant in.

She didn't need the plant. She needed Renee to come home.

*

If Renee caught Bryar's performance, no one was aware of it. But the next night, Constance was awakened from a sound sleep by a shivering body crowding into the narrow bed with her.

"You reckon it snows when it's barely autumn?" Renee whispered.

Constance shifted onto her side and drew the frozen child closer. "It wouldn't surprise me. I'm not used to – *yow!*" Renee's feet had found her legs, sending shafts of ice through her shins. Now thoroughly awake, Constance chafed the girl's skin, getting her circulation going. "Where have you been?"

"Think I'd be anywhere *they* could find me?"

"No. But I was worried."

"That's dumb." Renee's voice was already fading. She had needed a warm nest to sleep in, and now she was taking full advantage. "I can take care of myself."

"I know you can. And I can worry."

Under the covers she felt Renee shrug. "One or two knew where. They'd never tell." Her stomach let out a loud protest.

"Oh? Who?" Another shaft of jealousy visited her already over-taxed heart. "You're hungry."

She caught a mumbled, "I been eatin'," and then nothing. Her child was asleep.

In her bed. With her.

*

A different picture presented itself the next morning. Renewed, Renee started squirming long before Constance, unaccustomed to sharing a bed, much less to the emotional upheaval of the girl's return, was ready. She nudged Constance to wakefulness. "Come on. I gotta show you sumthin'," she said, seemingly oblivious to the chill in the room.

"Later."

"Now. Then you'll see."

See what? But Constance recognized the futility of delay. Blearily she shoved her arms into a woolen wrap, her feet into a pair of boots newly acquired, in anticipation of still colder days to come.

Renee opened the door cautiously, studied the empty corridor a moment, then slipped out, making for her own room next door. She barely touched the door, opening it just enough to view inside, then pushed it open.

Constance stood in the doorway and felt her insides sink. Renee's room was a disaster, in what had to be a deliberate act of destruction. Her treasured stack of mind maps had been shredded, the fragments tossed in the air to land where they might. Her mattress was half off the frame, her scant clothing pulled from the wardrobe. A pool of ink lay by her worktable next to the shattered ink pot. She found her voice and whispered, "When did this happen?"

Renee was almost nonchalant, but under the attitude Constance sensed she was shaken. "Found it like this last night. It'd been fine up to then. They got no time for my drawings, say I shouldn't mess with 'em. Wastin' time when I should be workin'." She stooped and began picking up the fragments of her hard work. "Dal, he's gonna be mad."

"Mad at them, not you. He's not alone." Constance took Renee by the shoulders, lightly so she wouldn't feel trapped, and looked her in the eye. "They'll never get you. We won't let it happen."

"Looks like they ain't gone away yet. They find me, you couldn't stop 'em."

"We'll see about that." Grimly, she joined Renee in tidying the room, leaving the map fragments to the girl. Later she would find a box for her to put them in, keep them safe.

The Weavers had released the shield around the buildings just yesterday; the energy required was too great to maintain it for any length of time. In that short time, the bastards had been here, and no one had been aware. The risk to Renee...

After breakfast they would meet with Arwen, begin figuring out ways to keep her child safe.

Chapter 31

Meade awoke with more optimism than she was used to and began the process of rolling out of bed. She had evolved methods of seeing to her own needs, but it was slow going. Dal or one of the Healing assistants – senior apprentices who soon would leave for their journey year – occasionally helped her to the dining hall, but usually she got a tray of food in her room. For someone who loved the social aspects of life at the Motherhouse, it made for a barren existence.

Today promised to be different. She expected Dal mid-morning, with Renee in tow. She hadn't seen the two together since the girl's training began; her mind teased her with speculation about how they interacted. Renee was a regular visitor, but their time together was mostly 'girl time'. She knew little about things other women took for granted, and for whatever reason didn't feel comfortable talking to Constance. So, they discussed skin and hair, how to decorate the plain tunics they all wore, and – what concerned her most – what it was like to become a woman. She knew the physical basics but had no role models for living the changes her body was going through.

Or how those changes would affect her relationship with boys. Meade smiled, remembering the hair cutting incident. It would be fun watching Renee mature and blossom.

Sitting on the edge of her bed, she donned the tunic conveniently placed on the covers. A small table placed within reach held a jug and a comb. She splashed water on her face and began pulling the comb through her short hair.

Dal arrived a few minutes later, carrying a tray. "I intercepted the runner from the dining hall," he said. "Do you want a hand over to the desk?"

"I've got it." An exaggeration, but Meade had made the one-step journey from bed to chair often enough by now, and she was sick of always needing help. She rolled herself to the end of the bed, then executed a step-lunge maneuver that placed her squarely in position to sink into her chair. She peered under the withy-woven dome covering her breakfast. Scrambled eggs, sliced tomatoes, an abricoe pastry. Next to the plate stood a small carafe and even smaller mug. Caff, thank the Aura. Meade focused on her meal.

"Today's going to be an experiment, you understand." Dal sounded unusually tentative. Meade got it; he was worried she might have her hopes too high.

She nodded and went on consuming her egg and tomato.

"Renee's never tried anything like this. Neither have I. I'm not sure how well I'll be able to convey what I sense, whether she'll understand enough to build her diagrams."

Meade swallowed. "Her drawings are fascinating. She puts detail in them she couldn't possibly know. Somehow she intuits what's needed to fill in gaps."

Dal gave her a smile. "Do you think she'll intuit what's going on with your energy?"

Meade polished off the egg and moved on to the pastry. Her mouth full, she shrugged.

"You seem upbeat this morning."

She paused to swallow. "At least it's something different. I'm going out of my mind, trapped here."

Dal nodded. "I imagine."

"No, you don't." Meade's voice was sharp; these days her mood changed in an instant. "You can't. You've never been a prisoner. And frankly, imagination's never been one of your strong points."

Dal didn't flinch. "True enough. Enjoy your breakfast. We'll work in the small healing room."

"Outdoors?" she asked hopefully.

He shook his head. "I want an environment with as little external stimulation as possible. We all need to focus. Anyway, it's raining and cold."

Meade merely nodded as she picked up the caff pot. She would rather be outdoors; it felt safer somehow. But she was growing used to not having things go her way.

*

Later, Meade settled herself on the raised cot, Dal assisting. She wondered how long this experiment would take. The beds in the treatment rooms were hard and wouldn't be comfortable for long.

Renee stood to one side, shuffling her sandals against the wood floor. The sandals had been a compromise, once even Renee agreed it was too cold to go barefoot. Getting the girl into boots... well, she would leave that one to Constance. The shuffling sound was going to grow irritating before long. Meade bit her lip, reminding herself not to snap at the girl, who, after all, was one of her most loyal visitors.

Dal draped a woolen blanket over her. "Are you warm enough?"

"I'm fine. Let's do this."

"Have a seat, Renee. You know what to do."

Unusually quiet, Renee settled at the table in the corner. In front of her lay several clean sheets of paper, each with a crude drawing of a human shape. Dal had assured Meade that he and Renee had been over what would happen and what her job would be, but the girl looked anything but confident.

"We'll smooth your energies first, as much as I can," he told Meade. "Then I'll start feeding my impressions to Renee. This is only our first try, so don't expect too much."

Meade was far from over-optimistic. As best as she could tell, this was an awkward scheme that put pressure on Renee while being unlikely to yield positive results. She had even considered refusing to participate, but ultimately decided to go ahead, since Renee seemed to be keen to try. But this morning the tension on the girl's face was palpable, as if Meade's entire recovery rested on her slender shoulders. Attempting to reassure her, she said, "It should be fascinating. No one's ever tried to diagram energies before. We sense them and know when they're tangled, but we've never looked for patterns in them."

In other words, if this didn't work, it would be Dal's fault, not Renee's. But of course, fault didn't play into this experiment.

"Relax," Dal commanded. "I'm starting."

Meade winked at Renee, then closed her eyes. Her energies wouldn't smooth completely, she already knew that, but restoring order to the flows not caught in the knot was so relaxing. She felt herself sink into trance as Dal's hands hovered over her, gently tugging and straightening.

Chapter 32

Arwen walked into the meeting room with less than her usual energy. Many things were going well at the Motherhouse, but more were not. Her mandate was to create and maintain equilibrium—somehow. The council, the men and women sitting around the table waiting for her, represented one of her primary tools.

As she took her seat, she surveyed them. To her right, Daren, head of the Healers' guild, brought an active mind and solid understanding. On her left, Fergus, head of the Bards' guild, kept them all from growing too serious while still providing unexpected insights the others missed. Cynth, a no-nonsense Healer, relied on for recognizing hard facts but with little imagination for creative solutions, sat to Fergus's left. Hector, another Bard, occupied the foot of the table. As head of the apprentices' school, he might provide valuable insights into one of their impending problems, Renee. He had replaced Quinn on council a few nine-days ago.

Arwen missed Quinn, a Scribe with a daring approach and ruthlessly analytical mind. But Quinn was far away with the newcomers on the Adventurer. No one expected her back anytime soon.

The arrival of the Adventurer had contributed to the problems rampant in the Midland. As far as Arwen could tell, the settlers had kept a low profile and integrated well into their immediate neighborhood, but that did nothing to mitigate the paranoia stalking the roads and tracks. Weavers returning to the Motherhouse reported hostility, suspicion, and occasionally violence, even against themselves. The unwritten covenant guaranteeing Weavers safe passage throughout the Midland in exchange for their services, no questions asked, was falling apart.

As well, Renee, Constance, and Meade's injury each presented a challenge, as did the continuing effort to recover from the earthquake, establishment of trade routes far to the south, and Borgonne, the civilization on the other side of the hills, with whatever possible threat it might represent.... A general malaise pervaded not only the Motherhouse but all the Midland, like an infection.

Having organized the morning's agenda in her mind, Arwen brought her attention back to the room. The dining hall had provided caff, tisane, and nut pastries. Fergus was already munching; Cynth poured a tisane. Arwen sensed the tension around the table, nothing unusual anymore. The council worked well together, but there was no denying they were all on edge.

She settled in her chair, aware of all eyes on her. "Let's get started."

Fergus spoke up immediately. "Dal's working with Meade this morning. Any word?"

"No," Daren said. "Don't get your hopes up. Today is an experiment, nothing more. I don't have a clue how you could describe the energies we sense, so whether Dal and Renee can produce anything effective... I think it's doubtful. But we can hope. I hate to see Meade so diminished."

Nods around the table followed his words. Meade was among the most popular of the Weavers, and everyone grieved to watch her struggle.

"That's not the most important issue at the moment, though." Arwen reached for the caff pot and poured herself a tiny mugful. She sipped, then said, "The fact that those horrid people got into the guest lodge and invaded Renee's room is truly scary. It makes me question our safety. All of us."

"Coupled with the recent assault on the main north road," Daren put in. "Johann wore his Healer's sash. There was no provocation or justification for such an attack. Our world isn't what it used to be, and we've never developed defenses against physical violence."

"It's always happened," Cynth said, "but very rarely."

"How is Johann?" Hector asked.

"Recovering in Salberg. Concussion, but thankfully nothing was broken."

"Unlike the attack out in the northwest," Fergus added. "Pushed over a cliff? Poor guy's been laid up for nine-days now."

"I heard he's on his way home?" Arwen asked.

Fergus nodded. "Slowly. There are still decent people out there who remember what we mean to them."

Others reached for drinks and pastries as the council reviewed the events and indications of unrest in the Midland. One thing sure, Arwen thought as she listened to the others, everything has changed.

"Back to the agenda," she said. "First is Renee."

Hector shot a wry smile around the table. "She's unique, that one," he said. "She's everywhere at once, you can't pin her down. I wanted to get her into some of the apprentices' classes, at least teach her to read, but she's too unfocused."

"Constance has no control over her?" Cynth asked. The two women had never warmed to each other, Arwen knew, and wasn't sure if she heard criticism in Cynth's voice or if it was her own interpretation.

"Maybe," she said. "In a crisis, Renee turns to Constance. But we have problems there, too. I don't want to put too much responsibility on her yet."

"She still feels guilty for Meade, according to Dal," Daren put in.

"How do we protect Renee?" Arwen asked before the conversation could lose focus.

Fergus scoffed under his breath. "Tie her down?"

Arwen glared. Insouciant, Fergus took a bite of his pastry.

"Is she aware of the danger she's in?" Daren asked.

"I'd say so," Arwen said. "She's terrified of them, according to Constance."

"And she's not a child anymore," Cynth said. "She surely recognizes the need to stay close. To not wander off on her own."

"Good luck on that one," Hector said.

Cynth waved a quelling hand at him. "To stay with adults, stay close to the Motherhouse—"

"She has a lot of friends in the village. Not to mention Socksy." This time it was Fergus who interrupted.

"Then we must ensure she never travels between the village and the Motherhouse without an escort. That's when she's most vulnerable, I'd say."

"Or when she's alone in her room," Arwen said. "We know now that the guest lodge isn't inviolable."

"Could we keep the shield up around the guest lodge?" Fergus asked.

As the only Scribe present, Arwen seemed to sag a little as she shook her head. "We exhausted the power of the Scribes, doing what we did. The lodge isn't small... no, we can't handle it. We don't have the numbers or the energy."

"That was pure spite," Hector said. "Just because. Anger, frustration at not getting what they want. Perhaps it was their last kick before clearing off."

"Move her into Constance's room," Cynth said.

Everyone paused to think that over. "It might help, at least for night times," Daren said. "The problem is, we can't monitor anyone every minute of the day, much less Renee."

"Have we learned anything about where those people went?" Fergus asked.

"No," Arwen said. "It's almost impossible, tracking people who aren't Weavers. But so far, no one in Stanstead or Hallan has seen them."

And if Renee's relatives had left the environs of the Motherhouse, they would have to have gone through Stanstead or Hallan. Unless they dared to take the track north. But in that case Ezra would have notified them, surely. Arwen frowned. Ezra, the Old Man, had been in failing health for some time. Another worry.

"I think the best we can do is sit down with Renee – and Constance too – and let them know where things stand and what little we can do to defend her," Daren said. "We're trying to put limits on a young woman with a mind of her own, and we all know that won't work."

Indeed, it wouldn't. The main function of the Motherhouse, besides providing a home base for the Weavers when they came off the road, was to train apprentices, generally between thirteen and nineteen years old. Everyone there had experience with headstrong, opinionated teens.

"There's one other possibility," Fergus put in. Being a Bard, he waited until the room quieted in anticipation, then said, "Move them both to the Scribes' lodge."

His idea was received with consternation. "They're not Scribes," Cynth pointed out, stating the obvious.

"Constance will be," Daren said, but a frown creased his forehead. The suggestion, while practical, broke with centuries of protocol.

"Arwen?" Hector said. Ultimately, the decision would be up to her and Dorcas, the head of the Scribes' guild.

"It could work," she said. "Constance is close enough that we're sure she'll qualify for the sash. And Renee... well, she doesn't have traditional Scribe's powers, but she certainly has *something*. And that's what Scribes' guild has always been for, to catch the exceptional ones who don't fit anywhere else."

"The guild lodges have residual shielding, so it would be safer," Daren said.

"Yes." Arwen gave it another minute of thought, then nodded. "I'll take it to Dorcas, but I think this may be a solution. In the meantime, move Renee in with Constance."

"I'll see to it as soon as we're finished here," Cynth said.

Arwen left a pause while the other council members shuffled around, stood and stretched, or reached for the refreshments in the middle of the table. Then she waved them back to attention and said, "Moving on, the next item is sustained help for Stanstead. They still have only apprentices for village healer and apothecary, and Dal isn't going to be amenable to returning any time soon. Any ideas?"

Arwen settled back to listen as names were proposed to provide Healer support to the broken town. It would be a long meeting. If only she were twenty years younger.

Chapter 33

"I *knew* it wouldn't work. I *knew* it was a stupid idea."

Constance watched from the safety of her desk as Renee, ranting with frustration, kicked at the leg of the bed with a sandaled foot, then prowled the room – their shared room now, since earlier in the afternoon, although not all Renee's things had been moved over yet. Renee had just come in; Constance hoped Dal had excused her in time to get some lunch.

"Did you manage to diagram anything?"

"Fat lot of good it did." Renee paused long enough to open the leather satchel that had become her constant companion since Constance found it in the textile building and presented it as a means to store Renee's drawings and tools. "It's just stupid. *Stupid.*" She pulled out a couple of sheets of paper and threw them in Constance's direction.

The sheets fluttered to the floor, nowhere near her desk. Renee shrieked in pure frustration before fetching them up – causing some damage – and thrusting them at Constance.

It was quiet for a blessed minute while Renee closed the satchel and resumed her prowl, and Constance studied the drawings. For once, the paper wasn't seconds; that small fact pointed directly to the importance the Motherhouse as a whole placed on this experiment. A basic body outline filled each sheet. Renee's diagrams looked like nothing so much as unconnected, mostly parallel straight lines drawn in a child's coloring book.

Renee sank into a dejected puddle on Constance's bed, the one closest to the worktable. The crew shifting furniture from Renee's room to hers had made an effort to create personal spaces, Constance in one corner, Renee's bed and a place for her worktable in another.

"I see lots of lines, but nothing connecting them. You usually have bubbles, intersections."

"Weren't none, were there." Renee's contempt for the process was absolute.

"What did Dal say? Perhaps he didn't know that's what you'd be looking for."

Renee gave an indignant and very unladylike snort. "He knew. Said he could only tell me what his hands tell him. It was up to me to sort it out. How'm I supposed to do anything with *that*?" she flung a hand in the direction of the papers.

"Some of the lines are thicker. Could that be a clue?"

"Or maybe it's just the ink, or the stupid pen, or two lines on top of each other."

"Renee. Take a breath."

The girl quieted, the furious energy draining away. She sat, hunched and limp, in the middle of the bed, looking down between her crossed legs. Constance waited.

"How am I supposed to know? Dal's no help. I done it just the way he said, but he told me it's nothing like what he feels in his hands. He thinks it's rubbish."

Constance heard the hurt in Renee's voice and said, "I doubt that. He just doesn't know how to interpret this any more than you do."

"But what am I gonna *do*?" Renee wailed. She pitched onto her side and huddled in a miserable ball on the bed.

Constance thought, rallying all her problem-solving skills. "I agree, it looks meaningless, but perhaps it isn't. Think back, try to remember when Dal sounded intense, where he seemed excited or – I don't know – more absorbed or something. Any clue to tell you which lines, or groups of lines, were the most important. Did the energy ever curve? If it's tied in a knot, I'd expect it to, but he might have forgotten to convey that. He was in that weird Healer's trance, remember."

"What's convey?" Renee mumbled.

"Carry. Maybe his words didn't carry everything he meant to say."

"Doubt it." But the frown on Renee's face and far-off look in her eyes told Constance she was taking in her words. Thinking.

"Problems aren't always solved in an instant, you know," Constance said. "Sometimes you need to turn off your mind and get away from it for a while. How about we walk over to the river before lunch?"

Renee sat up abruptly. "The river. That's it, ain't it? A river." She swung her long legs off the bed and headed for the door. "I need my table."

She was gone before Constance could say anything, so she left her own worktable to follow Renee into the corridor. By the time she caught up, Renee was in her old room, struggling to move the heavy desk.

"I know you ain't gonna let me work over here, right? So, I gotta get this thing shifted."

Wooden legs grated on the floor as she pulled one end in a semi-circle, then moved to the other end. No doubt Renee would drag the table, a little at a time, all the way to Constance's room.

"This is a job for two." Constance positioned herself at the other end. "We'll probably have to turn it on its side to get it out the door."

Working together, they shifted the table, tucking it in the corner by Renee's bed. She darted back for her chair. Her old room now was mostly empty, only a few odds and ends remaining from her numerous collecting excursions around the Motherhouse environs.

"It's all about flowing, see." Renee placed the chair just so, snatched the diagrams, and emptied the contents of the satchel onto her table. "Got a different kind of connection. Don't bother me."

Constance bit her tongue and turned back to her own work. The girl's head bent over one of the diagrams as she chewed on the end of the wooden pen, already lost in her patterns.

Chapter 34

Five days later, on a morning that had hinted at sun before delivering stinging rain pushed by a cold autumn wind, Meade smiled as she watched Constance cross the dining hall for tisanes. She had made a corner in the adults' section her home base for the day; the endless hours in her suite in the Healers' lodge or the healing rooms were driving her mad. Two men from the village had been deputed to assist her down the hill. The hall was noticeably warmer than the lodges; Meade relaxed as the warmth sank into her muscles.

Constance had come in a few minutes later. Neither had attempted to dodge the meeting, and the tension between them might be better termed embarrassment. Meade felt ashamed of her snappish behavior toward the other woman and was more than ready to end the awkwardness between them. Constance, she had heard, still labored under a blanket of guilt over the accident, but had persisted with occasional visits, made no less awkward by Meade's own mercurial temper. That took guts, she reckoned. Now the two of them were face to face on neutral territory for the first time in ages, inching back toward the incipient friendship they had forged in Stanstead.

Or so she hoped.

"Your being here – is it a positive sign?" Constance passed over a mug and sat across the table.

"Renee's on to something. Look." Meade wobbled up, keeping her hands on the table, and stood sturdily for a few seconds before easing back to the chair. "Dal still doesn't have a clue what she's talking about most of the time, but he got an inkling a couple of days ago. They did another mapping session, then he tried a Healing yesterday. It's not gone, but I can focus my energies a little better."

"Perhaps someone besides Dal could make sense of the diagrams? I already know I can't. These are even more complicated than the straightforward mind maps."

The term 'mind map' had been new to Meade, new to everyone for that matter, but had taken wings under the onslaught of Renee's intriguing, and frequently useful, diagrams. Rumor had it that the agriculturists in the village had modified their system of crop rotation, and the sheep and goats were following a different grazing pattern, all based on the maps combined with the agriculturists' more specialized knowledge of plant habitats.

"An experienced Scribe, maybe," she said. "They're used to those crazy weavings they develop. I guess you're working with those now?"

"Working is right." Constance grimaced. "Just a bunch of lines, but tracing them, defining the intersections, building on them... when you get down to it, I guess it's not much different from the mind maps. It just arises from a different source."

"The odd minds of Scribes," Meade confirmed with a grin.

The two women sipped the sweet tisane. It was nice to just be quiet with someone for a while, Meade mused, without being poked at or speculated about, although she sensed the tangle of uneasy energies swirling between them. *The joys of being a Weaver.* She heaved a barely perceptible sigh. Sometime in the future, once this horrible knot was disentangled and she was herself again, perhaps they could rebuild their friendship.

"I'm sorry," Constance said quietly, breaking their reverie. Meade could hear pain underlying her voice. "I never wanted anything like this."

Meade shook her head. "I'm the one who got in the way of an uncontrolled energy weave. It wasn't your fault."

Constance's earlier smile was long gone. "It happened because of me."

"No." Meade reached over and put her hand on the other woman's. "No one's fault. And today I'm out of the healing rooms, I've escaped Dal, and there's even hope it will all get better. Maybe soon."

They let silence fall once again, a comfortable silence. Meade glanced around. At this hour, the dining hall was quiet, only a solitary Bard sipping caff and playing riffs on his chitarre over in a corner. A group of Healers drifted in; one of them waved absentmindedly in their direction. Probably taking a break from the workroom.

And Constance sat with her, trying not to look miserable. She took the whole business of the knot in Meade's energies personally – too personally. Abruptly, a golden opportunity opened, one that might address two problems, Constance's angst and Dal's eternal presence. Without taking time to second guess herself, Meade seized it.

"You could do me a favor. A big one, actually."

Constance switched instantly to alertness. "Anything I can do. You know my capabilities aren't—"

"Oh, you'd be capable of this." Meade grinned. "I'm not talking about Entrée. No," she emphasized, the grin fading. "This is more personal."

She stopped to gulp at her tisane. She felt like a traitor, but really...

To Constance's wary expression, she said, "The thing is, Dal is driving me crazy. He never lets up. He's there constantly, questioning me, poking at me, scanning me. Really, I can't stand it anymore."

Now Constance looked puzzled; a frown creased her brow. "But what can I do?"

"You can get him off my back," Meade said bluntly.

"How? I barely know him, and he doesn't have much use for me."

Meade's grin returned. "Don't believe that. He's never been one to show what he feels, and you're a woman. You'll find a way." The grin fell away. "If you don't distract him, eventually I'll say something I'll regret. Dal and I have always been close, but these days I long to... I don't know, send him back to Stanstead maybe. He's obsessed, and it isn't even his problem. If anyone's going to solve this, especially given the challenge of interpreting Renee's diagrams, it'll be a Scribe, not a Healer." She leaned forward. "Please. You couldn't do me a greater favor."

Constance squirmed; Meade wondered why. Dal wasn't *that* intimidating. If anything, Constance was the more formidable of the two.

But she said, "I'll do what I can. Maybe he just needs to hear a fresh opinion."

"Or maybe..." A possible cause of Constance's unease came to her in a flash. "Maybe he needs something else to distract him."

Constance flushed, but to her credit she didn't look away. "I'm not the right person for that."

"I'm not so sure." Meade picked up her mug of tisane. "I suspect you might be the perfect person."

*

When Constance left Meade that morning, her only thought was how she would handle the promised conversation – confrontation? – with Dal. She had assiduously avoided him for weeks, beyond the occasional polite nod when their paths crossed, and she would far rather keep it that way.

Well, it was a problem she could postpone. Her time with Meade had left her unsettled, despite the overall conciliatory tone of their chat. Her priority was to shift her few personal belongings to the Scribes' lodge. Renee had already removed her own bundle of possessions, an easy task since the girl had even less than Constance did, and barring some secret stash over in the barn with the horse, everything she valued traveled with her in the battered satchel.

Then it was back to the workroom to do battle with another weave. Discipline, Dorcas called it. And it certainly exercised her mind in a new way. Given the blustery weather, the teaching workroom in the Centra didn't sound like such a miserable place to be.

But after a futile hour or so, her concentration everywhere except on the new weave, she gave up and stretched. Her eyes needed a fresh focus, if only there were something more inspiring than the stone walls and scuffed wooden floor to gaze at. She wondered what the time was, and how long it would be before the lunch bell sounded... assuming she even heard it from behind the stone walls.

"Use your abilities," Dorcas would lecture. "You don't need to hear the bell with your ears. You'll know when it rings, just stretch yourself a little."

She stretched, as well as she could. No bell.

The weave wavered in front of her. It was just lines on a paper, but they did this sometimes, almost as if they were alive and shifting. She hastily moved her eyes away. Sometimes the sheer weirdness of life in the Motherhouse, with strange energies and talents swirling around her – through her – was just too much. No one back home would believe a word of it.

Home. Life on Terra had been increasingly fraught, politically, environmentally, and personally, but Eurocorp was home. She had been able to walk into town, enjoy the occasional treat from the numerous shops, sit in an outdoor café – under the screens, of course – and enjoy a cappuccino. On the good days, trouble had seemed so far away. But here, all was cold and austere. There were no shops, not a one. No variation in the clothing, little variety in the food. And the Aura... well. She wished she didn't believe it, but there it was. She had healed a plant; she had walked a weave. It was real, unless they had some mysterious way to tamper with her mind. But that, in its own way, would be just as odd.

Restless, Constance rose from her chair and paced the small room. Then she snatched up the sheepskin vest she now used to stay warm – minimally warm – and headed out. Fresh air would clear her mind.

She had taken no more than a half dozen steps from the Centra when she collided, literally, with Dal. She stepped back. So did he. His tight mouth and rigid posture, beyond his usual air of remote disdain, told her something was bothering him. There was a pause she could have done without before they both started speaking.

"Are you looking for Meade?"

"Have you seen Renee?"

It took a moment for the words to make sense. "Wait," Constance said. "Isn't she with you? She had a lesson this morning, didn't she?"

"She did. She left a message. Urgent business, something about that horse. I suspect even the Aura can't keep up with her." Dal wore his irritation like a cloak. Constance had gathered through the Motherhouse grapevine, which was so ubiquitous that even she, a newcomer, was part of it, that Dal found his work with Renee frustrating and intriguing in equal measure. He wasn't amused to find his student had escaped.

"And she's not there? You've checked the village? She didn't say anything to me."

The struggle to keep his irritation in check at her question was evident by the tight set of his mouth. "Of course. They haven't seen her."

Reality sank in. Renee was missing. When Constance met Dal's eyes this time, there were no sparks, no instant electricity, only well contained panic.

"Notify Arwen," he said. "We'll put out an alarm. Then go to the dining hall, collar everyone you see. Grab the workers in the distillation hut to help. I'll go back to the village and start the search."

They stepped around each other, for all the world like partners in a formal, old-time dance, and went their separate ways. Constance forgot all about lunch, the wavering weave, the cold. She would check with Meade first, then do all she could to track down her child.

*

Constance had been assisting Dorcas to work her magic, attempting to track the girl. Mid afternoon, groaning with fatigue and an aching back, she had been granted a break, and had just entered the dining hall when Renee wandered in, her face innocent. "What's going on?" she demanded.

Arwen, who had been sitting with Meade over a tisane, stalked across the floor and lit into the girl with a cold fury that sent a chill up Constance's spine. "What were you thinking? Don't you realize the entire Motherhouse has been looking for you? Haven't you been told not to go wandering off? Are you blind to danger?" Arwen's chest heaved as she fought to catch a breath, betraying her agitation.

Renee looked bewildered. "I left a message."

Arwen stared at her, speechless, then strode to the door where she jerked the pull to summon a runner kid.

Renee spotted Constance. "What'd I do?" she demanded. "This whole place has gone nuts. I left a message. I said I'd be back." She turned to Meade, who looked limp as relief washed over her. "Why's everyone all crazy?"

Constance said nothing. She folded her arms around the child – who was now almost as tall as she, and arguably no longer a child.

Renee squirmed free. No one would ever hold her for long. Constance shook her head, sharing Arwen's reaction. "You scared us. No one knew what had happened to you."

Renee gave a loud, frustrated sigh. "There was a goat birthing, out in the far field. Liam came and told me. So I left a message with Amalie and went. Like always," she added with emphasis. "I ain't done nothin' wrong."

Now that Constance could breathe again, she reviewed the sequence of events from Renee's perspective. She had gone off with her friend. She had left a message. "You might have provided more information. Even the village didn't know where you were."

Renee was working her way out of the awkward discussion and toward the serving line, where slices of cake with abricoes were stacked on the counter. "I missed lunch," she reported. "I'm hungry. You want anything?" Her fast look took in both Constance and Meade but skipped over Arwen.

"Please," Meade said faintly.

Constance gave a terse nod.

The runner kid came into the dining hall. Arwen spoke to him, then returned to Meade's table. "Calling off the search. I have to go."

Constance watched Arwen leave, then sat in her vacated chair. "Renee means a lot to you," she said to Meade. "Are you okay?"

"I'm a little shaken. No, make that a lot shaken. She's so much fun to be with. I mean, just imagine being a girl without any idea what it means to be a woman. She soaks up everything you tell her."

Constance didn't reply, but pondered Meade's statement. Renee, fun to be with?

Perhaps that was the difference between a friend and a parent. And one way or another, she had been assigned the harder role, the one designed to keep the wayward, uneducated, and headstrong girl on a straight path to responsible adulthood. Meade, she knew from Renee's occasional comments, taught her about relationships and what Constance dismissed as 'girl stuff', hair styles, skin care, and such. Heaven knew she couldn't explain relationships in the Midland. After the relatively rigid social-sexual mores of Eurocorp, she still found them bewildering. For instance – not that it mattered – how many people at the Motherhouse, women or men, had Dal taken as lovers? Sometimes the dribbles of information over the grapevine just couldn't be believed. Could they?

So, better to leave that to Meade. All Constance had to do was become a full-fledged Scribe as well as a full-fledged parent, avoid Dal and that unfortunate spark of recognition between them while still honoring Meade's request, and at the same time figure out her purpose in this new life. Piece of cake.

As if timed to her thoughts, Constance looked up to see Renee receive a ferocious hug from one of the cooks. Then she came over with three large pieces of the abricoe cake. They sat together, no one speaking, as they devoured the treat.

Interlude

"I hate him," Renee grumbled.

Constance turned from her desk to face Renee's corner of their shared room. She had heard the pen hit the table and shuddered to think of the spattered ink. But she kept her voice mild. "I notice you're doing the work he assigned."

"Yeah, well, it'll help, won't it? Nothin' to do with *him*."

'Him' was Dal, who had been so irate at Renee's defection, he had assigned an afternoon's work, carefully tracing out the alphabet over and over. Dal had it in his head that Renee needed to learn to read. Constance wasn't so sure, given the almost total absence of books. Renee, however, seemed taken by the idea, no doubt finding interesting patterns in the set of symbols that would unlock the mysteries of the written word.

Back at the Adventurer, Kiril was working to solve the problem of supplying cheap, abundant paper and ink. Having seen his drive, despite his failing health, Constance didn't doubt his eventual success. But she had begun to wonder what strengths of an oral tradition might be lost once the folklore could be written down.

The immediate issue, however, was Renee. And Renee was determined to master the letters. The current problem, Constance suspected, was the brilliant sunshine outside; the girl had always resisted confinement, especially on a day like today.

"How much more do you have to do?"

"Enough to take *forever*." Renee stood and threw herself on her bed with full drama.

"Too much to finish after supper?"

Renee frowned at her. "You'd let me off? If I promised?"

"Make it a double dog promise." An odd phrase she had learned from Renee, meaning a big promise that couldn't be broken, like crossing your heart back on Terra. Constance had no idea where either expression might have originated. What did dogs have to do with it? Or crosses?

But Renee now looked doubtful. She shifted her gaze to the paper on her table, then to the window, almost as if she was torn. Constance wisely kept quiet.

"Maybe... how about I went out just for a while? I wanna see the new kid."

"Find someone to walk to the village with you."

Renee's eye roll told Constance the warning was received with contempt. "I ain't dumb. You think I want those people to get their hands on me?"

"No. I'm sure you don't." She waited.

"Okay," Renee grumbled. "Double dog."

Constance smiled. "Go on then."

To her credit – and Constance's surprise – Renee took a few minutes to find a rag and wipe the spatters of ink from her worktable. Then the girl galloped out, all long legs and enthusiasm, eager for the afternoon's adventure.

Constance sighed and returned to her own studies, wondering if she had ever had so much energy, so much zest for life.

Chapter 35

On a bright autumn afternoon a few days later, freed from her lessons, Constance called at the Healers' lodge, hoping to find Meade. The conversation in the dining hall had encouraged her to believe their friendship could be revived, so a visit on this rare morning with no duties, no lesson with Dorcas, no recent rain, and sunshine was an opportunity not to be wasted.

The entrance to the Healers' lodge was imposing from the outside, a stone arch at the end of a winding path through the physick garden where at midsummer the air hung weighty with the overpowering scent of the herbs. Today, although the sun shone, the garden had a look of finality as it settled in for the winter. The lobby proved to be undecorated wood paneling, doors left and right, stairs to the upper floors. The Healers' lodge was one of the few buildings she had seen in the Midland with three floors.

The lodges were sacrosanct, only the initiated allowed in. It made the fact that she and Renee had been welcomed into the Scribes' lodge all the more remarkable.

Or, she thought grimly, it meant they recognized her as a Scribe in training. And Renee as a child at risk.

She shook her head, clearing her thoughts, and presented herself, then waited while the woman at the desk sent a runner kid to find Meade.

Off the child went, up the stairs. A minute later, she came back down, shook her head in the direction of the desk, and disappeared through the right-hand door.

The girl came back. "She's there. Says the lady can come on through."

"Thank you." The woman on the desk smiled to the kid, then turned to Constance. "Down the hall, last door at the very end."

Constance spoke her thanks as well, then began her first foray into the Healers' lodge. In character, it differed markedly from the Scribes' lodge. It felt more... organic, she decided. Instead of stone walls, here the warm, polished wood seemed to pulse with life. Windows punctuated the wall on her right; a couple of closed doors, presumably to Healers' suites, lined the left. The door at the end stood open, and from it she heard a light feminine voice. And then another, businesslike, definitely masculine.

She paused before entering, calling out to let them know she was there. She couldn't avoid Dal completely, especially in light of her promise to Meade.

The two Healers faced each other across a large, high wooden table, dried plants in front of them, waxed linen bags piled in the middle. At harvest, every Healer in the Motherhouse had been in the fields for the late-season herbs, which now had been dried and must be processed into either glass bottles with alcohol or these little bags carried by those traveling from hamlet to hamlet. Tedious, Constance would have thought, but

Meade and Dal both seemed to be enjoying the process.

Meade looked over her shoulder as she came in. "Hi. Pull up a seat."

Dal said nothing but dragged a stool from the wall to a place next to Meade.

"I didn't mean to interrupt. I just thought it'd be nice to have a chat." Constance perched on the stool, looking at the mess of dried herbs on the table.

Meade seemed cheerful, as if a weight had been lifted. "I can't stay here much longer. It takes all my concentration to stay balanced. But it's just so good to work with these." Her hand brushed the pile of herbs in front of her, spreading them slightly then gathering them up again. "It's in our blood, the smell of them, the awareness of their properties, how they support us."

Dal smiled slightly. He had yet to look at her, Constance thought, although that might not be true, because she hadn't dared more than glance at him. "I'll take you over to the healing rooms," he said. "You do look a little tired. You should rest before we have another session."

Meade deflated, sagging a little and losing her sunny mien before straightening and narrowing her eyes at Dal, her face tense with determination. "You know what? I don't want another Healing session. I'd rather sit outside in the sun, visit the dining hall, do ordinary things... like maybe do a Healing for someone else? It's been so long. I think I could sense energies." She hesitated. "Whether I could pull it off, though..."

"No," Dal said firmly. "You need all your strength for your own Healing."

Constance caught a flash of anger in Meade's voice. "And you don't trust me to try," she stated flatly.

Dal finished scooping his pile of herbs into the little bags. "Don't do that to yourself," he said, his voice flat. "We've been through this."

"And maybe she's been through this enough," Constance cut in. "Maybe she needs to do normal things for a while. Something you don't seem to have much awareness of." She muttered the last words, but Meade heard her and grinned. She wasn't sure if Dal did, as his expression was unchanged.

He switched into teacher mode – or what Constance privately thought of as hectoring mode. "You know we have to move as quickly as we can," he said, addressing Meade and ignoring Constance completely. "We can't let the energies become rigid."

Meade started to speak, but Constance got there first. "And in your opinion, your so far ineffective methods are the only option to keep the energy flexible. Do you even know that's true?" she asked, gaining passion as she went. "Everyone says what happened is unique. Meade loves people, loves the outdoors. Are you so damn sure those things won't do as much for her energy as your supposed Healing?"

Dal's nose went a bit higher in the air at the word 'supposed'. "You are no Healer. And you aren't much of a Scribe. Let those who know what they're talking about do the talking."

"Dal."

They both turned to Meade. Constance heard something she hadn't heard before in that lilting voice – steel. "My whole instinct is to follow what Constance says. My body has improved, but only a little. And I swear my aura is shrinking under this regimen. She's right."

The silence in the room weighed heavily around them all. Meade had had her say, Dal said nothing at all, and observing this, Constance felt any possible words clog in her throat.

Then Meade turned her attention to the remaining pile of dried herbs before her and began shoveling them into bags. "I'll have this done in a minute," she said. "Dal's commandeered one of our wheeled chairs for me, so perhaps you could push me over to the dining hall? It's downhill, so it doesn't matter so much that they don't roll very well."

Constance had seen no sign of rubber on this backward planet; naturally, the wheels were wooden. "I'd be happy to," she replied.

Meade settled in to complete her work. Constance fought the urge to squirm under the weight of displeasure filling the room. Dal said nothing more, but tidied his part of the worktable, labeled and stowed his collection of herb-filled bags, and left the two women alone, the set of his back radiating displeasure.

Just as he crossed the threshold, Meade caught Constance's eye and winked.

*

"Let's go over there," Meade said, pointing to their left.

They had just begun the descent from The Healers' lodge to the dining hall, following the path alongside the slope of land they called the amphitheater. Fifteen paces or so from the bottom of the slope, a level place provided a meeting spot for students and full-fledged Weavers alike, conversing or merely soaking in the sun.

The chair stopped. Constance demurred, "I can't push this contraption across the grass."

"I hear you," Meade said. "But you know what? It's not that far. If you helped me, I bet I could get there." She twisted in the chair, looking back at Constance. "You don't know how much I've longed for something like sitting on the grass. The sun... we've never formally explored its healing properties, but I suspect they're there. To feel it on my skin again, and not have someone harrying me off to my room or one of those blasted treatments."

Constance wasn't convinced, that was clear. "I don't think I can support you very far. You're more..."

"Say it. Robust?" Meade felt her grin surface. "I've never been all that slender, so I don't mind. Let's try, anyway. There are enough people around, if I get into trouble one of the apprentices can rescue me. Please?"

She hadn't meant to plead, but she would, for the freedom of the amphitheater instead of that chair on the porch of the healing rooms, or even the dining hall. "Have faith, Connie. Let's do this."

After a pause that tested Meade's nerves, Constance said, "I'll try."

She had caught Constance's grimace at the use of the nickname, but really, her proper name was hard to say with its accent on the last syllable. Anyway, didn't she realize having a nickname meant people liked you? Nobody bothered to give a nice nickname to someone unpopular.

Constance nudged the awkward vehicle closer to the verge and got a wheel onto the grass, which provided an adequate brake. Then she walked around to stand in front of Meade. "How do you want to do this?"

"Give me your hands to start with." Oh, the feel of the warm breeze on her face, the sun on her head. She took a breath, breathing it all in. "Bliss."

Constance held out both hands, visibly bracing herself. Meade cautiously put her feet down and leaned forward, then lunged, heaving herself toward Constance and onto her feet. She felt the other woman's hands tighten as they both faltered, but miraculously she stayed upright.

Unstable, weak, but upright.

Their eyes met for a moment. "It's only a few steps," Meade said, reassuring herself as much as Constance.

"Eight or ten, I'd say."

"More, with my weak legs. You're radiating your thoughts all over the place. Haven't they taught you how to shield your mind?"

She felt the barrier go up. Constance might be a Scribe, but the whole business of the Aura was still unnatural to her. Oh, well. This wasn't for Constance, it was for her. Her day, her adventure.

And wouldn't Dal have a fit if he knew?

She changed her grip to clutch Constance's upper arm, turned so she faced the grass, and cautiously took a step forward.

It worked. She risked another.

After four of these tiny, tentative steps she felt herself tiring and stopped, grateful for the solid anchor of Constance's arm. She closed her eyes, inhaled the grass, the sun, and let it flow through her.

"Again. Almost there."

Even shielded, she felt Constance's concern, but that didn't matter. The object was to get from here to there, and so far it was working. She inched along, barely able to keep her legs beneath her but determined to have this treat, a few minutes on the grass in that flat place, enjoying the perfect autumn day.

And somehow it worked. They made it to their destination before Meade's strength – which she knew had been more a matter of will power than of muscle power – gave out completely. She let herself collapse as gently as she could, Constance bending down with her, onto the earth.

Oh, the earth. Her hands brushed the grass, releasing its aromas. Beside her, Constance sat gracefully – the woman was so elegant. Like Dal, in fact. They both made Meade, in her low moments, feel like an awkward bumbler.

"You know what would make this perfect?" she asked. "A pastry and caff. A triumph like this calls for pastry and caff."

Constance got it – somewhat to Meade's surprise. "I'll fetch some. Don't go anywhere."

Meade hesitated, then laughed aloud. Constance, making a joke? "For a pastry, I won't budge."

Constance worked her way downslope to the dining hall, while Meade lay back and hiked up her skirt, letting the sun caress her legs and regretting it really was a little too chilly to remove her clothes completely. She might sense the healing from the sun, but pneumonia was a reality. And Dal would murder her if she let herself get sick as part of an effort to get well.

*

Back in her room in the Scribes' lodge, Constance took a break from her studies to muse on the afternoon, a couple of hours lounging on the grass with Meade, chatting or being quiet, soaking in the still autumn air. It had been healing for them both. Meade had shown an improved strength in her legs as they finally made their way back to the rolling chair, although not as much as she knew Meade had hoped for. And for herself, well, it was one of the very few instances when she had experienced uninterrupted hours to enjoy the day. Dorcas and Arwen both had crossed the green at different times and noticed her, but neither had approached.

On the other hand, Dal had intruded, spotting them on his way from the healing rooms to somewhere. As he had begun to climb the slope, Meade, who happened to be sitting up at the time, called, "Leave me alone." As evidenced by his scowl, Dal didn't like it, but he turned on his heel and headed downhill.

"Do you know how to do this stuff?" Renee's voice cut across her memories from her corner of their shared room. "'Cause it's hard."

Constance looked up. She and Renee had been companionably quiet together, each absorbed in her work, and she had paid no heed to what Renee might be up to, assuming – inaccurately, as it turned out – that she was devising yet another version of Meade's energy scans.

"How to do what?"

"This." Renee waved a scrap of linen at her. On her desk lay a knife and a tangled pile of red threads.

Constance got up and crossed the room to peer at the fabric. Renee had been... embroidering? Surely not.

"I got this one," she said, gesturing at what appeared to be an identifiable, if somewhat lopsided, flower petal. "But there's this other one for the stem, and I can't make it work." She tossed the fabric onto the desk and crossed her arms. "It's all stupid."

Constance picked up the discarded fabric and studied the remainders of several attempts at stems. "I've never done anything like this," she murmured. "It wasn't encouraged, unless you were going to adopt it as a career. No time for—" She bit her tongue. She had almost said time for trivial activities like making pictures with needle and thread, which would have resulted in Renee sulking or storming from the room, and probably not speaking for days. Constance attributed the tempestuousness her child exhibited nowadays to puberty. The horrid family who had come searching for her had placed her age at fourteen, which was at least two years older than she had originally thought.

Slowly, she was learning to respect the activities of this strange world, where the work was never-ending just to survive, yet people found time for such amusements as embroidery.

"Where did the thread come from?" she asked, realizing suddenly that in a world of neutral linen, she had never seen such vibrant color.

Renee shrugged. "Textile building. Meade says most women have a tunic they keep just for themselves, and they fancy it up. Make it special, like for holidays. She showed me how."

"I don't suppose she drew you a picture?"

"Yeah," Renee grumbled. "But I still don't get it."

When she extracted and proffered the crumbled second of paper, Constance studied the loops and dots. It looked like the stitches formed a chain, out and in, out to catch the loop, in again..."

"I think I see," she said. "Whether I can do it is another thing."

"Show me," Renee demanded.

Constance shifted her chair over to Renee's side of the room, so they sat side by side. Slowly, with something of a death grip on the crude needle, she began.

After two loops, Renee snatched the fabric from her. "Got it," she crowed. "Watch." And after a single false start, she produced a chain of her own.

Constance retreated to her own desk, her own work. But after a few minutes Renee appeared at her side and actually gave her a quick shoulder hug. "Thanks," she said, without even her usual reluctance to acknowledge when anyone did something for her. Then she barreled out of the room, fabric in hand, presumably heading for the Healers' lodge to show her results to Meade.

Alone, Constance put down her own work and allowed herself the luxury of taking time to reflect on that hug, the exuberance behind it, and Renee's plunging headlong into new skills. The skills related to growing up. The girl was gone, a gangly teenager was emerging. What the next years held was anyone's guess.

*

All good things must come to an end, Constance reflected that evening as she approached the dining hall, where Dal hovered at the entrance. From the way he tracked her progress, there was no doubt in Constance's mind he was waiting for her.

He stepped in front of her before she could brush past him. "She's too fragile for outings like that. Can you really be so little aware—"

But Constance had had enough. "Today was just what she needed," she snapped back. "She'll be tired tomorrow, but the improvement in her strength, not to mention her willingness to work toward a cure—"

"You're no judge." Belatedly they both realized he had grasped her arm. He dropped his hand, but only to make a frustrated fist.

Her ire equaled his. "And you're forgetting one thing. I may not have your Auric endowed Healing powers, but I was a doctor on Terra, a medic on the Adventurer. I know more about medicine than you ever will. Give Meade time for a good rest, and I'd bet my life she'll be stronger, healthier. Not to mention having a better attitude. Unlike her attendant Healer, I might add. Now, if you don't mind..."

He let her brush past him, then stopped her with a word. "Connie."

She turned.

"This isn't personal." If she didn't know the man better, she would swear he was blushing. But maybe it was the failing light. "What happened in Stanstead... we're both better served by forgetting it. Or at least not letting it get entangled with our lives here."

Oh, she knew. She could live another lifetime or two without having to deal with the potential consequences of that meeting of eyes. The feelings it had evoked, the physical reaction, still haunted her memory more frequently than she liked, triggering bodily sensations she had done her best to put behind her.

At least it was on the table now. And for once, she agreed with Dal wholeheartedly. "My thoughts, too. Now, if you'll excuse me..."

This time he let her go uncontested. It was inconvenient, Constance thought, that their short conversation, the touch of his hand on her sleeve, had brought it all back. But now, she thought as she entered the dining hall, she had tools. Not for nothing had she been learning Scribes' techniques at mind control. Dal might as well not exist.

Chapter 36

The weather turned that night, the mild autumn displaced by the cold winds carrying the scent of winter. Later, Constance would remember the feel of the day, the way a cold wind worried the leaves into whirlpools, the eerie light, the louring clouds that seemed to have a greenish tinge, portending icy rain or even snow.

There had been no premonition, beyond the ominous change in the weather. Nothing to suggest Renee might be at risk. Still basking in the glow of her afternoon with Meade, Constance awoke feeling sanguine about life and her future. By mid-morning, that had been shattered.

Dal turned up in the Centra, interrupting her work with Dorcas, fuming, based on the thin line of his mouth, but with lines of worry etched on his forehead. "Do you know where Renee is?" he demanded. "She promised she would be there for another mapping, but she isn't. No one's seen her. Again."

The room went quiet. Constance could say nothing. Her heart had dropped to her stomach under the weight of impending disaster. "The kitchen?" Dorcas asked.

"No," Dal said. "Not the kitchen, the Scribes' lodge, the village. She hasn't been with Meade. Did she say anything, anything at all to suggest where she might be? I never expected her to run off and miss a session with Meade."

Constance took a breath and got control of her voice. "No. She was gone when I got up." Hearing how weak the words sounded, she added, "She often is. She goes to the village to ride Socksy and visit with her friends. Not alone, someone comes to pick her up."

Dorcas sighed with frustration, then rose and made for the door. "Arwen needs to know. We'll activate our tracking and call for search parties. It's only mid-morning, she can't be far." She stood and left, her purposeful tread in wooden clogs sending a hollow echo into the room.

She could be far, Constance thought. Those terrifying people... they would have had time by now to find the back routes, the animal tracks, the hiding places. They had her girl, she knew it to the very fiber of her being. Panic gripped her in one terrifying instant. Her mind altered, it seemed organically, to focus on one thought only, one point in the cosmos that was Renee and her own need to reclaim her.

Before she could follow Dorcas, Dal grabbed her, swinging her around. She collided with his chest; he held her there. "No," he said, reading her mind. His hand softened on her arm, the other moved to her back. "*Think,* Connie. You'd slow them down. We'll find her, but your place is here."

She barely registered the comfort of his arm round her. Yanking back from him, she snapped, "My *place* is with my child."

As she raced from the room he shouted, "Don't be *stupid.*" She ignored him. Supplies... she would need supplies. Stanstead was the most obvious destination, the best place for them to hide. And they almost certainly came from somewhere near the town, given where Renee first entered her life. She had learned enough, she would be able to track them... Food. And something warm. One of those hideous waterproof cloaks that stank of sheep.

And quietly. They would try to stop her. Dal would try to stop her. She couldn't let that happen. Dried provisions were always available for anyone to take. And a cloak hung abandoned on a hook in the Scribes lounge.

Her girl. She had to find her girl.

Chapter 37

Constance hadn't seen a soul all day, not since she turned the corner at the Bards' lodge and struck out on her own toward Stanstead. As the light began to fail, she was forced to accept she had walked as far as she could; the blister on the side of her foot pained her too much to continue, and she wished she had paid more attention to the walking lessons first Agnes, then the various teachers in the apprentices' class, had tried to pound into her. The icy rain presaged by the clouds had arrived, and the lanolin-infused cloak proved inadequate to keep her dry. She had forgotten to pack a waxed linen tarpaulin for a tent, and her boots were heavy with mud and slippery on the rain-soaked track. She was sure there had been a checklist for journeys, back in the class, but she had dismissed the information as irrelevant to her, and too hard to memorize given everything else she was trying to cram into her head.

Deeply chilled, her fingers and toes frozen, she worked her way down one last forested slope before coming to rest in a more open, grassy valley. The forest frightened her, ominous in its darkness, so she couldn't stop there. No shelter was visible anywhere other than a spreading conifer that blocked some of the downpour. Hard against the trunk until she realized water was running down it from the branches above, then a little ways out with nothing to lean on, she huddled in the cloak, one leg thrust out awkwardly to avoid pressure on the blister. Medicine... she needed an ointment and a sterile way to lance the blister or she would never be able to walk tomorrow.

Her mind in a dark, despairing place, Constance realized that she had neglected to pack a lot of things, including a selection of medicines. And in the cold reality of twilight, rain, and plummeting temperatures, she grasped – belatedly – that her entire hasty flight from the Motherhouse had been a mistake.

Stupid...

But Renee...

Sunk in misery to a state of semi-awareness, in the gloom she didn't even notice a dark, cloaked figure approaching. Not until he stood over her, gazing down, did her senses prod her to full wakefulness. She looked up from under the hood of the cloak, resigned to whatever happened next, too defeated to argue.

She couldn't see his face, but there was no mistaking his voice. "You're an idiot," Dal said, his carefully neutral inflection conveying no hint of what he was thinking. "But at least you picked a halfway decent place to stop. Didn't it occur to you to build a circle of protection? They do keep the rain out, for the most part." Then he followed his own advice, constructing the energetic circle around them both. Constance watched from under her drooping hood, fascinated in spite of herself. He moved smoothly, making the required gestures with his hands, intoning words so quietly she couldn't hear them against the backdrop of the downpour. Agnes had done the same, during the long walk from the Adventurer. The circle cast, he busied himself erecting a shelter.

He didn't speak again until he had a small fire going and had placed a cup of hot tisane in her shaking hands. "You'd warm up sooner if you took off those wet clothes."

Her voice was small; under the sound of rain pounding the ground outside the circle, she could barely hear herself. "I brought a change, but I think it's wet."

"No doubt. Your entire pack is wet." Dal's voice had the tight timbre of a person holding onto neutrality with an iron grip.

She sagged, if possible, even more. "You're right. I'm an idiot."

"You care that much."

She didn't answer. After a while, Dal produced a small, but hot, meal. Gradually, her shuddering stopped; her clothes steamed in the heat from the fire, and the warm food eased her body if not her concern for Renee. Constance found herself tongue tied; the torrent of feelings around Renee's disappearance and the shambles of her ill-conceived mission left her incapable of sorting out what she felt, how she should react.

As they settled for the night side by side in the small shelter, she in his dry sleeping sack, he making do with her damp one, Constance experienced a moment of dizziness. When she opened her pinched-shut eyes, she realized some maturation seemed to have happened, some ripening of her Scribe's abilities, because she suddenly became aware of the man beside her, beyond what she might have expected given their strong physical attraction. She felt the hard wall, the shape and nature of the screen he had clamped down around his mind.

Thus reminded, she restored her own shields, then set the intention to sleep. Irrationally, though, she found herself longing for a relaxation of those shields. Shut out, she had never felt so lonely.

*

Despite Dal's best efforts, it took them closer to five than the usual four days to reach Stanstead. Constance refused to allow herself to moan about her ongoing battles with blisters and aching muscles, but there was no question her physical misery colored the trek. At least the weather turned, the rain replaced by brisk, sunny autumn.

Dal, also, never complained, beyond telling Constance the search party from the Motherhouse would beat them to Stanstead by at least a day, more likely two. "Not that you could have handled the northern route anyway," he pointed out. "It's shorter, but much rougher than this one."

By the end of the second day, they had used up all possible topics of conversation, which really were limited to the trek, Constance's ongoing physical challenges, and Renee. Constance, for her part, considered the silence a blessing. If she could just turn her mind away from Renee for a while, perhaps she would be able to use the time to come to terms with the changes in her life, feel more grounded in what was now her uncomfortable reality.

Or maybe conversation simply proved impossible, given the ongoing sexual awareness between them.

As she walked and reflected, Constance did her best to utilize what few practical lessons she had retained from her classes with the apprentices – paying attention to her surroundings and walking style, holding her stomach at bay long enough to assist Dal in preparing a small animal he had caught for their evening meal, tending to her physical ailments. During the long walks, she reviewed and occasionally practiced the exercises Dorcas had tried to pound into her head. Dal made no comment on the random light balls hovering in front of her in the middle of the day, the odd spider webs of weaves that had no purpose, and kept his own mind thoroughly shielded from her probes.

Unfortunately, those efforts sank beneath the weight of her fruitless worry about Renee.

*

They arrived to learn the team, four from the Motherhouse plus two Weavers who chanced to be in Stanstead, already had a plan to leave the next day, divided into three parties. In the meantime, they were preparing for days on the trail and fanning out to search throughout the slowly rebuilding town, questioning anyone they encountered. So far, no one had seen a group matching the description of Renee or her relatives.

Dal refused to let Constance go with them. Citing her own stupidity, he brought an assortment of healing salves from the healing room and sat her on the side of her bed. Half an hour later he had lanced, cleaned, and poulticed her feet. "Don't move until I say," he commanded. "Once the poultice has done its work, I'll put on a salve and bind your feet. But it'll be a couple of days yet before you can walk any distance."

From the door to her room – in the guest lodge as the Scribes had no lodge in Stanstead – he turned and said, his voice hard, "I mean it."

Sighing, Constance collapsed back on the bed. Now she was stuck in Stanstead while others searched. *Useless.*

But not totally. A day later, with the help of a cane a kind citizen found for her, Constance hobbled across the square – now bright, clean stone, a far cry from the dilapidated remains of a makeshift hospital she had last seen – when she caught a glimpse of dark rags darting around a corner.

Her newfound Scribe's senses told her, beyond a doubt, the quickly disappearing figure was the female, one of Renee's kidnappers. Constance couldn't have explained how she could be so certain, but working on conviction she left the cane propped against the wall of the administration building and crept after the woman.

She lost the trail, no surprise as she and her quarry delved deeper into the outlying streets of the town, but not before she had gained a good impression of the direction the woman was heading – toward a hamlet Constance knew, the one with the safe water. With that information, they had a better chance of finding Renee. For once not deriding her own abilities, she hastened, as much as she could on her hobbled feet, back to the square to find Dal.

Chapter 38

Constance and Dal, accompanied by an elderly Healer named Peter who chanced to be in town, left Stanstead before dawn on the third day. Dal had done one of his intense Healings on her feet the night before. Despite the considerable relief that brought, her legs and ankles ached as she stumbled over wheel ruts on the track to Little Hutt. She bit her lip, said nothing, and carried on. The possibility of being sent back was much too real.

Dal and Peter both wore Healers' sashes, the green cutting across their chests like armor. She had no sash. Although she had used an apprentice Healer's sash for her walk from the Adventurer, it appeared the Scribes allowed no such designation. Either you were a Scribe, or you were not. No apprentice status allowed. The absence of that simple, crudely dyed piece of fabric increased her insecurity as she plodded along after the men.

Little Hutt was nondescript. A few mud-colored structures surrounded a small central plaza, the well situated in one corner. Behind them were a stable and shacks – workshops and residences, Constance knew from far too many previous visits. It was still early, but several of the buildings on the plaza had opened their doors, including the tiny dining hall. They paused there for food, and to ask whether anyone recognized the description of Renee's kidnappers. Toward the end of a meager breakfast of lentils and corn bread, a hunched, elderly man approached their table. "Heard you're looking for that Levi and his," he said, chewing on the end of an unlit pipe. In a detached part of her brain, Constance wondered what he ever found to smoke, as tobacco appeared not to exist here.

"That's their name?" Dal effortlessly assumed leadership. "Two men, one younger, his name's Jimmie, and a woman."

"Yeah, and a kid. Girl, I think. Haven't seen 'em since summer. Ain't sociable."

"So we gathered. We have reason to believe the girl is in danger. Do you know where they live?"

"Nope. That Levi, he keeps hisself to hisself. Makes sure the others do, too." The man leaned against a wall, as if settling in for a good long chat.

"Perhaps you've seen what direction they go when they leave town?" Dal asked, clearly tamping down his impatience. Constance would have smirked, were she not suddenly terrified for Renee.

The man, however, was in no rush. "Yeah, I reckon. Not always the same direction, though. So who's to say which way's their camp? Hmm?"

"Camp?" Peter interposed.

The man shrugged. "Seems likely it ain't much more'n that. Look pretty rough, that lot."

"Surely one direction predominates." Dal always seemed to become more pompous when under pressure.

"Guess you mean which one they use most?" the man asked conversationally. "Yeah, perhaps.

They wander, you know. Forage, like. Rough-scrabble."

"If you could just—"

"Reckon I could. Could be wrong, though. Now, that kid as travels with 'em, she's around more. Maybe Pen over there's better informed, on account of she feeds the kid sometimes. Sad little scrap," the man added with a touch of compassion. "Always looks hungry."

And didn't she, back then, Constance thought as she waited for Dal to end his interrogation. One thing for sure, if Dal didn't go see the woman, she would do it herself.

"Thank you," Dal said stiffly. "Where do we find Pen?"

"Over there, like I said." The man gestured across the plaza toward a group of huts; this was not a prosperous village.

Dal nodded in acknowledgment and left, dropping his bowl and utensils in a bin for that purpose. He crossed to the huts, Constance and Peter hard on his heels, the man who had given them the information watching from the door.

"Oh," the woman named Pen said when they tracked her down over a cookfire. She looked like she should be rounded and content, if only life weren't quite so hard. "You must mean Nada. Always felt sorry for that little thing. Fed her up when I could, when that hulking boy wasn't with her. Work her something fierce, don't they?"

Impatient with Dal, Constance put herself forward. "We need to find her. We think she's in danger."

"I expect you're right. Their camp's thataway." She gestured to the south. "You'll get there before lunch. Place is a mess, filthy – sent my son out once to see if they's all right, after the earthquake. Turned him away right smart. Better they lived in town, worked like the rest of us, but I guess they go their own way. Gotta say, haven't seen Nada in a while. Sometime this summer, happen."

"Thank you." Dal once again assumed control. "We won't trouble you any longer."

"No trouble. Nice to see a new face. Don't get many strangers, now the water problem's solved over in Stanstead."

The woman gave them a largely toothless grin as they strode off, as fast as Constance's ailing feet allowed them, toward a narrow trail running south from the village.

*

"I don't like this," Peter said.

At first the trail had been easy enough, copses of trees punctuating rough grazing fields, but soon had disintegrated into a rough track which they followed until well past mid-morning, with no guarantee there was anything ahead or even that they were on the right path. Constance picked her way carefully, uneasy for reasons she couldn't put her finger on. Something about the land? Nothing seemed out of the ordinary, but everything felt... wrong.

Ahead of her, Dal and Peter moved cautiously, as if they were picking up clues she missed; they both had acquired the wary mien of animals sensing danger. As a Scribe, she should be able to sense things Healers couldn't... like a perturbation in the Aura that presaged danger. Wondering why she hadn't done so before, she cautiously lowered the shielding she now held around herself as a matter of course.

And there it was, so clear she could almost see it. Gooseflesh raised on her arms. She said, quietly, "Wait."

Perhaps the intensity carried where her voice didn't. Both men, several meters ahead, stopped.

She started toward them, then froze when a scream cut through the air.

Another. And then a laugh, humorless, male, and cruel.

"Renee," Constance whispered. All three of them turned left, toward the sounds. With Dal in the lead, they plowed through the coarse shrubbery lining the track, providing a boundary of sorts to the field on the other side.

No one spoke. Unshielded, she experienced Dal's grim fixation on their mission, Peter's fear, as if their emotions were her own. She was sure they equally sensed her terror for Renee, her determination to kill if she had to, to protect her girl.

The wonders of the Aura.

On the far side of the rough field, just before the land fell away into a valley, a copse, now denuded of leaves, offered scant cover. When they reached it, they dropped to the ground, inching forward with as little noise as possible. Constance cursed the long skirt that tangled with her legs.

A shack lay in the valley beyond the copse; Constance wondered how it didn't collapse. Renee and the younger of the two men stood near what appeared to be a pigsty; he had a grip on her arm. Her hair was stringy, her face filthy. In this cold morning, the tunic she wore was little more than a rag, and her feet were bare.

And she was shrieking like a banshee as she struggled against the man's grip.

The man abruptly jerked her closer, causing her to stumble against his chest. His free arm wrapped around her. "You're mine," he growled. "Pa gave you to me, and that's that. Stupid wench." He shoved her away, then smacked her across the face with his free hand. "And you're gonna learn to behave. I give the orders now."

The woman stood in the door, nodding. Her tunic was relatively clean, if a bit short. Constance guessed it was Renee's tunic, the day she disappeared. The thought of those *animals* daring to strip her girl, steal her clothing—

Dal signaled for them to shift back, fully out of sight of the shack. Below them, the noise continued; Renee would never give up without a fight.

That brute intended to possess her, *rape* her, control and destroy her life. Constance obeyed Dal's command, but every fiber in her body wanted to run into the clearing, smite the brute with some horrible, nasty power. Never had she been so possessed by rage.

A safe distance from the edge, they hunched together in the undergrowth. "We need to let her know we're here," Dal said, his voice so quiet as to be almost nonexistent, "so she'll be ready. They probably lock her up at night, and there's the possibility she'll be forced to spend the night with that man."

Peter nodded. Constance listened. Her synapses fought to shut her brain down, protection from the overload of traumatized feelings. She ordered herself to pay attention, maintain a clear head.

Dal looked squarely at her. "Neither Peter nor I have the ability to bind him or otherwise incapacitate him. Do you?"

To her credit, she didn't blurt out that she could barely make fire or walk a weave, never mind anything like using the Aura to tie someone up. Instead, she delved deep inside herself, exploring the interface where she and the Aura intersected. Could she?

No. It would be foolhardy to place the whole of their rescue attempt on her untested powers. She shook her head, mute.

"The other option is to wait until she's sent on some errand. They can't spend all their time down there, and they can't watch her every minute. I think we should go back to Little Hutt for help. From the way they were talking, this family isn't popular, but Renee has some support."

There was a shout down below, then silence. Constance's blood ran cold.

"Could we buy her?" Peter asked. To horrified looks from both Constance and Dal, he elaborated. "Barter? Is there something we have that they want? Something worth Renee to them?"

They all sat quietly for a few moments, thinking it over. Dal was about to respond when, instead, his hand went up, signaling quiet. Constance heard it then – footsteps on the track.

Very slowly, all three of them shifted deeper into the copse, taking as much care as they could to be invisible, make no noise. Peter flattened onto the ground, Dal plastered himself to the far side of a tree trunk. At a little distance from them, Constance got a group of thin trees between herself and the footsteps and hunched over, her hood over her head.

Two voices now. In a piece of appalling luck, they had left the track and were walking across the field, talking about plowing and planting, come spring. At least the younger man was no longer with Renee. Every muscle frozen, she listened in terror as the voices grew closer.

A new sound... a muffled sneeze. The voices stopped, then the rustle of footsteps grew closer.

They had been found.

"Whaddaya think, Pa?" A sound in the underbrush, a groan. Stretching out with her Auric connection, she realized that Peter had been kicked in the side. More rustling suggested he was pulling himself – or being pulled – to a sitting position.

"Spy, I reckon. Plannin' to steal Nada away."

"Want me to put a pitchfork through 'im?"

She could smell the men, smell the fear in Peter... or perhaps it was her own.

"Best not. One a them witches, ain't he?"

"Them that put high ideas in Nada's head, eh? How about I rough him up a bit and send him packing?"

"Let's just have ourselves a check around first." The footsteps crunched in the undergrowth.

Constance's eyes were squeezed closed, her limbs shook. She had never been so terrified.

"And just lookee here." A shuffle indicated Dal had been found and dragged over to where Peter sat.

"Can't keep 'em, worse luck. And can't kill 'em." It was the younger man. "They'd hex us, sure as sure."

"Reckon we've got ourselves a problem. Get up, you." More shuffling suggested Peter had been hauled to his feet. "Let's take 'em back, see if Pam's got any ideas."

Dal spoke, his voice tight. "We're Healers. We have immunity from harm. But if you've any illnesses or wounds, we can help. Just let me get my remedies."

The younger man snorted. "And have you poisonin' me with magic? Move, you."

"Hang on, Jimmie," the older man said. "Might be something useful in that there pack."

More shuffling, a groan from Peter. Constance wondered if he was hurt, and if Dal would be given a chance to Heal him.

She listened to the four of them crossing the field to the track, leaving her alone. Once the sound of their footsteps died away, she inched back to the far side of the copse and looked down over the ramshackle farmstead. There was no sign of Renee.

Chapter 39

There seemed to be no choice but to walk back to Little Hutt for help. That Weavers could be manhandled in such a way horrified her, despite constant concern and warnings floating around the Motherhouse community, but she recognized her own relative helplessness. At least the men would be closer to Renee and perhaps let her know help was on the way. As adrenalin drained away, her body felt awash with weariness, but she checked the copse, located Peter's travel pack – they must have confiscated Dal's – and tucked it deeper into the woods before leaving.

*

Little Hutt proved to be less than cooperative. "We don't mess with Levi's family" pretty much summed up the reaction. "Always was strange, that man, even as a young 'un," one helpful woman informed her while serving a meager meal in the dining hall. "He don't welcome interference. Not much we can do."

"They've stolen a child and taken two Healers," Constance replied with some acerbity.

"They won't hurt your friends. Just scare 'em some."

"But Renee..." At the blank looks on the faces around her, she amended, "Nada? I think that's what they call her."

The speaker nodded. "Levi's sister's child. Always was a wild one. No one wanted to take her on, but they've kept her fed and sheltered, best as they can. If she wants to leave, she'll find a way."

Constance was left alone with her stew and dry corn bread. Her thoughts turned dark; she recognized a lust for vengeance and struggled to put it behind her. Even if there was no immediate assistance available, she might well need these simple people before Renee and the men were secured. If nothing else, she recognized her utter incompetence when it came to making a camp or feeding herself.

As she hunched over her meal, then gathered what she could from the dining hall's limited supply of dried travel rations, the skeleton of a plan began to form in her mind.

*

Back at the copse, with twilight approaching and her target below, thoughts swirled in her head, only occasionally linking into coherent sense. There were too many unknowns. One thing she was sure of, though, she would not leave Renee with those people another day, not after witnessing how she was treated. She had retained a small piece of meat from the stew and saved half of the bread, thinking ahead to a defeated-looking dog that stalked the property. Would it be enough to pacify the animal? And the bigger question – could she muster her shaky Auric powers in her own service?

She settled down to wait, a half-formed plan never leaving her mind, and devoted herself to practicing some of the minor skills she had more or less mastered over the preceding months, weaving and twisting energy. A rummage through Peter's pack produced nothing she recognized among the dried herbs and potions he carried, but she cautiously explored the field behind her and found a plant, still bearing leaves but now dry and brittle, that she remembered from her classes. She focused and did her best to infuse it with greater healing powers before pouring a little water from her water skin into her bowl, using some of her energy to heat it, and immersing the plant to make a tisane and a poultice. The resulting mixture would be saved for Renee, who would need it more than she did. She could withstand a scrape or two.

Below her, she caught the occasional sound of daily occupation, a shout, the squeal of an axle in need of lubrication, the sound of pounding which might be grain being prepared for baking. The woman appeared, dragging a goat behind her, and commenced to milk the beast, with no discernable effort at sanitation.

The late afternoon inched on and chill ate into her bones. She diverted some of her practice to keeping herself warm, sending small shafts of power into her hands and feet. Her linen tunic provided no warmth, and she had been reluctant – foolishly, she now knew – to switch to the rougher, scratchier woolen ones. Her rain cloak helped, as did the sheepskin vest Dal had forced on her before they left Stanstead. All the unwonted exercise of the day, tromping to Little Hutt from Stanstead, then three trips between the hamlet and her copse, had resulted in new aches and blisters; helpless to change her physical pains, she resolved to ignore them.

With dusk, light appeared in the shack, probably a cookfire based on the smoke leaking from cracks in the walls and roof. Levi and Jimmie crossed the barren frontage and went inside.

Renee walked between them, head down, one arm locked in Jimmie's giant paw. Constance hadn't seen Dal or Peter all afternoon.

She left her lookout and followed the track, assuming it would provide the simplest access to the dilapidated homestead. It took her down, past several sheds and haphazard piles of scrap wood, ancient farming implements, and what smelled like a latrine. She tucked behind the nearest of the sheds, watching. By now, night had fallen, but her Aura-enhanced senses let her see enough not to stumble into a building or a pit.

And thank god – thank the Aura – for the apprentices' class, where they had refined her night vision.

There was no sign of the dog, but after a time Jimmie emerged carrying a deep bowl of something that smelled like it had once been edible. He circled the far side of the hut; Constance risked shifting from her lookout to watch him. He struck off down a path leading into scrub. After a minute she heard the squeal of wood against wood, a shuffling that suggested a door opening. Very faintly, Dal's voice.

Whatever he said, it had little effect. "Enjoy yer night," Jimmie chortled. Then a series of slams and gratings suggested the door had again been closed and locked. The hulking boy emerged and made for the door of the hut; Constance pressed herself back into the shadows, for all the world like a heroine in the spy movies Omar had been so fond of.

Chapter 40

When it appeared obvious that the family were in the hut for the night, probably enjoying something marginally tastier than whatever slop Jimmie had delivered to Dal and Peter, Constance crept slowly around the far side of the clearing, fighting to keep her heart out of her throat. The near constant noise coming from the hovel covered any sound she inadvertently made; Levi's family was anything but quiet. The squabbling rose and fell but never ceased completely. Although she distinguished few of the words, she did hear Renee's voice in among the others, just as contentious.

At the hut she raised the bar slowly, hoping to minimize noise, and murmured, "It's me."

Dal was the first to emerge. She had never seen him so disheveled, with cobwebs in his hair, his tunic and trousers filthy. Peter stumbled out after him in no better shape, moving carefully, a hand to his side. A sour smell from the interior of the hut told her all she needed to know about its condition.

"Broken rib?" she asked in a whisper.

Peter shook his head. "Bruised badly, though. Dal did a healing, so I'll be fine."

"We need to plan," Dal said. "Should we go back in?"

Peter and Constance both recoiled at the idea. Even at the risk of being heard, whatever confab they conducted would be held outdoors.

Dal nodded. "Behind the shack, then." He led them around the building.

Peter spoke first. "We've been discussing this. Our best hope for getting Renee is when they send her out on some errand."

"Which may not be tonight," Dal added.

"We should get out of here. Go somewhere we can keep warm. This weather portends snow." Peter shivered; Constance suspected he was not as hale as he pretended to be.

Dal clearly agreed. "I hate to say it, but I suggest we go back to Little Hutt. They'll have some sort of guest accommodation there. If nothing else, they'll let us sleep on the floor of the dining hall."

"Have you seen my pack?" Peter asked Constance.

"In the copse. It's safe."

Of one accord, the three set off to skirt the clearing once again, making for the track leading back up to the main trail.

They were almost directly opposite the hovel when the door opened. They froze. Jimmie appeared, herding Renee ahead of him. Constance caught the tail end of his diatribe. "... get them pigs fed. Don't trust you further'n I'd throw you, girl, and don't you forget it." He gave Renee a shove and watched her slouch off toward the pigsty from his place in the doorway. Then he turned and ambled toward the latrine. Constance couldn't see Renee's eyes but recognized the body language. She was on the alert, looking for escape.

Perhaps it was the change in the pattern of shadows as Jimmie moved away from the doorway, but something alerted him. His head went up. There must have been just enough light from inside the shack for him to realize his prisoners were on the loose. He bellowed, "Pa! They's out!"

Levi appeared, shoving Jimmie out of the way and stepping into the clearing. "Girl! Get yerself back here!" he shouted. The woman appeared in the doorway as Levi and Jimmie charged across the clearing, heading in their direction.

They had spread out, with Peter and Dal ahead of her. Renee vanished into the darkness. Levi came straight at Constance, his stench preceding him.

None of them bothered to run. In the darkness, and given their unfamiliarity with the terrain, they stood little chance of escaping.

"Well, well, look here, Ma. Seems as there's another of them devils." Levi's hand gripped her arm, pinching. Constance flinched.

Jimmie herded the two men back into the pool of light in the clearing. "Now what?" He kicked at Peter's shin; he stumbled and groaned.

Constance thought her knees might collapse, but Dal remained composed. "You're making a mistake. We want only to go our way peacefully."

Levi ignored him. "Well, Jimmie, guess we've got us a female for practice, afore ya take Nada there. Get the hang of things."

"I like it." Jimmie approached her, slowly, swaggering.

Her blood ran cold.

A tornado came out of the dark in the form of Renee, hurling herself at Jimmie and screeching, "Don't you dare!" She understood street fighting;

her knee made solid contact with Jimmie's arousal.

He howled, swung around, and launched a fist at Renee.

Constance didn't think. She lifted her free arm. A rope of energy, so thick as to be almost visible, flung from her fingers, wrapped itself around Jimmie and flung him to the ground.

Jimmie moaned and sobbed, groveling in the dirt.

Renee ran to Constance's side. Levi released her arm and darted into the shack. Constance inched closer to Dal and Peter. All four of them began backing away, toward the track.

Levi reappeared at the door. He howled in fury and launched an object toward them.

An axe. Constance, still operating without thought, sent another bolt of power and shattered it in flight. Dal cried out. When she risked a glance, she saw him stagger.

"Go," Renee hissed. "Now."

Peter wrapped a supporting arm around Dal, who grasped his side and seemed stunned. They moved forward toward the road, using a large light ball Peter cast to assure their footing. Constance brought up the rear, keeping an eye behind her to be sure the family remained at the shack. As a parting gesture, she created a light ball of her own and hurled it in their direction. It wouldn't hurt them, but would intimidate.

By the time they got back to the copse, Constance was depleted. At her direction, Renee darted into the wood to retrieve Peter's pack and the cooking pot holding the poultice, then they continued down the trail to Little Hutt, Renee with an arm around Constance's waist, Peter still supporting Dal who stumbled more frequently as they worked their way along the trail.

They didn't make it far. "We have to stop," Peter stated. "There's more blood than I like."

"Over there." Renee pointed to a clearing a little way off the road. As they arrived, Dal slipped from Peter's grip and slumped to the ground. His face was twisted in pain and deathly pale.

"My pack," Peter said, his voice brooking no argument. "And litter, whatever you can find to make the ground softer. Moss, if there is any. Water, we'll need water. A spare tunic, clean if you have one. We need rags and bindings. Fast!" he snapped, then bent over Dal, beginning the scanning she had witnessed other Healers use.

Renee scrambled into the surrounding brush, leaving Constance to search her pack for a tunic. Others had camped here before; Peter suspended his ministrations to focus energy on the remains of an old fire, trying to get it to re-light. It smoldered, but no more. Constance added her travel pot to the small pile of supplies she was accumulating. Her water skin wasn't empty, but now that she could see Dal she knew it didn't hold enough.

Staying busy kept her from thinking. Because there was suddenly so much, too much, to think about...

Renee scurried back, her arms laden. She dumped the pile and began picking it apart, tossing small tinder on the fire, separating out the moss.

"Someone get this set up," Peter shouted. He tossed them the tarp they used as weather protection. "Open toward the fire. Dal needs warmth. Constance, get over here. Renee, the fire."

Both of them obeyed unquestioningly, although when she knelt beside Dal she almost wished she hadn't. A great gash tore through his side. Peter's hands were bloodied as he struggled to join the edges. "Keep the wound closed while I sew," he barked. "Rub your hands in that." He nodded at a little pile of herbs. "Sanitizing. Then put your hands where mine are. Did you bring water?"

She returned to her pack and brought everything. Wordlessly she handed over the waterskin and cooking pot, still holding the healing herb and tisane she had created so hopefully for Renee.

He sniffed at the mess in her pot. "Heal-all. Good, we'll need it. Right now, this is more important." When Constance hesitated, he growled, "Now, not tomorrow."

You're a medic. You're experienced. "Have you sanitized it?" she asked.

He gestured with his head toward several empty travel vials, but his focus never left Dal.

Her hands felt like custard, shaking and weak, but she rubbed them in the herbs, then placed them where he showed her. Peter produced a coarse needle threaded with a strand of linen. As he began stitching, Dal cried out, then fainted.

Over to their side, Renee produced a healthy blaze from the smoldering embers and nestled Peter's pot, now holding water, close to the fire. Then she began rigging the tent.

Constance held on for dear life, closing Dal's wound so Peter could stitch.

Chapter 41

When Dal's wound was closed and the heal-all poultice in place, Peter stood, a hand protectively on his side, and began the ritual to cast a protection circle around them. Constance watched, wishing for the first time it was she, rather than the Healer, creating the circle. She could see it appearing like a purple flame along the line he demarked, arching overhead as a purple mist. Should Levi and his family come in pursuit, they would be unlikely to locate them, even less likely to break the circle.

She felt the expected diminution of her Auric connection as Peter brought up the circle, and found the new experience uncomfortable. Most Weavers preferred not to cast a protection circle, she had been taught, for just this reason. It required a major drain on their own energies, and while it did serve a purpose, it also cut them off from much of the Aura. This circle was ragged; Peter must be depleted after working on Dal. She felt vaguely affronted he had not asked her assistance.

The circle in place and sealed, Peter turned to her, his face a mask of suppressed fury. "Can you tell me what in the name of creation you did back there?"

Constance settled near the fire and drew Renee close before answering. It took concentration to keep her voice calm and factual; nothing could control the shaking in her hands. "I don't know. It was instinct, I didn't plan it."

"A piece of that axe went straight into Dal's side. You could have killed him."

"But she didn't," Renee said. Her voice sounded by far the calmest. "And the axe would have sliced open one of you, sure."

Peter sank to the ground and placed his hand over the pot. "Almost hot enough. Tomorrow we must reach Little Hutt, and hopefully Stanstead. I'll go first and find us a donkey cart. You two stay with Dal."

Renee and Constance both turned to look doubtfully in the direction of the track.

"I know," Peter shot at them resentfully, as if the roughness of the trail were their fault. "But if we have to, we'll make a litter and carry him. This is bad."

Constance gave a minute nod.

Peter shut off further discussion. "We should eat."

Renee stood and rummaged in the two remaining packs. "Got a handful of trail bars." She passed the tough sustenance around and they ate, sitting in a gloomy circle around the fire. Then Peter rose and strode to the shelter, carrying the heated pot. "I'll stay with him. Tonight will tell the tale, whether he makes it or not."

Constance's head jerked up. Despite the evidence of her eyes, it had not occurred to her that Dal's wound was so serious.

"He'll pull through, sure," Renee stated. "We just gotta do some of that energy stuff, like with Meade." She cleared a patch of ground near the edge of the circle. Although she couldn't see it, possibly couldn't even sense it, she seemed to know not to cross the circle Peter had etched. She began drawing one of her diagrams, lost in thought.

"You're sure?" Constance asked, keeping her voice low so as not to disturb the men.

Renee didn't respond until the diagram was complete. "This here's the path, see? And there ain't no turnoffs. So you connect this to him, and he's gotta get better. 'Sides, Meade would never forgive him, if he didn't."

I might not either. Forgive him, or myself.

"Here," Renee said. "You put your hand on the path here, and do that energy thing. Let him know he's gotta use it."

Would her energy have any effect? Renee's faith in her diagram was absolute, and Constance had no doubt Peter had infused his herbal brew with all the Healing power he could muster. Surely Dal would pull through. The diagram meant nothing to her, but she placed her hands as Renee directed and pinned the path to her mind. Doing what Renee asked couldn't be that much different from tracing one of the weaves the Scribes used. She let herself sink into trance, doing her best to channel the diagram's energy, and her own, to the inert man in the shelter.

*

In the early morning, barely dawn, Dal was conscious, and there was no sign of fever. Between them, they had started him on the path to Healing. Constance and Renee tidied the waysite while Peter went into a Healers' trance to do more work on Dal.

Given his improvement, they agreed their best option was for all of them to make their way toward the main track. Peter took down the protection circle while Constance checked on Dal's stitches and Renee extinguished the fire. Dal insisted he could walk with help; Peter took one side, Constance and Renee alternated on the other. Progress was slow through the pre-dawn, and Constance was acutely aware with every step they took that Levi and his family might be tailing them. But all was quiet apart from the expected sounds of birdsong and the gentle rustling of small animals in the brush. A layer of cloud obscured the dawn, but the air felt warmer than it had the previous night.

Somehow, they made it. Once the track improved to a proper trail, they hastily made a temporary camp and settled Dal – who by then was ghostly white – near their fire. Peter did another Healing, then set off to find a cart. However well Dal had coped with the trek so far, no one believed he could walk the rest of the way. The injured man fell into an uneasy slumber, while Constance and Renee huddled close to the fire.

"Your diagram," Constance said softly. "Is that what you're trying to do for Meade? Force her energies onto a path for Healing?"

Renee gave her an incredulous look. "Of course. What else?"

"But how did you know Dal's energies well enough to diagram them?"

Renee shrugged, as if her diagram were the most everyday thing in the universe. "Meade's been teachin' me. Most of us, the energy goes always the same. Dal's got interrupted by that cut in his side, and we need to get it back to where it belongs. Should be easy."

"So that's what Healers do, when they go into that trance."

Renee scrunched up her face, thinking it over. "Kinda. Only it's like they just know where the energy ought to be. Don't need maps."

"So, with Meade..."

"Big mess. Everything's too scrambled. Dal says we're gettin' closer. He's been learnin' to use my diagrams, that's what he told me. But we ain't got it right yet."

Constance couldn't help but notice that Renee's language had reverted during her days with her family. The girl really was a sponge; she had made enormous strides before the kidnapping and would no doubt return to better speech quickly.

"And you could diagram it well enough for me to follow it and send it to him."

Renee shrugged. "Sure." Then she looked down, drawing a pattern in the ground litter with her toe. "Leastways, I think so. I figured it couldn't be too far wrong."

"But if you can do that, and if I can follow it and send it to Dal...." She paused to consider the implications. "Then potentially any Weaver could be a Healer. Or at least assist." Assuming her work with Renee's diagram last night had had any effect at all.

"Hope so, 'cause he don't look so good now."

True enough, Dal seemed locked in an uneasy, possibly feverish, slumber. Constance crossed to him and touched his forehead. Cool, thank god, but a long way from healed. Overhead, the weak sun fought to break through the layer of clouds. It must be mid-morning by now; Constance's stomach rumbled, but they were out of food and had only enough water for Dal.

"Think we ought to try it again?" Renee asked.

She shook her head. "Not without Peter. I'd want someone more skilled here, just in case."

In case these erratic energies did harm instead of good. Like yesterday, that axe. Like Meade.

Renee fell quiet. Constance eyed her closely, reaching out with whatever energy she could command. Renee was in shock, coming down from the ordeal and the necessity of action that had driven their small band to this place. There was no water to spare, so she wrapped a blanket around the girl's shoulders, tucking it in well and adding a hug. "We're on our way home now. We're going to be fine."

Renee leaned against her for a moment, then huddled into her blanket. "Lots to think about," she said, dismissing Constance and showing gratitude for her concern at the same time.

"Okay. I'm here if you need me."

Or want me.

As they waited for Peter, Constance reflected on the strange manifestation of energy yesterday, wondering how she had created the rope-like flow, what it meant. But that wasn't a topic she could dwell on; it scared her too much. Instead she left the fire and paced a short length of the track, her arms wrapped around her for warmth and to keep her hands from shaking. She kept an eye on Renee but remained out on the track until they heard the rumble of a donkey cart.

That energy, the power in her, in her hands... this was deep, a part of her she had never known existed, and wasn't at all sure she wanted.

Chapter 42

In the dusk of Solstice evening, wrapped in her sheepskin-lined woolen cape, Constance walked across the Motherhouse green, now dusted by the first snow of the year. Around the corner, tucked between the dining hall and one of the apprentices' buildings, a bonfire held many of the students rapt; several were dancing to music leaking from the hall where the main celebration was taking place. Solstice was big here, one of the major celebrations in a world where agrarian concerns dominated. Constance appreciated the season and its celebration, even if she didn't share the enthusiasm.

The kids from the village hadn't arrived yet but were expected any minute – according to gossip overheard in the Scribes' lodge – with Renee in tow. The night they returned from Stanstead, Renee had climbed into bed with her and snuggled there until dawn, but since then her girl had spent the short days at the stables, riding and grooming Socksy or working on Meade's energy diagrams. She was never far away, and someone from the Motherhouse or the village always knew her plans – and accompanied her.

Stability, she thought. Stability and joy. Already the haunted look had left Renee's face. She would be all right.

Dal appeared at the door of the dining hall. Both he and Peter still took care in their movements but were solidly on the mend. She had seen little of him since their arrival at the Motherhouse, but understood he was occupied with his own Healing, and, as always, with Meade.

He saw her and stepped outside, apprehending her before she could enter the building. "A walk might be useful before we indulge," he said without preamble – and with a clear expectation she would fall in with his wishes. "It's hot in there, and the sheer quantity of food... we'll all feel sick before midnight."

She acquiesced without comment, accepting the inevitability of facing Dal and what still lay between them, sooner or later. Tonight, the thought didn't perturb her. Besides, a walk in the brisk air would feel good. It seemed she was growing accustomed to both the cold and the otherworldly existence she now lived. They turned away from the light spilling out the door, and she allowed him to set the direction, along the path circling the amphitheater.

They moved slowly. Dal held himself rigid, more so than usual, and once placed a hand on his side as if the wound had spasmed. When they reached the bench where Meade's energies had become so entangled, he used a mittened hand to dust the seat, then held out his other hand. She took it and allowed herself to be guided to sit beside him.

"I suppose Arwen's already spoken with you," he said.

Constance listened carefully. Perhaps it was the night, or the shared experience of rescuing Renee. Perhaps she was simply more in tune with the Aura than she had been back in Stanstead, when the attraction that flashed between them was so strong as to be almost visible. One way or another, she recognized the tension in Dal's voice. Whatever he had determined to say, it was no easier for him than for her.

She smiled to herself at the irony that Arwen, of all people, would provide a safe conversational topic.

The snow was beginning again, a light fall that melted on her face. She allowed the smile to emerge. "More testing, more training. It seems no one has ever produced energy like that. They want to know how I did it, and how they can do the same. I just hope it never happens again."

"As do I, but there's the lingering threat from the other side of the hills, not to mention growing unrest here in the Midland. One day, it might prove useful, if we can learn the technique. Willow told us the man she knew in Borgonne did something similar, but that was more like a force than a rope."

Constance shook her head. "I don't know myself how it happened. I'd wish it hadn't, but...."

"It saved us," Dal said bluntly.

That silenced her. They sat for a time, watching the flakes catch what was left of the light.

"And then there's Renee's diagram of me," Dal said. He had no clear memory of that night, but she and Peter had briefed him, and Dal had encouraged Renee to reproduce the diagram on paper. "Your arrival brought changes to the Motherhouse. New ways of thinking, new ways of practicing our craft."

She chose to pass over her own significance, if it existed. "Renee... I never understood what she was doing, not really. Or that someone could put their energy into it and use it to support...." Words escaped her. The matter of tracking Dal's energies seemed so personal, an invasion when she spoke of it.

"Meade's better, thanks to her. I suppose you know that?"

"We had a long visit this morning." The memory of that conversation, and especially of the hug at the end, warmed Constance. It had felt as if their derailed friendship had found a fresh beginning. She hoped so. Despite all the people she now knew around the Motherhouse, loneliness frequently crept in like a fog, suppressing what could have been a better time.

As had happened altogether too often, Dal read her thoughts. "It can be a lonely life," he said, then hesitated. "But you and I...."

Constance swallowed and turned to face him.

He continued speaking, although not with his usual assuredness. "We could be... I don't know. Your customs are different from mine. We both know what happened in Stanstead, but what happens next...."

Tongue-tied? Dal?

"Go on," she said, her voice carefully neutral.

"We could be more."

Another pause before she said, her voice betraying doubt, "We could."

He grinned, as if he were making fun of himself. "But you'd rather not."

"I don't...." He had called her bluff, although he might not know it. She drew a breath, one that stung with cold deep in her lungs. "It's my background, my life before I came here."

"And?"

Once, it had been about Pierre, her commitment to her marriage, her family. That seemed far away and long ago now. But there still remained.... At a loss for words, seeing more hazards ahead than she could name, she grasped the first stumbling block that came to mind, never mentioned or even thought much about in the last years but reflective of the overall panoply of her life, her ingrained beliefs and her memories.

"You all... you all sleep with each other. I can't do that."

Dal relaxed as he switched into lecture mode, reminding her how much more comfortable he was imparting facts. "It's the way of things, here. In general, Weavers don't form exclusive relationships. I tried once, and it didn't work. She resented the itinerant lifestyle, the things about the Aura I couldn't explain or divulge. We see more deeply, know what others don't."

"So, you share yourselves but don't commit. Whereas at—" She had almost said at home. But Terra wasn't home anymore. In fact, she struggled to make sense of her history in light of her new reality.

She sensed in Dal both an underlying annoyance at her assumptions and a need to make her understand. "It's not promiscuity, or not for most of us," he said. "There is a bond. Willow, for instance – she and I traveled together during her journey year. We became close, as you must if you take to the roads together."

"Meade, too, am I right? A lot of others. For me, it's different. I was married, back on Terra. One man." *Who stole my son, who betrayed me more deeply than I ever thought possible.*

"I've watched Willow and Joss together. It's a different kind of bonding, isn't it?"

She sighed, facing the reality of her marriage for the first time, and offered it to him. "Sometimes it doesn't work out, even when it's the norm."

Dal nodded, waiting. Below them, the kids from the village charged across the green in a noisy clump, radiating life. The light in the dining hall poured out as they hustled through the door. She knew with the certainty of motherhood that Renee was among them.

She turned back to Dal. "I don't share," she reiterated. "I can't."

"I understand. On those terms...."

"I know it may not last."

"It's Solstice," Dal said quietly. "A night of magic. I'd like us to be a part of that magic."

Pierre was the past, and much though it pained her, so was Omar, her cherished son. But now, consciously, she laid her life on Terra aside – and felt the heaviness that had burdened her heart for three years evaporate into the night air. Dal, Renee, Meade, all the others she had come to know... this was home now, here in this impoverished land, the bleakness of the Motherhouse in winter. And, however improbably, Dal was a part of it. "So would I," she whispered.

His face was gaunt in the faint light, reminding her again of his injury and the trauma they had faced together. He drew her close – as close as she could get, given the thickness of their capes. When he kissed her, when she felt his lips discovering hers for the first time, she let the last of her resistance go.

The night lay hushed, the snow falling around them, as they quietly entered a new, wondrous exploration, together.

Chapter 43

Trust Dal to convene a meeting the morning after Solstice.

Meade studied her companions in the healing room somewhat blearily. She hadn't stayed at the festivities too late – her minders saw to that – but once back in her room in the Healers' lodge, she had been unable to sleep. Too much excitement and rich food? True enough, but underlain with a tinge of disappointment. Solstice had always been a highlight for her, not only the revelry but also an opportunity for deep reflection about the year now gone and expectations for the year to come. This year, for the first time ever, her thoughts weren't positive. The recent past held a lonely trek, an earthquake, and the disastrous twisting of her energies, and the future held scant promise. The ongoing, tedious work to Heal her had yielded some positive effects, but there was no reason to think she would ever be fully cured.

Her companions also showed the effects of last night's celebration. Renee admitted to attending an all-night party in one of the student lodgings with a group of apprentices her age. Who could blame her? She was blossoming now, taller and with the beginnings of curves. Not that that would thrill Renee, despite her new interest in hairstyles and overall appearance. The girl was subdued this morning, undoubtedly tired.

And Dal... Meade wasn't sure where he had disappeared to last night, only that one moment he was there at the celebration, the next he wasn't. She wondered if he had returned to the Healers' lodge last night. Their rooms were on different floors, so she hadn't been able to check, not with her restricted mobility. But she suspected not. There was something about him this morning that told her he hadn't slept much. Dal was a man of angles, in his appearance as well as in his austere personality, but this morning she sensed a new softness, as if some of those hard corners had been filed down and rounded.

Meade turned her attention to the table in front of her. Renee was drawing one of her diagrams, right on the table, with a charred stick. "It looks so familiar," she observed. "Like something I've seen, but I can't quite place where."

"I thought the same," Dal said. "And we are familiar with it, in a sense. This is normal energy flow in a person, or so Renee assures me. She's pieced it together from what I've told her about your flows. Where they're tangled, she straightened them out. I hope that by scanning someone healthy—"

Just then, Daren stepped into the room. "Was this really necessary?" He slumped onto a stool. The morning after Solstice was rarely a good time for meaningful conversation.

"I need an experimental subject," Dal said. "And if this works, you'll want to see it." As head of the Healers' guild, Daren had been privy to all their efforts on Meade's behalf.

Renee put down the stick. "Best I can do."

"The same as you drew for me?" Dal asked.

"Think so." The girl yawned hugely. "Can I go back to bed now?"

"Give me five minutes. Daren, onto the cot, please. Fall asleep if you want to."

"Tell me again why I'm here?" Meade asked.

Dal smiled and pushed the hair back from her face, letting his fingers cradle her head for a moment and thoroughly shocking her. Dal was not known for overt displays of affection. "An approach we never considered. If this diagram is accurate, I want to use it for you to attempt to Heal yourself. Renee had Constance feed the diagram into me. Peter said he sensed the new energy, and it seemed to support his Healing."

"So," Meade said doubtfully, "you transfer the diagram into me, and my energies follow the paths in the diagram. And disentangle themselves. Is that even possible?"

Dal nodded. "That's what I intend to find out. But first I want to confirm the diagram. That's why you're here," he added to Daren.

"You're not changing anything, right?" Daren said as he stretched out on the examining table. "You're just seeing if my energies respond appropriately to the diagram. As if you were doing an energy smoothing, but via a different route."

"That sums it up. Ready?"

Renee shifted her stool into a corner, where she leaned her head against the wall and closed her eyes. Meade, on the other hand, wouldn't miss a moment of this experiment. Her restored abilities didn't yet extend to following Dal's work, but she watched, her Auric connection as active as she could make it, while Dal stood over the diagram and entered a Healing trance.

The room went silent. After a time, Dal put his hands on the diagram, but otherwise nothing moved.

"Ow," Daren said suddenly. "That pinched."

Dal immediately abandoned his trance, giving his head a violent shake to quickly ground himself. "Tell me where."

Daren sat up and pointed to a place on his right thigh. "Until then it felt like the usual process."

Dal gently shook Renee's shoulder. "Renee? I need your help."

"Oh... okay." The girl struggled to wakefulness and wandered over to the table. Dal explained what they had found, and she set to work, rubbing out lines with the side of her fist, chalking in new lines over the resultant smear. After a minute she said, "There. Might be better."

Dal gave her a smile. "Thanks, I'm grateful."

Renee nodded, already half asleep again, then retreated to her stool. Before Daren could settle back on the bed, her eyes were closed.

Meade watched the whole process, wondering what it would feel like to have this pattern of seemingly arbitrary lines fed into her body. Daren was relaxed, almost purring, much the way any of them felt during an energy smoothing. Dal was deep in his trance, but his head moved every now and then, as if he were nodding approval.

When he was done, he and Daren consulted briefly, then Dal offered her a hand. "Your turn."

*

Meade lay on the examination table. She had fallen asleep during the treatment, but before she lost consciousness, she had been aware of Renee's pattern overlaying her own energy flows. The lines, which had appeared random on the table, formed an elegant design. She sensed energy – her energy – following several of them.

Now awake, she opted to remain still, sensing the room, and more important, sensing her body.

Something had shifted.

She knew Dal was there, probably waiting for her to wake up and report. But Meade didn't want to report. She wanted to luxuriate in the slight release she sensed in her body. Something along her spine, something that had been pressing on her bones, was now lax.

A flow, it had to be a flow. One of the knots, perhaps one of the worst ones, had untied.

Poor Dal. After all his work, her body did it by itself, with support from Renee, the miracle worker.

Taking her time, she directed her senses along her other energy flows, something she hadn't been able to do since the accident. She stumbled on a couple of blockages, but they seemed to be minor ones.

She was Healed.

Slowly, she opened her eyes. From the amount of light in the room, she concluded she had slept for most of the morning. Well, it was the day after Solstice, after all. She was entitled.

She yawned and stretched, thinking how delightful it would be to tell Dal she would soon be whole again.

Epilogue

The first hints of spring appeared around the Motherhouse – a green weed at the base of a building, a touch of mildness in the wind. In all ways that mattered, Solstice had presaged new life. And not only for Constance.

She and Meade made their way toward the rock formation that provided a convenient seating area near the river, for those seeking privacy or a chance to commune with flowing water. The river wasn't in full spate yet; further north, it must still be frozen. Meade spread a quadruple-folded blanket over the stone seat. "Don't expect much from Dal at the equinox celebration," she said. "He's a lousy dancer."

"So am I. We'll applaud you instead." Both women settled on the blanket. Meade stretched her legs out in front of her, lifting them off the ground. "It's... well, it's just good to be whole again."

There was still some untangling to do, but for the most part Meade was restored. Equally important to Constance was the revival of their friendship. She expected to receive her sash as a fully trained Scribe sometime this spring, which in her mind legitimized their bond – Weaver to Weaver.

She had done it. Passed all the exercises Dorcas had set her, discovered new courage as she explored the weird world of Scribes, a world that could veer wildly from ordinary reality. Part of her shuddered at the thought, but as her confidence grew, her desire to *know*, to learn the boundaries of her new territory, only increased.

"Renee's got a boyfriend," Meade said.

Constance nodded. "Seems like a nice kid. I don't really want her to become a farmer, though."

"Did you stow her diagram in the Aura? I don't think we can make it any more accurate."

"Tonight. I want support for this one. We can't afford to lose it."

Renee's diagram of human energy flows had become the object of both study and practice in the healing rooms. Dal worked with it constantly, calling on Renee when he found a refinement or correction. Other Healers were learning the technique, and by next autumn they expected it to become part of the apprentices' curriculum. All the apprentices, not just those expected to become Healers, because Constance herself had proven that by using the diagram, any Weaver could smooth energies.

Or untangle them.

After a few minutes, Constance said, "I've got an assignment."

"So I hear. Any idea what?"

Constance smiled. The muscles around her mouth had ached when she started smiling so much. She was appalled now by how little use those muscles had had, before. "Sort of like a journey year, but without direct supervision."

"That means you're leaving."

The smile faded. "I'm used to it here. Out there in the world... I'm not easy about it."

"We were all ambivalent about leaving when we finished our training, but I guess it's even bigger for you. Don't worry, you'll be fine. And you always have a home here."

"I'm wondering about Renee."

"Yeah, so am I," Meade said. "I guess it'll be up to her whether she goes with you. In our terms, we'd say she's all grown up, so it won't be anyone else's decision."

Constance thought about what it would mean to take herself out into a world that still seemed alien, even with her newly honed powers. There was little point, now, in returning to the Adventurer, and she couldn't see them assigning her to a tour of villages, mining their biblios for data about the formation and evolution of the Midland culture. So, what would they do with her?

Well, she would find out soon enough. "I'm supposed to see Arwen after lunch."

"Don't sound like you're dreading it," Meade said. "Arwen's all right. Once you've proved yourself to her, anyway."

Constance shuddered. The sessions after they had retrieved Renee, as Arwen and Dorcas poked, prodded, and experimented to figure out how she had created those ropes of energy, had been grueling.

A bell rang in the distance.

"Food," Meade said. Constance had worked out that her friend loved to eat and had to restrict herself when she wasn't burning energy traveling.

They packed up and headed toward the dining hall, chatting about nothing much. Neither of them had mentioned Dal again, but now that her departure was imminent, Constance couldn't help but wonder how he would figure in her new future.

*

"Here's the plan," Arwen said. "The week after equinox, we'll hold your initiation ceremony. Then you're going to Colgate."

Constance frowned and glanced at Dorcas. She had heard of Colgate but couldn't remember where or why.

"You have abilities we haven't tapped, but that we need," Dorcas said. She settled comfortably in her chair, clearly content with the decision. "Logic, primarily, and organization. Trade with Borgonne will open up this summer via the new southern route, and Colgate is the closest town on our side. We need an administrator." At Constance's horrified look, she laughed. "It'll challenge your skills, don't worry about that. Some elementary Healing if nothing else. Colgate hasn't been on one of our traveling routes for some time. Besides that, though, you'll be going head to head with your equivalents from Borgonne – they call them mages over there, and their training is different from ours. We don't really know what to expect from them, no one's even sure yet if they can cross the hills to our side, but they're as keen as we are to open trade routes. We'll provide you with guidelines, so you won't have to make it up as you go. And, of course, you can always reach us."

Constance wasn't so sure of that. Her ability to communicate through the Aura was tenuous, at best.

"True, but it'll get stronger with practice," Arwen said.

Constance reminded herself to screen her thoughts better.

"But the deciding factor was the horses," Dorcas said.

"Horses?" Constance struggled to maintain the thread of conversation.

"That will be the main trade item at first," Arwen said. "Colgate's been getting ready for this for a year or more. That's where Socksy came from, you know, and Quinn's horse. They'll need someone to handle the trade. And equally important, they'll need support training the horses."

"Training?" Constance gasped. "But I don't know—"

Renee.

"She's going?"

"She's going," Dorcas said. "She doesn't want to leave Socksy or that young man, but she's ready."

"You haven't asked her," Constance said.

Their faces gave her their answer, but Arwen said, "She's going. Besides spreading her wings, she wants to be with you."

And I want to be with her. Renee's emergence as a teenager had been a wonder to watch. While the girl was still subject to occasional fits of pique and frustration, her transition to young womanhood had, overall, been smooth.

There was a pause while the three contemplated the work ahead, the new assignment.

"There's more," Dorcas said at last. "I think you'll approve. We plan to set up a new base in Colgate, a hub like we have in Stanstead. The southern part of the Midland has been underserved for years. This is our chance to correct that. It'll mean finding or building a suitable Weavers' lodge, a healing room..."

"You won't have to handle that alone," Arwen said. "We've already confirmed someone to take it on. Much though we'll hate to lose him."

"He's been here teaching for too long," Dorcas added. "He needs a challenge as much as you do."

Dal. She read it in the Aura. The three of them, almost like a family, beginning a new life together. And Quinn, her first friend on Newfoundland, far away but soon to be a sister. She wouldn't be traveling alone.

Constance closed her eyes, breathing in the new reality. Then she asked, "What do I need to do between now and equinox?" If the thought of leaving made her uneasy, the nine-day or so of work ahead, her last days at the Motherhouse, didn't daunt her. It was time she tried her own wings.

After all, she was a Scribe.

About LizAnn Carson

It's interesting, trying to condense who you are into a paragraph or two. I live in Victoria, British Columbia, a smallish city that's large enough to have all modern conveniences, but not so large as to have hours-long traffic jams or heavy-duty pollution. I can follow a trail to my local supermarket, or I can be downtown in twenty minutes.

Yes, I spend much of my time writing (and editing, formatting, critiquing for other writers, battling computer problems, and occasionally tearing my hair out). But beyond that, I enjoy a variety of crafts. I play early music on a baritone ukulele and struggle to produce attractive paintings in oil pastel. I walk a lot and enjoy weight training and yoga. Once, a long time ago, I owned a yarn shop, and for a while I taught English as a Second Language.

And sometimes, I just watch my cats sleep.

See more about my books in the worlds of both fantasy and romance on my website, www.lizanncarson.com.